Praise for

THE SCRIBE

"Talk about turning the ordinary into the extraordinary, Matthew Guinn nails turn-of-the-twentieth-century Southern history. Guinn captures the look and feel of Georgia perfectly. It's a whodunit with a twist—a heady mix of history, sizzle, punch, and danger. A definite keeper." **—STEVE BERRY,** *New York Times* best-selling author of *The Patriot Threat*

"A gripping tale that will have readers gasping, both in suspense and in horror. . . . [Guinn is] one of the most promising fiction writers in America today." **—JIM EWING,** *Clarion-Ledger*

"One of the most tense and exciting novels I have read in ages." **—DON NOBLE,** *Tuscaloosa News*

"So good. . . . Historical figures mingle freely with Guinn's own fully fleshed characters in a time and setting that make this horror story something much more than just scary reading at dusk." **—LAURA WADLEY,** *Daily Herald*

D0064188

ALSO BY MATTHEW GUINN

The Resurrectionist

THE
SCRIBE

A Novel

MATTHEW GUINN

W. W. NORTON & COMPANY
INDEPENDENT PUBLISHERS SINCE 1923
NEW YORK   LONDON

For information about permission to reproduce selections from this book,
write to Permissions, W. W. Norton & Company, Inc.,
500 Fifth Avenue, New York, NY 10110

For information about special discounts for bulk purchases, please contact
W. W. Norton Special Sales at specialsales@wwnorton.com or
800-233-4830

Manufacturing by Courier Westford
Book design by Lovedog Studio
Production manager: Louise Mattarelliano

Library of Congress Cataloging-in-Publication Data

Guinn, Matthew.
The scribe : a novel / Matthew Guinn. — First edition.
pages ; cm
ISBN 978-0-393-23929-4 (hardcover)
1. Police—Georgia—Atlanta—Fiction. 2. Serial murder
investigation—Fiction. 3. African Americans—Crimes against—Fiction.
4. Atlanta (Ga.)—History—1865–1898—Fiction. I. Title.
PS3607.U4856S37 2015
813'.6—dc23

2015013780

ISBN 978-0-393-35327-3 pbk.

W. W. Norton & Company, Inc.
500 Fifth Avenue, New York, N.Y. 10110
www.wwnorton.com

W. W. Norton & Company Ltd.
Castle House, 75/76 Wells Street, London W1T 3QT

1 2 3 4 5 6 7 8 9 0

for Amy Guinn Bowling

*The more intense is one's love for this planet and its
creatures, the greater is one's agony over the evil that
twists it. Sensitivity to evil is sensitivity born of love.*

—Jeffrey Burton Russell, *Mephistopheles*

*Il y a dans tout homme, à toute heure, deux postulations
simultanées, l'une vers Dieu, l'autre vers Satan.*

—Charles Baudelaire, *Mon Couer Mis à Nu*

*He sank deeper in the dark and the mist, aghast,
Alone, and behind him, in the eternal nights,
His wing feathers fell more slowly still.*

—Victor Hugo, *Et nox facta est*

Author's Note

ALTHOUGH SEVERAL of the characters depicted in this narrative were actual persons of the nineteenth century, I remind the reader that this is a work of fiction. In it, historical fact has been augmented with invented scenes of historical figures' "lives." I hope that this imaginative projection will be seen as an extension of these larger-than-life men's characters—and how they might actually have reacted to the fictional events herein.

EXILE

From the papers of Thomas Canby, detective,
Atlanta Police Force (ret.):

*Atlanta, in the years just after the war, was a hell of a
place. A third of the buildings still rubble but the people
hustling by them as if they didn't see, or as if it didn't matter anymore; the war was history. Streets bristling with
people and energy from curb to curb: peddlers, teamsters,
carpetbaggers (this before Vernon had gotten to calling
them "northern investors"—with a straight face), and the
shell-shocked planters who'd gone bust, come into town
from the outskirts to find out there was nothing here for
their kind, just like before. And as ever the trains burning
through town down the middle of streets, scattering mules
and wagons and men or running them clean over if they
didn't scatter. Ashes everywhere.*

But that was before. By the time I was back in '81 the men I had fought with in the war had all long gone home up north. But I thought of them often that fall. I thought of them because I had first seen that kind of darkness with them and now I was alone to see it, again. Should say, I suppose, that I was driven to join up by something akin to that darkness, on a fool boy's errand of vengeance, after my father's death in the siege of '64. In the war we'd brushed up against it, passed it in the night or faced it down in the scalding daylight of a pitched battle at Bentonville or in the shady occupied streets of Columbia, where the civilians would cut their eyes away from you like convicts do, because they know what you're capable of. That you can get away with damned near anything.

We never called it by its name but we knew it by sight. Some men went home tainted by it. I surely thought I did.

But what I learned in Atlanta in '81 was that what we'd seen was only the shadow of evil, its coattails at the most. When I really saw it for the first time clean and clear it was not a shadow. No fleeting glimpse. It was in the flesh, real as dirt and cold as gunmetal—a vortex wanting to pull you down. Like the draw of cowardice in battle but twice as strong.

All of this clear in hindsight, of course.

But in Atlanta, in 1881, the only thing that seemed clear was that the vortex knew my name. Canby, *it said.* Canby: *you are* mine.

September 29, 1881

CANBY SIGHTED DOWN THE RIDGELINE, DOWN THE crest of the low mountain tufted with crimson and gold trees and fringed with outcroppings of granite, toward the afternoon sun. By his estimate he had an hour of daylight left, maybe a few minutes more, before the sun would drop behind the ridge and the valley would fill with the deep and sudden mountain dusk. Time enough to get back to his tethered horse at the Old Branch Road, if he could finish his business here first, time enough maybe to have a sip of whiskey back at the jail before heading home to his dark house. Except for one thing: he realized with a sinking feeling that the ridge in front of him was not Sugar Mountain. Not a single of the dogwoods that bloomed white each spring and had given the mountain its name dotted the steep slope. It was maybe Catlick Mountain, maybe Little Roundtop, he couldn't be sure. He was lost.

"You damned city-bred fool," he muttered.

Canby looked down at the ground, at the tracks that had led him here in a circuitous path of the animal's own devising.

They were large prints, the pads of the big cat's paws spreading out as wide as a man's hand. He had half hoped to lose the trail that had started back at John Peake's bloody pigpen, but the ground was still soft from an autumn thunderstorm and the prints were fresh.

That afternoon, at Peake's farm, Canby had said, "You know, there aren't many of them left this far south."

John Peake had leaned over the rail fence and spat in the road, too close to Canby's boot.

"Well, that's a pity, ain't it?" Peake said. "But ain't going to be none of my pigs left by the next sheriff's election."

Peake had held Canby's gaze for a moment. "You let me know if I'm going to have to go after him myself." And then he had turned and walked back to his barn with the pigs behind him sniffing at the mud of their pen, licking at the blood trail of their lost member.

Canby looked down now into the hollow below him, at the gathering shadows there. He was thinking of turning back to follow his own trail through the falling light when he caught a flicker of movement below.

He lowered himself to one knee and brought the Winchester up carefully, until his left elbow rested on his left knee and the rifle's bead was out front of him, steadied by his body and ready. Slowly, he pulled the hammer back on the rifle and sighted among the rocks, his eye and the rifle's sights moving together. He caught it again, the slow and careful motion, almost tentative, like a tree limb dipping in a breeze. A patch of fur among the granite, picking its way toward the spring that flowed between the boulders fallen from the higher slopes. He waited a full minute, until the cat's shoulder came clear of the rocks, and then squeezed the trigger.

The boom of the .44-caliber shattered the forest quiet and he saw the cat jerk as though it had been kicked, then disappear behind the rocks. He levered the spent round out of the chamber and sat down with his back against a tree. While he waited for the ringing in his ears to subside he tried to remember how long it had been since he'd last fired a shot at someone else's behest and found that he couldn't, which he took to be a good thing. After a few minutes the noise in his ears quieted and when he heard the caw of a crow somewhere overhead he rose and started down the hillside.

His feet slipped and skidded in the rocky soil and once he had to reach out and catch the limb of a laurel to keep from sliding hind-first down the mountain. When he reached the hollow's bottom he could see a splash of blood on the rocks by the creek and he knew by the size of it that the cat could not have gotten far. He knelt by the spring and ladled cold water into his mouth with his cupped hand until his throat ached, giving the cat a bit more time, remembering what he'd seen done to Peake's sow.

He rose and stepped across the stream, then climbed over the jumbled rocks. The cat lay on its side a few yards away, amid a drift of fallen leaves, the neat hole of the entry wound on its upturned side leaking viscous blood. He watched it long enough to see that the chest was not rising or falling with breath, then moved to it.

He poked it twice with the tip of the barrel, gently, before he knelt beside it.

"*Felis concolor*," Canby said, hearing the echo of his father's brogue in his own pronunciation. "You were a thing of beauty." He reached out and stroked the cat's tawny hide, feeling the fur bristle beneath his palm.

The cat twitched and raised its head in a single motion, then swept a paw, listlessly, across Canby's forearm. His arm burned instantly and he pulled it back, his eyes cutting to the cat's face. Its lip pulled back in a weak snarl, exposing a long canine tooth, then its head dropped to the rocks and the eyes glazed.

Canby looked down at the four furrows on his arm. He leaned the Winchester against a rock and pulled his handkerchief from his back pocket and began wrapping the wound, knotting it tightly to stop the blood. When he was satisfied with his work he looked at the cat again, then at the sun dropping behind the ridgeline. A crow flew across it, ink-black against the crimson. He turned back to the cat and stared at it for a long moment, then began gathering what rocks he could lift to cover it. As he worked he saw the blood beginning to seep through the handkerchief, a dark spot of its own against the white bandage that glowed in the gathering dark.

It was past six when he got back to Ringgold. He could smell supper cooking in the houses, the good smell of plain food drifting out over the dirt road that wound down from the mountains and through the center of town. As his horse ambled past the Winfield house and the little clapboard church, he saw that a lamp was burning in the sheriff's office and knew that his deputy, Anson Burke, was waiting for him there.

Canby watched Anse through the window as he tied the horse to its post outside. He was tilted back in Canby's chair with his boots propped on the desk, immersed in the Sears catalog as though reading Scripture, his face beatific in the light of the lamp. Canby smiled as Burke licked a finger delicately and turned a page. A cat burglar could drop a copy of the Sears or Montgomery Ward catalog on a front porch and count on getting ten minutes' jump on Burke. Leave one in an outhouse, Canby thought, and his deputy might not emerge for a week.

Yet Canby had also seen Burke subdue more than one belligerent mountaineer with a single quick blow. Slow to anger, Anse was, but once his ire was raised it struck with an efficiency that could drop a man cold as a hammer before his body hit the ground. One of these was knocked so insensate that he soiled himself while Canby and Burke were carrying him back to the jail to sober up, then, on waking late the next morning to see Anse entering his cell with a cup of soup, had repeated the performance.

Burke looked up from his book slowly as Canby came through the door.

"Evening, Anse."

"Evening, Sheriff," Burke said. He dropped his feet from the desk and leaned over it with the catalog in hand, pointing out one of the shotguns drawn on a spread of the sporting goods pages.

"Look here, Sheriff. I've got my eye on this double-barreled Lefaucheux," he said, sounding out the French very slowly. "Three percent discount if you send them cash."

"Get the Pieper instead," Canby said, putting the Winchester in the gun cabinet next to the door. "Rifle and a shotgun side by side. Hard to beat."

"I would," Burke said, his face coloring, "if I had twenty-four dollars."

Canby felt his neck burning. His own Pieper hung in the cabinet next to the Winchester, though he'd been no closer to a twenty-four-dollar budget when he got it than Anse was now. He'd confiscated it from a pimp called Big Slim Gourley in Atlanta's Shermantown district in '76. He locked the cabinet and turned back to Burke, bent over the catalog with him. Burke's dirty fingernail was poised over the Lefaucheux. The catalog called it a "high-grade import." Canby was doubtful of that, at eight dollars.

"They'll ship it out to you for approval if you give the express agent a dollar. Can you believe that? Have to give them a dollar to look it over in your own house. Like they don't trust you not to steal the damned thing."

Canby looked at him wearily, thinking of all the swindles and petty hustlers he had seen—at least until he had come up to these mountains. "I guess times are changing, Anse." He sat on the edge of the desk and put a hand on Burke's shoulder. The deputy's eyes lingered for a second, as they often did, on the vertical scar that ran down Canby's left cheek. Then they noted the bloody handkerchief for the first time.

"Well, be damned," he said.

"Yep," Canby said, "where've we put the kerosene?"

Burke's eyes hardly left the bandage while he busied himself getting the canister of fuel. They widened when Canby pulled the sticky cloth from the wound, peeling it by degrees from the long gashes.

"Hell, Thomas, did you wrestle it?"

"Thought he was dead," Canby said, pouring kerosene on the cuts and wiping them clean with the bloodied handkerchief. The kerosene burned deep. "Fetch me a bedsheet, would you?"

Burke came back with a sheet from the jail's single cell, tearing it into strips as he walked. He looked out the window into the dark. "Have you brought it back?"

"I buried it."

"Folks'll want to see the carcass."

"Is my word not good enough?" Canby asked. His eyes burned brightly on Burke's face until the older man looked away.

"Sure, sure," Burke said, not sounding so. His eyes still on the black window, he said, "Mountain folk are different, Thomas. It's not personal, but you ain't from around here. Some of these families been here a hundred, hundred and fifty years. You got to ease into their trust."

"I thought I'd've eased in after nearly four years."

Anse smiled. "You still on Atlanta time. Four years ain't a drop in the bucket up here."

Burke yanked open one of the desk's drawers and pulled a

bottle of Jameson whiskey from it, along with two glasses mottled with fingerprints. "I'm grateful for your bringing this up from town," he said, offering Canby a half-filled glass. "Beats the hell out of anything that ever came out of Gilleland's still." He raised his glass to Canby and said thoughtfully before taking a sip, "I haven't passed blood in months."

"To your health, then," Canby said, raising his glass.

There was a single knock at the door and then it opened, the lanky frame of John Dodson nearly reaching to the top of the doorway. He had taken off his shopkeeper's apron and was hatless. A supper napkin hung from where he had stuffed it into the pocket of his striped pants and he held a yellow telegraph paper in his left hand.

"This just came over the wire for you, Sheriff," he said.

"Come in, John," Canby said. "Like a drink?"

"Wish I could. I'm already in a bad spot for leaving in the middle of supper." He held the paper out to Canby. "It's from Atlanta."

Dodson studied Canby's face as he read the message. "Atlanta. Don't they even stop to eat down there?"

Canby spoke without looking up. "Not if they can help it. They eat standing up, walking." But his voice trailed off when he saw the telegraph was from Vernon Thompson, his old sergeant. Vernon had made chief the year before Canby left the force and Canby had never quite adjusted to the news of his old mentor presiding over the department, knowing what he knew. How Vernon could be among them without being of them was a mystery. Canby read:

VERY SENSITIVE CASE DEVELOPING HERE [STOP]
NEED AN OLD HAND WITH NO CONNECTIONS
TO CURRENT FORCE [STOP]

"Can you believe all them words? A telegraph that long costs something," Dodson was saying. "They spend money like they'd as soon burn it."

SUSPECT THAT PERPETRATOR MAY BE INSIDE
MAN [STOP] CANT SAY MORE OVER THE LINE
[STOP]

"You going to wire him back tonight?" Dodson asked.

Canby shook his head. "You go on back and finish your supper, John. I'll come by in half an hour, if that's not too late."

Dodson shot Burke a look before he turned to go. "Goddamned Atlanta," he muttered as he shut the door.

Canby stared at the telegraph's last lines.

MEET AT POWERS FERRY SIX OCLOCK WEDNES-
DAY [STOP] KNOW YOU WILL BE RELUCTANT BUT
NEED HELP [STOP] YOUR FRIEND, V

Canby read the telegraph over once more before wadding it into a ball and tossing it into the cuspidor. Burke was looking at him expectantly.

"Nothing to fret over, Anse," he said. "Just an old friend saying hello the only way he knows how." He picked up the bottle of Jameson and poured them each another round. He grimaced when he tossed back his glass, whether from the burn of the whiskey or the thought of his reply to Vernon, he was not sure. But he knew that when he stopped by Dodson's store, Dodson would make him tap out the message himself. The language was not the kind Dodson cared to have sent out on his line:

VERNON [STOP] GO TO HELL

TWENTY MINUTES LATER Canby stood on the board porch of the sheriff's office, watching Burke make his way down the dark street. He saw Burke list sideways and worried that the big man might have started on the Jameson before he returned from the mountains, but as the deputy moved on he could just make out a dark pile of horse manure that Burke had weaved around. Canby looked up and saw that the sky was overcast, no moon and no stars. This street so dark, he thought, because it had no gaslights, had only the lamplight from the houses to illumine it.

As the sound of Burke's padding footsteps on the dirt road faded, Canby turned back to the office door and shut it tightly. The door had no lock, the jail's only keys being the two that opened the cell and the barred gun cabinet. He jingled them in his pocket and thought about going home, lighting a lamp, and pulling down one of his father's old books, maybe Marcus Aurelius, and reading until he felt like sleep. *You will find rest from vain fancies if you perform every act in life as though it were your last*, that had been one of Angus's favorites.

The words sounded in his head as he walked down the wooden steps, thinking of his itinerary for tomorrow, the last day of September. There was one property line dispute to be presented before the county judge first thing in the morning, then the monthly trade day that afternoon. If he could get through the day without locking any of the local farmers up for public inebriation, he and Anse would probably spend the evening at the jail playing dominoes. It being payday, he supposed he would break out another bottle of Jameson around dark.

Canby stood in the middle of the quiet street for a moment, looking up at the gray clouds scudding across the sky, the dim hulk of the mountains in the distance, then walked quickly to Dodson's store. He knocked on the glass of the double doors before letting himself in. Dodson, who had been drowsing at the telegraph table, sat up and looked at him through tired eyes.

Canby wrote out his message longhand on the form and gave it to Dodson. The storekeeper's finger began tapping out the message, the clicking key's rhythm insistent and sonorous at the same time. While Dodson worked, Canby counted out change on the form, dropping the coins one at a time on the paper.

ALL RIGHT THEN [STOP] BUT NO POLITICS

As he put the last nickel down on the table, Canby saw Dodson glancing at his forearm.

"Damn," Canby said, looking down at his arm. In spite of the kerosene and the fresh bandage, the blood had started to flow again.

SUMMONS

October 3

CANBY WATCHED THE LAST TARDY STUDENT DISAP-
pear into the Vinings schoolhouse, the door slapping shut
behind him, before he stepped out of the sycamores where he'd
tied his horse. He crossed the dirt yard out front of the white
clapboard building and sidled up to the closest of the windows.
Looked inside.

She was at the front of the room, harried he could tell by
the milling students, the boys especially slow to settle down,
to take their places at the desks. A row of Latin conjugations across the slate blackboard behind her, legacy of what
Angus had taught her, taught him, in the little schoolhouse
on Whitehall Street, in the way back before the war. She had
always been the better student, *il migliore*, his father had loved
to say. Now she shuffled the papers on her desk, stacked them,
and held her hands out for the students to come to order. A
white blouse with the collar up to her delicate chin. Chestnut
hair pinned atop her head. Eyes flashing green as she smiled
at her scholars.

His plan was to watch her for a while, as he'd watched her candlelit house last night, grateful that no suitor came calling before she snuffed the lights at ten. To watch and see whether he could tell, in the daylight, if she carried any bitterness in her face, the resolute cast of defiant disappointment that was the lifelong portion of a jilted Georgia lady. He thought her better than that. Hoped he would be confirmed and that he could wait out here until she dismissed the students for lunchtime, to have a word before he went down into Atlanta.

Inside, Julia had quieted the students and stood in front of her desk with a little girl standing before her, facing the class, Julia's hands on her thin shoulders. "This is Lauren Clay," Julia said. "Who just came up from Savannah. Her father works on the railroad."

The little girl nodded at her new classmates, shy, solemn.

"Tell us something about yourself, Lauren."

"My name is Lauren," the girl said, her speech impaired, the *r* in her name slurred. One of the boys snickered and Julia shot him a fierce look.

"I swap my *r*'s for my *w*'s," the girl said as she looked around the room. "It's something I've been working on."

Working said as *wuwking*, straightforward and earnest. Canby saw that Julia's eyes had misted as she patted the girl's shoulders.

"Spoken in the voice God gave her," Julia said as she guided the girl to her desk, "and not a thing wrong with it."

And then Canby saw that Julia was looking through the window at him. He nodded to her through the glass and she nodded back just as slowly, studied him a long moment before moving back to the front of the room to begin her lesson.

He decided then that he would wait there until lunchtime. Thought that it might be prudent, though, to greet her from the saddle, sitting his horse in the dirt yard, lest she emerge from the schoolhouse bearing a poker or skillet to launch as a missile his way.

He walked under the shadow of Vinings Mountain, her voice clear behind him as she led the students through their recitations, to the trees where the horse waited. Her voice faltered once and he stopped in the silence, listening, until she resumed the lesson.

He could not say whose work was the more important, hers or his own, he thought as he put his boot in the stirrup and climbed into the saddle. Yes, he thought, on considering it for a moment. Yes, he could.

UNDER THE NEARLY full moon the Chattahoochee glowed silver, pale light winking from the chop of its currents and eddies. As Canby stood on the northern bank and rang the bell for the ferry he could see across the way the dim outline of the black police hansom, lit by its two flickering lamps, and, faintly, the red ember of Vernon's cigar flaring and ebbing in the night. He watched as S. W. Power poled the raft across the river, the current tugging against the ferry's creaking guide rope. Power and the raft moved over the silvery surface of the water as though crawling across the surface of the moon.

How different the landscape was here, Canby thought, even this far out of the city, from the true mountains to the north. This was where the Appalachian Range ended, winding down to a series of ridges that stretched in a long slow descent to Atlanta. The mountain at Vinings the last of them, five miles behind him now. When Julia had set her scholars free for the lunch hour and stepped out on the schoolhouse's little porch, he felt as though he had been frozen in amber, in time. She had just looked at him sadly, her hands on her hips and Vinings Mountain looming behind her.

"Four years," she said.

"And two months."

"Not nearly enough letters."

"I'd have written more if I'd had better news to relay."

Julia had sighed and come down the steps. He tethered his horse and they walked slowly down to Stillhouse Creek, under the canopy of sycamores that grew on Vinings Mountain. He saw that their leaves were beginning to yellow, to turn gold against the scaling ivory bark of the trees. Canby told her of the message from Vernon Thompson, explaining the prospects he saw in it.

"I have a chance to clear my name. *That* would make me fit as a suitor."

Julia had stopped along the trail, shaking her head. She'd reached up and touched the scar on his cheek. "They'll burn you again," she'd said.

The ferry banged against the upstream pilings of the dock and Canby led his horse onto it, patting the animal's neck to calm it as the raft moved with the currents. He paid his fare and noted that Power had aged a great deal in the years since he'd last seen him; his hair and beard had gone nearly white and his eyes were red-rimmed. Yet still he seemed to have the strength of a vigorous man, Canby thought, as he leaned against the pole and moved the weight of two men and a horse against the current, toward the other side. As they drew closer Canby saw the butt of Vernon's cigar arcing through the dim light, followed by the hansom lurching as he climbed down from it.

"Thomas Canby," Vernon said, walking to the river's edge. "Back from the dead."

"That's not exactly how I'd put it," Canby said, taking his hand. Vernon's handshake was almost weak and he winced under Canby's grip.

"See you're shaking hands like a country boy now."

"And you, like someone who shakes hands all day."

Vernon nodded and put his arm around Canby's shoulder, turning him toward the hansom. He whistled loudly and the door of Power's store swung open, a uniformed officer coming out of it. "Maddox, tie Canby's horse on the back, will you? Thomas, I believe you remember Maddox."

Canby nodded to the burly captain. "Good to see you, Thomas," Maddox said as he took the reins.

Canby did not answer, only climbed into the hansom and waited for the others. Vernon spoke quietly with Power for a moment, then the two men laughed at something Vernon said. Canby felt the hansom shift as Maddox climbed up to the seat in back.

Maddox cracked the reins as soon as Vernon was settled

on the seat beside Canby, steering the horses east on the old Stone Mountain road. Canby looked at Vernon's profile in the flickering light.

"Decatur is our first stop."

"Decatur? That's way the hell out of town."

"More time for us to talk. Have I mentioned that you're looking well?" Vernon said as he pulled a fresh cigar from his coat pocket. He offered it to Canby. Canby shook his head. Vernon put the cigar in his mouth and struck a match on the bottom of his shoe. In moments the cab was filled with smoke that collected up against the roof and hung there before wafting out into the night. Vernon began to cough, a deep hacking. He pulled a handkerchief from his pants pocket and spat into it.

"Too many cigars," Canby said. "Your voice is beginning to sound rusty."

Vernon nodded, his face still red. "You're right. But it seems like they're the only thing that gives me real pleasure anymore." He waved a hand against the smoke. "Beside the point. You seem well, Thomas, and I'm glad of it. The mountain air must agree with you."

"It does."

"But God, what do you *do* up there?"

"What if I told you I went to the woods because I wanted to live deliberately?" Canby said, wondering if Vernon would catch the reference.

"Bullshit. You ran away, though I can't say I blame you much. Quoting Emerson don't make it any truer."

"That was Thoreau, his protégé. You should read the book about Walden Pond."

Vernon waved a hand absently. "I live in Atlanta," he said. "I can't imagine it up there—what do you do besides chasing poachers? I'd bet your biggest case has been a sheep-mounting farmer's son."

Canby could feel the color rising in his cheeks but he fought it down. "Do you know what I have found out up there, Vernon? I like it."

"Sure you do," Vernon said, then caught Canby's eye and held it in the steely way that had ended so many interrogations over the years. "That's why a single telegram brought you all these miles. And back to Atlanta."

Canby looked away. He counted five breaths before he spoke. "Tell me about the case."

"Certainly. No offense intended, Thomas." He put a hand on Canby's knee, patting it. When he spoke again his voice was lower, difficult to hear over the creaking of the wheels. "We have a madman on the loose."

Canby laughed. "For that you want me back? Since when is a madman in Atlanta cause for concern?"

But Vernon did not smile. "I've seen the victims, Thomas. And I've had some nightmares since." He shook his head slowly. "What does that tell you?"

"A great deal."

"Right. As it happens, I found the first of them myself."

"You did?"

"I did. Tell that to anyone who thinks the chief spends all his time in the office. Do you remember Alonzo Lewis?"

"The barber? He was doing very well for himself, last I heard."

"Very well, indeed. Last year he expanded his shop, hired six new barbers, and took up most of the business space in the Markham Hotel. Eighteen chairs in all. He also owned half the real estate in Summer Hill. Two entire blocks of rental property east of South Pryor Street. Even had a loan business, conducted under the table and off the books. He was in all likelihood the richest Negro in Atlanta."

"Was?"

"Was until the late evening of September seventeenth, or the early hours of the eighteenth. I went to his shop in the Markham before opening, as I do for my shave every Friday, and found the door unlocked. He was inside.

"No cash taken from the box, although I counted nearly two hundred dollars in it. And Alonzo's body on the floor in a pool of blood the size of a billiard table, cold as a fish."

Canby nodded, piecing the details together. "Lewis kept no rough company, did he? And the Markham is not a place where your criminal element could pass freely. Too much traffic, and too much of it upscale. And no robbery. There's no clear motive."

"You haven't gotten too rusty chasing cattle. No motive except for this: I said Alonzo's body was on the floor. His head, however, was on the marble counter, swaddled in towels. He still had his spectacles on and the razor that had done the work was arranged around his neck like a bow tie. There was a letter, an *M*, carved into his forehead, Thomas."

Vernon traced the letter in the air with his cigar. "All my years on the force, all the wives beaten, all the suicides and poisonings, I've not seen anything like that."

Canby thought he could feel the temperature of the night air drop.

"I'm surprised you haven't read about it in the papers."

"No one in Ringgold reads the Atlanta papers much. Least of all me."

Vernon nodded. "Well, that's not the story you'd have read, anyway."

"And why not?"

Vernon's face took on a nearly weary cast. "I have been getting pressure, Thomas. If you did read the papers, you'd have heard about the cotton fair the city's putting on. In fact, you'd have *been* hearing about it. International Cotton Exposition, they're calling it. Henry Grady's been crowing about it in the *Constitution* for months."

"You know my opinion of Grady."

"Indeed I do. But it's not just Grady who has skin in this game. It's to be the biggest thing Atlanta's ever seen, that Georgia's ever seen. Dozens of the city's prominent men have invested in the exposition—Negroes among them. Alonzo was one."

"And so . . ."

"And so I took the cash out of the box and, God forgive me, put Alonzo's head back with the body. Then I grabbed the first boy I saw on the sidewalk and sent him for Jim Fitzsimmons. Stood watch out front of the shop myself until he got there. So the coroner got to the scene before anybody else on the force, before Alonzo's people came in for work. We arranged a towel around Alonzo's neck and reported it as a slashed throat. Fitzsimmons did the embalming himself."

"But the *M*, you couldn't make that go away."

"No. I had a probable scenario, though. Fitzsimmons and I figured some drunk peckerwood in town for the expo dragged himself back to the hotel while Alonzo was closing up shop, wanting a shave, and Alonzo sassed him. This old boy, not being as progressive as an Atlanta citizen, didn't cotton to it, so he took Alonzo's own razor and did him with it."

"And then emptied the cashbox."

"Why not? There would be no witness."

"What about the *M*?"

"Alonzo was a mulatto, you could tell it by a glance. Our boy from the outlying districts didn't care much for this black man, nearly as white as you and me and wearing a gold watch chain and cuff links, telling him when he could or couldn't get a shave. He was mad as hell, and inebriated, and thought he'd make a point."

"That is complete hogwash."

"It certainly is. But Henry Grady was glad to help out on that one. And so that's how it got reported."

"He's got a precedent of publishing lies."

"Grady's got the best interests of Atlanta in mind. Always has."

"I hope you'd make an exception to that in my case."

Vernon looked uncomfortable. "He erred there. We all do, sooner or later. I hate it that the stakes were so high for you. But we have an opportunity to set that straight now. You see, Thomas, every spare man on the force will be out at Oglethorpe Park, covering the exposition. This is the first real chance I've had to bring you back. Now we have a good shot at trying to right things for you."

"I'm not at all sure of that."

"I am," Vernon said. "Sure as I can be." He pulled an envelope from his vest pocket and handed it to Canby. "Your retainer. And you'll have quarters at Hannibal Kimball's new place. It's straight-up first-class. European fixtures, water closets, even heated water in the baths."

Canby squeezed the envelope. It was thick. "Two hundred dollars?"

"Thereabouts," Vernon said. He tossed his cigar out the window. "I know you've never cared much for procedure, Thomas, because you know as well as I do that procedure can get your neck wrung in a town like Atlanta. Atlanta moves too fast to do things by the book. And God help us, when we found the second one Friday, we knew we were dealing with a different kind of beast."

Canby found himself leaning forward in his seat as Vernon told him of the events of Friday night, when L. J. Dempsey's wife had grown concerned about her husband not being home in time for supper, as was his custom. It being payday, however, she gave him an hour, after which she folded the tablecloth over the meal she had prepared and walked through Jennings-town to Dempsey's office. She let herself into the office at seven o'clock and found her husband of fourteen years sprawled back in his desk chair, his throat cut.

Canby raised his hand. "Not severed this time?"

"Just cut, with a week's worth of cash payments for burial insurance stuffed into the incision."

"Burial insurance, you said. Was Dempsey also a Negro?"

Vernon nodded.

"How much money do you figure he had?"

"The city records show he paid nearly as much in taxes as Alonzo did."

"Had he invested in the exposition as well?"

Vernon nodded. "Quite heavily."

"Another *M*?"

"No. An *A* this time."

"So there will be more."

"Until he finishes this goddamned spelling bee of his."

Canby thought about crimes of passion, the only kind of crimes in his experience that did not somehow revolve around money. But the disfigurement of the bodies, the elaborate violence involved, was no typical kind of passion.

"I figure we've got a serious disagreement running in our Negro community."

"That could be," Canby said. "But I'm uneasy about the money."

"Ah, Thomas, that's your prejudice talking."

"You know it's not prejudice. It's pragmatism. You've just told me of crimes where hundreds of dollars were left at the scene. That makes no sense." Canby looked out the window, at the dark pine trees that lined the road like sentinels. "What rate of interest do you figure Alonzo charged his borrowers?"

"Enough to shame the Citizen's Bank, I'd bet."

"Can a Negro even sit down in the Citizen's Bank to make an application? Who is the black man in Atlanta who could afford to leave so much money behind?"

"These are new times for all of us in Atlanta, Thomas. There are more opportunities than ever before, for black and white. But we are now short two such affluent black men."

"Black *and* white? That's your political side talking. I know you better. I remember the walkout you led when the Republicans tried to integrate the force back in Reconstruction."

"That was a long time ago. This is a different era. Just this week, in fact, we added our first Negro officer to the force."

Canby turned to look at his companion. "Under your watch? I can hardly believe it."

Vernon kept his eyes on the road out front. "I change with the times."

In spite of himself, Canby began to smile. "Vernon, you are always a step ahead of me. When would I begin working with this man?"

Vernon reached for another cigar. "Tomorrow."

"And you called me down from Ringgold because no one on the force will—"

"I sent for you because no one else will work with him," Vernon said, lighting his cigar.

"Did you hire this man of your own volition, or was there pressure from elsewhere?"

"Does that make any material difference?"

"No, it does not. I just wish you'd done it at my urging, years ago."

Vernon continued to look straight ahead, his eyes narrowing. Canby studied the older man's profile.

"I wonder from whence it came, this pressure," Canby said.

"These days, most any question you ask, the answer is, the exposition. That's all I'll say on it."

Canby nodded. He knew Vernon would not be pushed any further. "If there is a Negro murderer, it makes sense to track him with one of his own, doesn't it? For public perception among the blacks, at least."

"This man is no common Negro," Vernon said. "I do not like him. He operates on some other kind of currency. Never been in a lick of trouble. Doesn't even drink, so far as I can tell. I'd not have known of him at all except he's been the janitor at the station nearly two years."

"A model citizen."

"He would be, but he's got these notions. Never just pushing a broom, without his ear is cocked for police business. Always listening in. And now, first week with a badge, he turns out to be the first of us on the scene at Dempsey's murder. Tell me that is not suspicious?"

"A good detective would have been there."

Vernon grunted, then turned and looked Canby in the eye. "Who do you think was the boy out front of the Markham?"

Canby felt the skin of his neck tightening.

"Atlanta ain't that small of a town, Thomas," Vernon said.

THE DECATUR INN was aglow with light as the hansom pulled up to it, the horses' shoes ringing on the cobblestones of the drive as Maddox guided them under the inn's porte cochere. Vernon stepped out of the cab quickly and held a hand out to Canby.

"Do we have an understanding? Can I tell the men inside that you're on the case?" Vernon smiled.

Canby thought he could sense another shift in the temperature of the night air, but he quickly dismissed it as the sensation of his own blood rising, perhaps his old ambition stirring again. "I suppose you can," he said. "Anything to help an old friend."

"Oh, I don't suppose I'm much of a friend, Thomas," he said as he dusted off the shoulders of Canby's coat, his smile fading, "or I wouldn't have brought you into this vile business." He put an arm around Canby and guided him toward the door.

Vernon made his way deftly through the crowd of cooks and waiters in the kitchen, propelling Canby through the white uniforms and black faces, past steaming pots and blazing cookstoves, toward the sound of dozens of men's voices in the dining room.

"Who's in there, Vernon?"

"Atlanta's first citizens. Prominent businessmen, mostly. A few others."

"What kind of others?"

"First we enjoy a fine dinner with these good men of the city, then an after-dinner drink with the Ring."

Canby stopped short. "You told me no politics."

"You have to *navigate* a city like Atlanta, Thomas. And that means politicians."

Canby looked out one of the kitchen windows toward the portico. Maddox was gone. He could just make out his own mare, trailing the hansom on its tether, moving out of the light of the drive.

"Shall we?" Vernon said.

The inn's banquet hall was packed with bearded and flush-faced men bent close to one another to be heard over the din. Vernon pointed out two senators—John B. Gordon and Joseph Brown—both of them stern-looking and huddled cabalistic in one corner of the room, their beards nearly touching. Canby saw that the governor, Alfred Colquitt, was here, too, holding a glass of champagne and talking with a man Canby recognized after a moment as Samuel Inman, the cotton broker. The men had hardly aged since Canby had last seen them on the streets of the city. If anything, they looked more vigorous, Brown's white beard excepted, and more prosperous than before, as if time stood still for men of such means and allowed them to gather more power to themselves.

A Negro waiter offered Canby a flute of champagne on a silver tray, but he declined and requested whiskey instead.

"Whiskeys to be served after supper, sir, with coffee and liqueurs."

"Fine, then. Nothing, thanks."

"You are on the job, after all," Vernon said, taking a flute from the tray and raising it to his mouth.

Canby did not reply. His attention was fixed on a man standing nearby, just the profile of his roundish, clean-shaven face visible. The man was holding forth theatrically, moving his arms as he told a story Canby could just hear over the babble of voices.

"So there I was, down in Tallahassee, waiting for the results of the recount. Everyone thought the election would go to Tilden, of course, but we were waiting for the announcement from the Florida canvassing board to be sure. Well, by the time they'd announced Hayes as the winner I was already in my buggy hightailing it to the telegraph office. We were there first and the *Constitution* had the news as soon as the *New York Herald*, by gracious."

"Go on, Henry. Tell them the best part."

Henry Grady smiled. "Well, we'd scooped the others, all right, but I wanted to be certain the *Constitution* got her due. I spent the next half hour transmitting pages from a spelling book."

"He did it to tie up the line, you see!"

Grady sipped from a glass of iced tea while he waited for the laughter to subside. "The boys from the *Chicago Tribune* have never forgiven me."

But the smile faded from his lips when he turned to see Canby glaring at him from across the room.

Canby was starting toward Grady, pulling against Vernon's hand on his arm, when a tall man in a white suit began tapping a butter knife against a glass. The sound carried over the din clearly and the men began to quiet.

"Gentlemen!" the man said. "May we take our seats? Bishop Drew will convene with a prayer."

Vernon led Canby to the table, taking seats for them next to the tall man.

"Robert," Vernon said, "may I introduce Thomas Canby, who has agreed to help us?"

Canby took the man's hand and found his handshake as strong as a country man's. As they sat and the bishop began his prayer, the man leaned in to Canby's ear and whispered: "This could take a while. Drew is the head of the Georgia Diocese. One only attains such a position by praying ardently and at great length."

Canby smiled and looked up at the bishop's smooth face, his eyes shut tightly, like those of every man around the table save his new acquaintance.

"What is it that you do, Robert?" he whispered.

"Oh, I own a couple of cotton gins. But my heart is in the new industries. My chief concern is Dixie Light."

"Dixie Light? Then you are Colonel Robert Billingsley. I should have known your face. I beg your pardon."

Billingsley smiled. "Think nothing of it. I try to stay out of the papers as much as I can. I'm certain you understand that."

Canby looked over at the man sharply, but his smile was kind enough to make Canby see that the comment was not intended as a barb. As the bishop continued his prayer, Billingsley leaned close to Canby's ear.

"I've talked with Vernon about you at length. He and I both see this case as an opportunity for your vindication. What happened in '77 was inevitable. The Radicals had to go. But it was unfortunate that you got swept out with the trash. It must have been extremely difficult for you to endure."

Canby looked into the man's clear blue eyes. "They ruined my name."

Billingsley nodded slowly, his eyes sad. "Perhaps with this case you shall get it back."

"Amen," Bishop Drew said.

"Amen," Billingsley echoed.

A half dozen waiters stepped forward from their places

against the walls and began removing the covers from the tureens at each man's place. The scent of turtle soup filled the room as the men fell to their food, and Henry Grady rose and began to speak.

"Let me begin my remarks by saying good evening to all of you collectively," Grady said. "I hope you'll forgive me if I go on at some length tonight. I would not talk so much, gentlemen, except that my father was an Irishman, and my mother was a woman."

Grady smiled at the laughter around the table.

"I have been asked to discuss the prospects for our International Cotton Exposition tonight, and I do so with an energy and optimism greater than I have felt in years."

A man near the head of the table snorted. "Tell that to the exhibitors. A third of the buildings aren't even framed up yet."

Grady shook his head, still smiling. "Let us not forget what that entity we call the Atlanta Spirit can accomplish. And what it can accomplish in a short time. Our story begins with the Atlanta Spirit, which lifted us, phoenix-like, from the ashes of a devastated city and brought us to this point, whence we will stage an exhibition fit to astonish the nations.

"I remind you that after General Sherman left our fair city in ruins, Atlanta's treasury had in it the grand sum of a dollar sixty-five," Grady said, nodding to the rueful chuckles around the room for a moment before smiling and adding, "and that was in Confederate currency, gentlemen."

Grady held his hands out for quiet.

"Our city was then overrun by Reconstruction. You know the story well: scalawags, carpetbaggers, and Radical Republicans dictated the lives and fortunes of white southerners anxious for peace and the return to prosperity. When the earnest Atlantan sought an honest government and the opportunity to regain his fortunes, his beseeching was answered with an upstart government riddled with corruption. Graft and embezzlement, even outright extortion, became the rule of the day. Alongside the Radicals, Negroes came to hold high office, woefully unprepared for such office in the best of cases, illiterate to the point of imbecility in the worst."

And the old guard of the Ring, Canby thought, found itself on the outside for the first time. He studied the faces around the table, how they followed Grady's account of their ouster. They must have felt like they'd been gelded.

"The siege of Atlanta had been terrible, the burning of our city the most trying of tribulations," Grady went on. "But we soon learned that the worst was not over. Our darkest hour stretched out into a day, then into a night.

"But as we know that every night has its dawn, so came a new era for Atlanta. The men we came to call the Redeemers roused themselves to collective action and accomplished in a few short months what would have taken years had they not been moved, together, by the Atlanta Spirit. And the new constitution of 1877 set things right once again."

Canby grimaced at the mention of '77. He couldn't help himself.

"The Negro, the scalawag, the Radical, were swept out of office and white southerners once again claimed their birthright. Many of those good Atlantans are gathered here, in this room, tonight."

Grady paused long enough to take a sip of tea. The waiters came forward again, removing the tureens and replacing them with plates of oysters. They handled the china almost silently and Canby wondered what they were making of the speech.

"And now we face a new challenge that promises further glorious results," Grady resumed. "Our International Cotton Exposition was conceived on a scale unseen thus far in the United States, and particularly in the South. It is the South's first world fair. We have set aside nineteen acres in Oglethorpe Park for the site. We are completing twenty-seven buildings on those acres, including a model cotton factory that is to be thoroughly modern, down to the latest items of technology— the newest gins, the freshest patents. We have sold nearly two hundred thousand dollars of stock in the exposition, including a pledge of two thousand dollars from our friend William Tecumseh Sherman. There is even talk—this should not leave this room, gentlemen—that General Sherman might make a personal appearance at the exposition. All of this accomplished in one hundred working days. Gentlemen, that number alone speaks volumes about Atlanta. *One hundred days.*

"So I urge you not to despair over the state of the I.C.E. at this early hour of the exposition. Though we are on the eve of our debut, and our hopes have thus far exceeded our returns, we have no cause for despair. I say it is time once again to summon the Atlanta Spirit and save the hour."

There was only the sound of silverware for a moment after Grady sat down. Canby pushed his dish of oysters away. Slowly, a small man with spectacles and a black mustache rose and gently placed his folded napkin on the table.

"I cannot match Mister Grady's oratory, so I will try to stick with simple facts," he said in an accent too clipped and swift to be local. "The exposition opens in two days. We expected crowds of thousands for our preview days; our total attendance has been just over one hundred. Our subscription of stock has been excellent, but our revenues may never earn out that money. We will need to keep the exposition open for a year at this rate if we hope to break even. We are at present nearly a quarter of a million dollars in debt."

There were murmurs of assent mixed with a general grumbling of disagreement. Grady rolled his eyes. "A year!" someone cried. "Sit down, Greenberg."

Greenberg nodded and looked down at his plate as it was replaced, silently, by one of the waiters.

"I will sit down. But first may I remind you of the Greek myth of Atalanta, one of our city's namesakes?"

Someone groaned, but Greenberg pressed on. "Do you remember it, gentlemen? As the Greeks tell it, she was known for her speed. But she was defeated in a race when three golden apples were thrown at her feet and she stopped to gather them up. Three golden apples—a distraction that drew her from her main purpose. Have we committed our Atlanta to a similar fate?"

Greenburg seemed shocked by the sudden silence that greeted his question. Canby knew then that the man must indeed be a late arrival to Atlanta, for since his own childhood he had been raised among a tacit but bedrock understanding that disparaging capital in Atlanta was anathema. He saw that

Vernon was looking at Greenberg almost sadly. Billingsley's expression was inscrutable.

Greenberg pushed his spectacles up on his nose. "What I mean to say, gentlemen, is that we have perhaps overreached with this project. Think of the terrible toll if our venture fails. Why must we insist on competing with older and more established cities? Do we aim to become the next Boston, the next New York?"

But Greenberg's voice was drowned out as the room burst into violent debate, with Grady trying in vain to quiet the men. The uproar continued through the main course of venison and pheasant, diminished only slightly over the cheeses and ices, and then carried on through the last of the desserts. Nothing was resolved.

"WE SHOULD HAVE given that Jew the bum's rush," Senator Gordon said as he cut the end off a cigar. "Who invited him, anyway?"

"I did," Grady said, looking for once a bit sheepish. "Greenberg opened the new pencil factory on South Forsyth Street, John. The Georgia Pencil Company. He's going to be a prominent citizen, like it or not."

Canby studied the faces of the men seated about the small round table. In the long minutes since the parlor's paneled pocket doors had been pulled shut by the last of the waiters the room had begun to fill with clouds of cigarette and cigar smoke—and worse, with the backroom talk of men accustomed to making decisions by secret quorums such as this one that would affect thousands. Canby decided he had sat among the members of the Ring for as long as he could without speaking.

"Where's he from?" he asked.

Grady looked at him directly for the first time. "Brooklyn, New York, originally. He spent the last few years in England learning the manufacturing trade."

"Another fairly recent arrival, then. Like yourself."

"I've always said that if a man has ability, Atlantans do not care if he was hatched in a stump. But no, Mister Canby, Leon Greenberg cannot claim an Atlanta raising, like you. He is, rather, someone who has come and *stayed*."

"I would have stayed," Canby said, hearing his voice trail off. "Perhaps you'll drive him off, too, in time."

"Gentlemen," Billingsley said, his voice conciliatory, "what's past is past. Our interest is in the present, and the future." He leaned over his crossed leg to snub his cigarette out in an ashtray on the table and nodded to Hannibal Kimball.

"Mister Canby, as director general of the Cotton Exposition, I thank you for accepting this assignment," Kimball said, "and I give you my personal assurance that the members of the Ring will compensate you generously for your time and expenses." He slid a key across the table to Canby. "That is for your suite at the Kimball House, sir. A sixth-floor penthouse. All expenses will be handled by me personally."

Canby looked to Vernon. "Will I not be back on the city's force?"

"None of this is on the city," Vernon said. "You're off the books."

"We want this handled as expeditiously as possible, Mister Canby," Kimball said. "Chief Thompson has fashioned the title of special inspector for you. He tells me there is no precedent for such a position on the force, so you will have carte blanche as to how you proceed. But your progress must be, as I said, expeditious.

"The concerns voiced by Mister Greenberg this evening are legitimate. The exposition is in dire straits. Men stand to be ruined if attendance is not robust. I have invited the governors of every state in the Union to attend for a day in November, and as Grady said, General Sherman has indicated that he might join us as well. Those will help, but they are weeks away. And they will do precious little if word spreads that we have some kind of maniac at large in the city. Already the Negro community is in an uproar. There are intimations that they will not support the exposition so long as these crimes remain unsolved."

"Hang the niggers," Gordon said. "It was foolish to count on them in the first place. What Negro would pay to see a cotton exposition after he's been picking it all day?"

"Regardless," Kimball said, "we are in a delicate situation that must be resolved."

"Mister Grady has agreed to cooperate fully in his coverage of your investigation," Billingsley said. "Care will be taken in how this affair reaches the public's eye."

Canby smiled at Grady, who seemed suddenly engrossed by a pattern on the table's surface.

"I have your word on that? No meddling?"

Grady scowled. "None. But I'm on record as saying you're not the man for the job."

"Hell, yes. I second that," Gordon said, looking around the table. "This man served in the goddamned Union army!" Gordon turned his fierce face to Canby. "I mean no personal insult, sir."

Vernon stood and put a hand on Canby's shoulder. "I vouch for Canby. He will see this through."

"Damn it, Billingsley," Gordon said, craning his neck toward the older man, "you were there with us at Gettysburg! I can handle reconciliation so far, but—"

Billingsley's eyes were clear through the smoke as he leveled them on Gordon. "I was there, and I saw blue dead on the field as well as gray. Let the dead bury their dead, I say. This matter has already been decided."

"Indeed, it has," Kimball said, rising wearily from his chair. "Business is business. And this is big business." He nodded to the men around the table. "Gentlemen, good night. Mister Canby, good luck. Atlanta has placed her trust in you."

The others stood, too, and began to file out of the paneled doors, hands on each others' shoulders, voices sliding easily back into the tone of cultivated banter common to Atlanta's men of means, as though there had been no tension in the meeting, as though the success of this and every future venture were ultimately assured.

As he followed Vernon out of the smoky room, Canby could already feel it—the sense of being carried on a tide to a destination beyond his choosing. It was, at its core, the same feeling he'd had through his time in the army: the sense of being propelled into another action by the wills of men removed from the fray, who would never be touched by the dirty work of its execution. That these men chose to give it a name as benign as the Atlanta Spirit did not change the nature of the tide. He knew that by any name, it was power. And that its undercurrents were ruthless.

October 4

THE MORNING SUN SHONE INTO THE VALLEYS
between the buildings of downtown, glowing brightly on the
window glass as it crept down the stories toward the street
vendors setting up their wares on the board sidewalks. Canby
watched the inching progress of the light from his penthouse
window, trying to take in every detail of the city. From the top
floor of the Kimball House he could see nearly out to Ken-
nesaw Mountain, and from there and from every cardinal point
of the compass he could see railroad tracks emerging in the
distance and winding their way down through the hills toward
Atlanta, light glinting off the hard-polished steel of the rails.
Terminus had been the city's original name, because all the rail
lines ended here. Even the streets, in their motley arrangement
that defied the grid of city blocks he'd seen in other towns,
followed the rail lines in a crooked, crosshatched patchwork of
lines. And all the lines met in the building across Pryor Street
from the hotel, in the roundhouse where they terminated in a
convergence of metal that marked the city's center, its heart.

He liked Atlanta best in this light, the morning light that promised bustle and energy, hope for the day. It was the light that had greeted him and Angus each morning as they walked down Whitehall Street to open his father's little school. Angus would throw open the school doors and light the woodstove as Canby washed clean the slate board and they readied for the arrival of Angus's pupils, the day's work waiting to begin. In the early morning, in Atlanta, one felt that all things were possible.

He had not felt such promise last night, riding in from Decatur. Stone Mountain had loomed like a wall of iron off to their east, its vast face glowing dull gray in the moonlight. Canby had turned the conversation back to the new detective, the black man. Vernon's great experiment, or else gamble. A striver, Vernon called him, who scrimped his janitor's pay for tuition at Atlanta University, taking a class or two as often as he could manage. The son of slaves and born one himself, but ambitious: the type that might have a long-simmering resentment for the likes of Alonzo Lewis or L. J. Dempsey.

"You've helped him along quite a bit in that regard, haven't you?" Canby had asked. "You gave him a hell of a promotion."

"Indeed. He is the first of his kind. We'll turn up the heat on that kettle and see if it boils."

"*If* he's the killer."

Vernon had lowered his hat over his face and leaned farther back in his seat. "If he's not," Vernon said, "he'll make a hell of a decoy, won't he?"

Then Vernon had dozed, letting the champagne and the rocking of the hansom take their effect on him, leaving Canby to muse over what kind of black man might inflict such ruinous violence on two of his own. It struck him that what Vernon took for gut instinct could well be nothing more than ingrained prejudice. In Vernon's early years in the department, the officers were paid for each arrest they made. You did not need a crystal ball to guess which section of the segregated jail stayed the fullest in those days.

Then, as they crested the last rise of the Decatur road and headed down into town, Canby had watched the lights of smokestacks coughing soot and fire into the night, seen the sign at the city limits that read WELCOME TO ATLANTA. WE HOPE YOU'LL STAY AWHILE. Vernon had stirred when the horses' hooves began to clatter once the road gave way from dirt to macadam. Gaslights began to appear, flickering atop their poles along one side of the street.

Canby turned from the window at the sound of a knock on the door. It was nearly a morning's walk from one end of the suite to another, he thought, as the knock came again. His feet seemed to sink into the thick Brussels carpet as he picked his way around one piece of walnut furniture after another toward the door. When he opened it, the heavy door swung smoothly on its brass hinges.

A black man perhaps ten years his junior stood in the doorway, dressed in a simple suit of sage linen and with a matching hat held across his chest.

"Cyrus Underwood, sir," the man said, nodding.

Canby studied him for a moment, noted the smoothness of his cheeks, the cast of his eyes. Gauging whether they held any of what he had come to call the night sickness in them. Then he held out a hand. Underwood took it, uncomfortably.

"Come in, then."

"Can't come in the room, sir. Rooms in Kimball House are whites-only."

"Horseshit. Come in and wait while I get myself together."

Underwood stepped into the room, looking it over as he shut the door behind him. His eyes lingered for a moment on the sheet draped across the sofa where Canby had slept and on the pistols laid out on the coffee table in front of it. He watched as Canby strapped the holster holding his .32 Bulldog revolver across his chest, then pulled up his left pants leg and fitted a Colt's New Line pocket revolver into his boot.

"How many do you carry?" Canby asked.

Underwood shook his head. "They haven't issued me a side-arm yet, sir."

Canby paused in pulling his jacket over his shoulders. "You have a badge, don't you?"

"Yessir," Underwood said, holding it out proudly. "But Chief Thompson says we're to take things in stages. Right now I've just got a badge and a whistle."

Canby said, buttoning the jacket, "Perhaps we'll see about that today."

But then he thought about the telegram that the hotel steward had awakened him to read a half hour before, its terse description of the whore who'd been butchered in an upstairs room at Mamie O'Donnell's last night. That was to be their first destination today. And about Vernon's description of the two victims who had preceded her, the chief's suspicions of Underwood. He studied the black man as they left the room and made their way down the hall to the lift.

By the time the lift operator had shut the metal grate and the lift had groaned into its downward motion, Canby had qualified his misgivings. As they trundled down the dark shaft, passing one richly carpeted floor after another, he thought that if what Vernon had telegraphed about the new victim's body was true, the issue of arming Underwood was superfluous. If this Underwood were the man capable of such work with a knife, he had no need of a gun.

THEY WAITED AT the intersection of Pryor and Alabama streets for fifteen minutes as Canby tried in vain to hail one cab after another as the hacks spurred their horses past the white and black men standing together on the corner. Finally, Canby stepped out in front of an empty carriage, the driver already shaking his head as he drew back on the reins to avoid running him over.

"Can't carry colored."

"Today you can," Canby said. He held his badge out, close enough for the man to see its number—000—though he knew that the hack would not recognize it as the chief's own.

"Ain't going to do it, Officer. I got a regular clientele won't ride with me if I do."

Canby looked the carriage over closely. "Where's your license tag?"

"It's in here in the toolbox somewhere," the man said, beginning to look uncomfortable.

Canby scanned the light globes that framed the driver's seat.

Both of them were unmarked. "Why is your license number not painted on your lamps?"

The man shifted on his seat. "Been meaning to get to that," he muttered.

"All right, then. We'll have to impound this vehicle. Officer Underwood, you take the reins."

"You can't do it!" the hack cried. He seemed genuinely bewildered.

"Of course I can. You're in violation of a city ordinance. You could lose your license, as well," Canby said, "if you have one. Regardless, the cab gets impounded until the next court session."

"What about my horse? You going to impound him, too?"

Canby thought it over for a moment, then pulled the Bulldog from its holster. "No," he said as he cocked the hammer back and placed the barrel against the horse's broad forehead. "I'm going to shoot the fucking horse."

After that, the driver had set his horse in motion and Canby and Underwood rode in silence nearly to Wheat Street before the younger man spoke.

"This has been a rare morning for me, sir," Underwood said.

"How's that?"

"Well, it's not yet nine o'clock and I've already been to the top of the Kimball House and ridden near a mile in a car that ain't colored-only."

"Sounds like the start of a good day."

"Begging your pardon, sir, you don't act like you were raised in the South."

Canby studied the buildings outside for a moment before he spoke. "I was raised in it, but not of it. My father was from Ireland. He brought me up to think it is unnatural for one human being to own another. I suppose you could have called him eccentric."

From the corner of his eye, Canby saw the beginnings of a smile on Underwood's face as he turned to the window.

But he was not smiling as they saw the garish façade of Mamie O'Donnell's saloon loom above the street in front of them. Canby knocked on the roof of the cab for the hack to stop, then stepped out onto the clay road and studied the crowd of Negroes milling about the front of the place. Word had apparently gotten out and the community had gathered in collective witness to another murder of one of their own.

The saloon had once been a grand old house at the city's outskirts, but had been converted by gaudy signage and knocked-out walls to serve its present purpose. It was situated precisely where the macadamized road ended and the red clay road began, at the limits of white Atlanta but not yet into the Negro settlement of Shermantown—the perfect locale for collecting girls of either race and at a proper yet not inconvenient distance for the city's businessmen to come and go with discretion.

The Negroes seemed to be in restless motion, now surging toward the saloon's porch, where a giant of a man stood yelling at them to go away, then falling back when he reached for the bullwhip looped at his waist.

"Y'all get your asses on home!" the man shouted, his face reddened. "Ain't nothing to see, anyway. Get back!"

Someone in the crowd said something about the dead girl and the man uncoiled the whip in an instant. It lashed out over the crowd and snapped on the top of a head. Canby saw the black hair glisten a second later.

"Who's next?" the man bellowed.

Canby walked to the porch steps wearily, the Negroes parting to make way for him, and the hack forgotten as the driver pulled away without accepting payment from Underwood. Canby had worked another case here, a murder-suicide, back in '73 that still haunted him. Climbing the steps, he felt the weight of the saloon's history descend on him. He heard Underwood's steps behind him come up short as Canby faced the giant white man on the porch.

The man snarled at Canby through a beard streaked with tobacco juice. "What the fuck do you want? We're closed till sundown, partner."

Canby nearly reeled at the odor of rye fumes the man breathed out. He showed him his badge and the man backed up a step.

"I'm here to see the nothing that's here to see."

The man shook his head. "Mamie says only the chief himself comes through. No flatfeet."

"This is Vernon Thompson's badge. Stand aside."

The man crossed his massive arms across his chest, the bullwhip drooping alongside his leg. "Mamie said—"

"Aren't you Monte Amos? Jack's boy? You haven't turned out to be much."

The man spat on the porch boards and wiped at his beard with the back of a hand. Then he looked at Canby through watery eyes. "Yeah, I reckon I could have been an officer like Daddy. Or a detective on the take."

Canby took a deep breath and leaned in close. "If you make me bring Chief Thompson down here, I guarantee you'll spend the rest of the year locked up for prostitution, pandering, and whatever else I dig up inside."

Amos's stare faltered. "Be careful what you ask for, mister. You don't want to see it." His eyes were red-rimmed—more red, Canby realized, than from drink alone. After a moment, he straightened up and stepped out of the doorway.

"Nobody never could tell Thomas Canby what to do," he said. "You go on in and take your nigger-boy with you. I got a wager one of you'll come out screaming."

CANBY FELT a great inrushing of breath the moment he threw open the door, like a punch to his gut. He regretted it an instant later as his lungs filled with the smell of the room, a combined odor like that of a charnel house crossed with a skinning shed, the biting tang of spilled blood mixed with decay.

The room was furnished in bordello red, with heavy velvet draperies on the windows and furniture in the same material— all of it a deep crimson that made it difficult to distinguish where the upholstery was unmarked and where it was splattered with the blood that had been slung across the boudoir.

The dead woman lay in the bed.

But, Canby saw as his eyes moved across the room slowly and he stood frozen in the doorway, she was also on the couch, on the rug, and in the washbasin on the lingerie chest. What lay on the bed was not only headless but also eviscerated. Even from across the room he could see into the gash in her abdomen and note that the dark cavity of her torso was empty.

Behind him, he heard Underwood cough dryly, a sound deep in his throat not far from retching.

"Are you all right?" he asked without turning.

"I don't think I'll ever be all right again," Underwood said.

Canby's eyes fixed on the dead woman's intestines, which had been draped on the back of a settee like streamers. Below them, in the center of the cushions, lay the heart, its arteries neatly severed. He thought the black object in the washbasin was her liver, but beyond that, there was a profusion of organs he could not name. He stepped into the room carefully, watching his feet, and motioned for Underwood to do the same. He knew already, with a sense of pity and revulsion that made his stomach churn, that he would have to lift the head from its place.

Strangely, in this room awash in blood, the girl's hair was unmatted. It still glowed softly in the light of the gas lamp, lustrous, in black ringlets. It covered her face, which was buried in the intersection of her legs.

Canby gripped the curls, his fingers tightening reluctantly on them, and lifted. The hair came away in his hand. He stepped back quickly, nearly dropping the hair, and looked down at the scalp. But in place of a glistening skull he saw tufts of kinky hair, cut short. He turned his hand over and showed Underwood the inside of the black wig, its web of netting, then handed it to him. Underwood took it and held it between thumb and forefinger.

Canby sighed and put his hands on either side of the woman's head, over her ears. One of them was sticky with blood. With his eyes averted, he lifted the head, heavier than he would have expected, then looked around the room for a suitable place to set it. None seemed fitting. He was loath to approach the chest of drawers with the liver sitting dark and slick in the wash-bowl, so he put the head on the couch, tilting it back against the buttoned cushion.

From its new perch the head stared back at them balefully. The eyes, Canby thought, were nearly unbearable. Such a mixture of horror and pain frozen in them.

Back in the war he had known the fear of battle and he realized with bone-deep certainty that it was nothing next to this. Nothing next to even the stories of the veterans who'd seen every battle. Staring down the maws of shot-loaded cannon, charging into the musket-bristling Hornet's Nest, could not compare to looking into the eye of the man who had done this.

And there, above the eyes, were two perpendicular cuts, forming an *L*. The flesh had already gone gray at the edges of the incisions, but the letter was clear, cut into the skin so forcefully that Canby could make out a scrape the blade had made on the skull beneath.

He lowered himself to a crouch and stared into the glazed eyes. They had been chestnut in color. Then he looked up at Underwood, gauging his reaction to the scene. His pallor was reassuring, but his own brown eyes were fixed on the body, on the dead woman's thigh, where Canby now saw that a bite had been taken out of the soft flesh high on the leg, the outlines of the teeth as clearly limned as a bite from an apple. Underwood turned, a hand to his mouth, and bolted out the door.

Underwood's foot slid at the doorway, his shoe slipping on the blood-soaked floorboards. After he was gone, Canby stared at the smear he had left, his eye lingering on the long heel-scrape in the dark crimson, with a deep pang of grief in his chest.

"You're looking well, Thomas," Mamie O'Donnell said, motioning for Canby and Underwood to take a seat as she settled herself on a long couch in her own rooms. She patted the cushion next to her, but Canby shook his head and remained standing. Underwood, though, sat and pulled a handkerchief from his pocket and dabbed at his face with it as the madam looked Canby over with her emerald eyes.

"And you, too," Canby said, "in spite of everything."

"Have you got yourself a sweetheart up in—where is it?"

"Ringgold. No."

"I'll mention that to Julia next time I see her in church," she said, her mouth curling into a roguish grin. Then the grin faded. "Not right, how you ran out on her."

"I know it," Canby said. His limbs felt weary but he would not allow himself to sit down in this room.

"You didn't have to ditch her when you ditched Atlanta."

"I felt like I did. Tell us what you know about the dead woman."

Mamie looked away from him, shrugged, and rearranged the shawl around her shoulders. "She was a new girl. Kept to herself, mostly, though I suspect Monte has been tapping her for free in the afternoons."

"Was he in her room last night?"

"I said in the afternoons. Monte knows not to leave the door at night unless I call him."

"And you did not call him last night? There would likely have been screaming."

"You think a whore screaming will draw a crowd? Honey, they get paid extra for making a ruckus."

Canby sighed. "Have you seen the remains?"

Mamie leaned back against the couch, grinning wickedly. "Can't stand the sight of blood, Thomas. Every time I see it, means no business for a week."

He crossed the room and gathered a fistful of her shawl in each hand. He drew her face up to his and whispered fiercely, "Let's take a walk down the hall. I think you need to see what's happened under your roof."

She squirmed until he let her go and she fell back to the couch, tugging the shawl back into place as if she were cold. "I don't want to see it. I can't."

She seemed to him, then, like the little girl he had known on Whitehall Street, before the war—small and vulnerable on the couch, despite all the cheap opulence with which she had surrounded herself. And beneath the bravado, he could see now, she was truly frightened. He breathed deeply through his nose before he spoke again.

"Tell us, then. Everything."

She stared at a point on the floor as she spoke. "I keep a close eye on my girls. They'll steal me blind if I don't. Her and Monte, I call that the cost of doing business. And they kept it to off-hours, I know.

"She had four customers last night, the last one at eleven o'clock. She was downstairs at the bar at last call."

"And after that?"

"After that, I don't know. Nobody saw anything, Thomas. That's what's got me scared. There was a crowd of men downstairs at closing time, but none of the girls remember seeing her go up with one of them."

"What can you tell us about them, the men?"

"I was with a customer. All I know is what the girls have told me. Businessmen, mostly. Monte saw them all out at midnight."

Canby felt his pulse quicken at the word *businessmen.* "White men?"

"It was closing time, I said. All the Negroes are gone out of here by ten on account of the curfew."

Canby turned this information over in his mind as a long silence hung in the room. After a moment, Mamie reached for a cigarette in an ivory box on the table beside her. She waited a moment for Canby to offer to light it, then shrugged and struck a match on the top of the box. She inhaled the smoke deeply. The process seemed to help her regain her composure.

"You don't approve of this, do you? This house, this life?"

"Hardly."

Mamie exhaled and stared at Canby through the smoke, her eyes piercingly green. "Then why did you take a fall for me four years ago?"

"I do not know. I suppose I hoped for a better return on it than this." He held her gaze until she looked away. She flicked ash from her cigarette and when she looked up again her eyes lit on Underwood and the coquettish gleam had returned to them.

"Mister Underwood," she said, "Thomas here does not think that a white woman should lie down with a black man. You still don't, do you, Thomas?"

Canby looked at the floorboards an instant longer than he intended to. Then he looked up at one of the draped windows, careful to keep Underwood's face in his peripheral sight as he did it. "No. I do not think so."

He thought he saw a flicker of emotion in Underwood's face, whether indignation or agreement or anger, he could not tell.

Mamie threw her head back and laughed. "Well," she said, "the first time made a believer out of me. Paul had a piece on him that would make a girl—"

Canby cut her off with a wave of his hand. "You had made good for yourself. A good marriage."

She rolled her eyes. "Yes. To an impotent planter's son, with a train of slaves in tow and debt up to his eyeballs."

Canby turned now to look at Underwood. "I knew Mamie O'Donnell when she was still called by her Christian name, Frances. We grew up together, Underwood, Frannie and I. With our friend Julia Preston, who lives in Vinings now. In the same part of town, and as classmates at my father's school down on Whitehall Street, until Frances married a wealthy man from Newnan named Pritchard Gorman. He built this house for her."

Underwood nodded cautiously.

"We were all proud for her. Immigrants' children rarely did so well. The Gormans weathered the war and even survived Sherman's siege, though they lost their slaves. All but one. Gorman's brother."

Frances O'Donnell corrected him with a long exhalation of smoke. "His half-brother. Paul's mother was a slave."

"And then in '75, Pritchard Gorman walked into this room with a Colt pistol and shot Paul five times. He saved the last bullet for himself. Frannie alone survived."

Frances's eyes were misty and distant when she spoke. "Paul loved to read. I taught him, even though Pritchard had told me not to. It was our secret. We were reading Walter Scott that day, *Ivanhoe*. What a story! The chivalry of it, Thomas. Love beyond time and place, just love itself!"

She rearranged the shawl on her shoulders and looked aside. "Next thing, we were in the bed. We stayed there all afternoon. I never heard Pritchard on the stairs."

"I have never understood why he killed himself," Canby said. "Surely he could have arranged a divorce, with a lot less scandal."

"Because he heard me, Thomas. He heard my cries, me calling Paul's name the way I'd once called his. It kills me to remember it now."

Canby shook his head slowly, but she was too caught up in

the memory to note the gesture. Her forgotten cigarette smol-
dered in one small hand in her lap.

"I loved them both. Why is that so hard for you to
understand?"

Canby nodded to Underwood that they should go. "You'll
not want to hear it, Frannie," he said, "but I pity you. I remember you in the yard of Dad's school. With Julia and the rest of
us. I remember all your red hair, how it flew behind you when
you ran with the boys—"

She rose from the couch in an instant, a full five inches
shorter than Canby but imposing in her fury, and struck him
across the face. The slap shook him to his boots. It took all of
his resolve to stand still after it, to keep his hands by his sides,
to blink back the water that started in his smarting eyes.

"Fuck you, Thomas," she said. "Fuck *you*." He could hear all
of the Dublin she had never seen in the accent she put on the
two words. "Whatever the hell did you ever do for me?"

"Not enough, I suppose."

He rocked back on his heels as she threw herself on the
couch. She covered her face with one hand, as if to conceal
it, and turned toward the lamp. He thought, as he left the
room, that the famed Mamie O'Donnell had given herself
over to tears.

HE MADE UNDERWOOD wait outside the dead whore's room
while he went inside it one more time, before the undertaker
arrived to begin the long job of piecing her together for whatever
sad, small funeral there might be. He imagined that Under-

wood was growing impatient waiting on him, yet he stood for a long time in the room, looking at the wreckage of the girl's body once more, then staring for long minutes out the painted-shut second-story window, at the unmarked expanse of bare clapboard that stretched down to the alley some twenty feet below.

Underwood was in the hall when Canby emerged from the room and shut the door softly behind him. The younger man said nothing as Canby wiped the blade of his Case knife on a piece of black satin he had picked up inside the room. Canby spoke softly as he folded the knife and dropped it into his pocket.

"I want you to go straight to the *Constitution* offices and have Grady send one of his stringers here to cover this crime."

Underwood began to speak but Canby silenced him with a raised hand. The hand kneaded the fabric deliberately for a moment before he spoke again.

"You bring him back and stay with him until he's through. The stringer has my approval to report everything he sees in there. He should note in particular the letter *U* on the victim's forehead."

"But, sir—"

"It's a *U* now, Underwood," Canby said, still working the cloth in his hand. "Let's see what our man thinks of that."

HENRY GRADY looked up from the stenographer's pad his reporter had handed him before hurrying on into the newsroom. He stared across the desk at Vernon, then down at the pad again, rubbing his smooth brow with one hand. Then he tossed the pad on the desk and looked again at Vernon. "I can't print this," he said.

"I realize it is graphic."

"I don't mean the grisly stuff. I mean the thing itself."

"Henry, you have a duty."

"I have many duties, Vernon," Grady shot back, "but none higher than my duty to Atlanta. Another horror story is not in her interest."

Vernon sat back, breathed in the air of the *Constitution* offices, the overwhelming odor of ink that pervaded the place, that seemed to have soaked into the very timbers of the building. "Not in the interest of the exposition, you mean," he said.

"I admit that another story like this runs counter to the spirit of the fair."

"Is that your opinion? Or what you've been told?"

Grady raised a hand full of telegram papers. "I hardly have room enough for the *good* news, Vernon."

"Run it on page four, then. Bury it in the back, at least. If Canby is right, our man will find it."

Grady shook his head. Vernon realized he had leaned forward in his chair. He sat back and took a deep breath. This feeling of being thwarted by the Ring was new to him. It, and the pungent odor of ink, was making his head light.

After a long moment, Grady said, "What about your black boy?"

"He's awfully suspicious."

"Giving him a badge couldn't have helped."

"It keeps him close."

"And this Canby. Why is it you insisted on him?"

"We did wrong by him in '77. We made a mistake."

"Mistakes are for my competitors to make. Bring me evidence and I'll print a retraction."

"He deserves another chance."

Grady had opened his mouth to reply when Joel Chandler Harris, one of the *Constitution* reporters, walked into the room and handed Grady a telegram. Grady scanned it quickly, then rose and retrieved his jacket from the coat tree in the room's corner. He was beaming.

Vernon returned the nod Harris had given him, studying the compactly built man. Harris's face was nearly as red as his hair.

"When will we have the next Uncle Remus story?" Grady asked, working an arm into his jacket.

"In time, Henry. Don't want to pump the well dry." Harris sighed. "I'm afraid that old slave is becoming the master of me."

Grady adjusted the rose that he kept in his lapel whenever the flowers were in bloom, a fresh one each morning. "Nonsense," he said. "Six thousand subscribers hang on his every word. How about another one with Brer Rabbit?"

"I'm sick of that damned rabbit," Harris said, turning back into the typesetting room. Vernon saw a silver flask protruding from his back pocket.

Grady frowned. Vernon knew how much he despised profanity. Knew, too, that the teetotaler hated liquor just as badly. In Harris, he tolerated the one and ignored the other. Harris was the best writer he had.

"You'll excuse me, I hope, Vernon. Pressing business."

"You'll consider running the story, won't you, Henry?" Vernon said, standing. "Right?"

Grady glanced into the next room, where the typesetters were at work, their fingers moving over the great banks of type like spiders, picking letters swiftly, silently, and slotting them into the press that would begin rolling out tomorrow's edition sometime after ten this evening. At midnight the paperboys would arrive, jostling like monkeys for their allotment of copies. The pace of the newspaper's day made Vernon weary; Grady thrived on it.

"How much control do you have over that man?" Grady asked from the doorway.

"Who? Canby? Enough."

"You're certain?"

Vernon nodded.

Grady walked back to his desk and picked up the notepad. He shook his head as he reread the notes there. "You'd better be," he said.

The clouds that had begun to gather on the western horizon were marshaling in earnest by noon, banding together in a long line the color of a bruise that seemed to billow as it moved toward the Chattahoochee River west of the city's border. Against their shadow, the gas-lit marquee of Lee Smith's Big Bonanza Saloon burned with defiant cheer, promising ease and comfort despite the darkening skies above. At night the marquee, with Smith's name emblazoned on either side, was visible from ten blocks away, making Mamie O'Donnell's place look like a backwater joint by comparison. On any day, even on the brightest noon, Canby thought, the marquee would have blazed over Decatur Street like something dropped from some more exotic locale, New York perhaps, into the midst of Atlanta's gritty railroad and business district.

He remembered the *Constitution* stories about the opening of the place back in '76, even remembering Grady's breathlessly reporting that the huge French mirror behind the bar had cost $2,500. That was nearly a career's salary for a policeman. But Canby thought he knew why Vernon had picked the Bonanza for their lunch meeting—he felt sure that, just like when Smith threw open his doors five years ago, cops still ate free.

He stepped through the vestibule into the cool shadows of the frescoed walls and his footsteps fell silent on the grass rug on the marble floor, into which had been woven BIG BONANZA in tall red letters. From the dining room came the din of perhaps a hundred voices, jumbled speech echoing off the marble. He scanned the faces at each table for Vernon's, or perhaps for that of some other member of the Ring that Vernon had also summoned. After a few moments, a clergyman in black— Bishop Drew, he realized after a second—stood up at one table and waved him over. Canby watched himself in the huge bar mirror as he walked closer to the table, feeling a strange sensation of closing distance on himself, until he noted that his own face in the mirror wore a scowling expression. With an effort, he composed it, as Vernon would have done.

"Mister Canby, please join us," the bishop was saying. He placed a hand on the shoulder of a portly man who had not risen from his seat. "Have you met Mister A. N. Wellingrath?"

"I have not," Canby said as the bishop's cool palm left his. The other man did not offer a hand, so Canby nodded to him, then sat. He did not look up again until he had arranged his napkin carefully in his lap. When he did his eye fixed on A. N. Wellingrath's cufflinks, which protruded from the sleeves of his coat. They were encrusted with tiny white diamonds—enough of them to look heavy.

Canby cleared his throat. "Are we waiting on Vernon and Colonel Billingsley?"

Bishop Drew took a sip of claret before he spoke. "I expect Chief Thompson will arrive soon. Colonel Billingsley has been detained by some of his northern investors. He sent me in his place."

"I didn't realize the two of you were associates."

"Oh, yes. He is one of my most prominent parishioners." He cut his eyes to Wellingrath. "We have yet to gather Mister Wellingrath into the fold."

Wellingrath snorted but made no comment, as if he hadn't heard. He motioned the waiter for another whiskey and Canby nodded for one himself.

"Let's get to it," Wellingrath said, fixing his smallish eyes on Canby. "Mister Canby, I won't bullshit you. I'm a cracker, purebred, out of Columbia County. We lived so far out in the country we had to go into town to hunt. I came to Atlanta right after the war, when I was through with my service, and I've never looked back."

"Mister Wellingrath is in the real estate business," the bishop said carefully.

"Damned right. This town is a gold mine, just waiting for

the big rush. The *big* rush, you see? And it'll come, you mark my words. What we've seen so far is nothing. Someday there'll be settled development all the way out to Buckhead."

Canby could not repress a smile. He thought of old Henry Irby's store—with its stuffed whitetail head out front giving the rough crossroads the name—and could not imagine anything more at the meeting of the Pace's Ferry and Roswell roads than the run-down clapboard pub. "And after that, Vinings?" he said. "It's hard to imagine many living a half day's ride from downtown."

"Don't smirk at me, boy. I've got over a half million in real estate to my name. Got a credit line with the Gate City National Bank for twice that"—Wellingrath glanced at the bishop, who looked intensely uncomfortable—"and you don't know shit from apple butter."

Wellingrath took the glass of whiskey from the waiter's hand before he could set it on the table. Sweat had begun to bead on his pink neck. Canby stared at his own glass for a moment, figuring that Wellingrath had gotten his start in the bad years, probably buying up land at sheriff's auctions or from war widows themselves, direct. Pennies on the dollar.

"And I'll tell you another thing before I shut up and let Drew take over. I told Billingsley to watch out for you," Wellingrath said, his drawl picking up speed. "Anyone who got into bed with the Union can't be much. Nigger-lovers, coon-humpers, scalawags, and damn Yankees, that's all the Union army was, I told him, down to the last man. But did he listen?"

Wellingrath glared at Canby as if to imply his presence was answer enough to the question.

"Strange bedfellows we are," Canby said, taking a careful sip from his drink. He and the bishop both seemed to be struggling for something to say next when Vernon slipped into the lone vacant chair at the table. The chief's eyes were on Wellingrath.

"A.N., you remind me of an overloaded boiler. One of these days you're going to blow your own gasket. Meantime, I'd appreciate it if you'd not insult my man." Vernon leaned on his elbows across the table. "If common decency isn't enough, just let the thought of your losses shut you up."

"All right," Wellingrath said, his features softening. "The money."

"Good, then," Vernon said. He leaned back and smiled at Wellingrath, at Canby. "Tell them what we have on the case."

Do the job, Canby thought. *Do the job and get the hell out of here*. So he began to talk.

Canby talked and did not let up until the sorbets arrived, taking them through each crime scene, through the state of the bodies, the linkages and discrepancies he could see between each murder. Before he'd even mentioned the dead whore's room, the bishop had pushed his plate of mussels away.

"He's trying to make a point, gentlemen," Canby concluded. "He has a grudge, some sort of injury he perceives that's been done to him.

"But I have to admit that these letters are a mystery." Canby felt a drive to keep his face on Bishop Drew's, away from Vernon's, as he spoke. "They ended in a *U*, which I've not been able to make much sense of."

"*Maul?*" the bishop asked.

"Could be," Canby said, feeling a stab of guilt at the lie he'd just told Vernon, the first he could remember between them. "Thus far it does not come together."

Vernon turned to the bishop. "Most of your murders are simple as can be, Bishop. Your motive's usually right in front of you. You've just got to figure out the history between the victim and the murderer—and it's almost always money, sex, or anger—and you're done. The history falls into place.

"The bad cases are the ones that don't show any history," Vernon said, and Canby found himself nodding along with him, warming to the familiar process in spite of himself—here and now, at least, where there was no blood or pain on display. He watched Vernon as he drew a cigar from his jacket pocket and clipped its end. "Remember, for example, the DeFoor murders?"

The bishop nodded. Wellingrath ordered another drink.

"That was a bad case," Vernon continued. He looked at Canby. "You were up in your mountain hideaway when this happened. Heads nearly hacked off in their beds."

The bishop held up a hand as if in anathema.

"Beg your pardon, sir. But that part of it was, from a detective's point of view, a help. We found the ax in the fireplace and their grandson confirmed it was theirs, had been taken from their own shed. What was troublesome, though, was the eighteen silver dollars left on top of their bureau, which had one drawer broken open. No robbery motive there, you see.

"We did find a broken window in the shed where the ax was, with a watermelon rind on the floor and, ah, human excrement with watermelon seeds in it. Old Man DeFoor's boots we found in a clearing by the river, like they'd been thrown aside.

As if the murderer had tried wearing them but they didn't fit. There was more, ah, evidence of watermelon next to them."

Canby took a breath while they waited for Vernon to deliver the verdict.

"So there was only one conclusion. A stray Negro had broken into the shed. Why he killed them, we can only guess that he was crazed—too crazed to notice the silver, and on the run from someplace bootless. Intending to walk a long distance, or already had come far enough that he needed new boots."

"Who was convicted?" Canby asked.

"No one," the bishop said quietly.

"We rounded up every Negro in north Fulton County," Vernon said, shaking his head. "Couldn't make it stick to any one them. Alibis—work or family—for near every one them. And the one or two who couldn't account for their whereabouts—the boots fit them."

Canby took a deep breath. "So the motive was what?"

"Crazed Negro, like I said."

"Did you question the grandson again?"

"We didn't see a need to. Those watermelon seeds told us what we needed to know."

"Vernon, when did you last eat watermelon?"

Vernon's face colored as he considered the question. After a long moment, he said, "But you would not find me shitting in a shed, Thomas."

"Because you have no need to. I wonder where the eighteen dollars ended up. Would they have been inherited by the grandson? The one with no crazed motive, I mean."

But Vernon's apparent discomfort in front of the other men made Canby want to move on.

"This case," Canby said, "is crazed, but crazed in a pattern. The common factor among the victims is their race and their prosperity."

Wellingrath gave the first indication he'd been listening by snorting. "You call a whore prosperous?"

"She was new, but she was popular. The doorman at O'Donnell's told me she'd been clearing fifty dollars a night. That's not money enough to join the Ring, but it's better wages than nearly every white man in the city earns. She'd have *been* prosperous, at any rate.

"So, if I am correct, race and prosperity trigger the motive. Our thoughts lead us instinctively to a black man as perpetrator. Perhaps jealousy in the case of Lewis, or a debt owed to Dempsey. But that could never give us a link to O'Donnell's. A black man could have killed the first two, but not all three."

The bishop's eyes flashed behind his spectacles. "You can't mean—"

"The killer may well be a white man," Canby said. He looked at Wellingrath. "A cracker, perhaps, somebody with a good deal of race hatred in him. Probably your lower-class sort of man, someone who could just get himself into the Kimball House but would not stand out in Jenningstown, walking through. Or maybe a foreman, a middleman for someone wealthier who has business in the Negro districts."

"But who also has enough money to pay the fare for your up-and-coming whore," Wellingrath said.

"You're right there. I have not yet figured that through."

"What about the letters?" Vernon asked, pulling on his cigar.

As he spoke, Canby found the sound of his own voice unconvincing. "The carving on this last one seemed to have been done in more haste than the others. Perhaps he was interrupted in his work. He may have intended to complete the letter as a *D*."

It made things worse that Vernon seemed not even to suspect the lie, so he pressed on.

"*Madness*, perhaps? He could carry it in a number of directions," Canby said, thinking instead of *malice, malignant, malevolent*. "Or maybe just *mad*. Maybe he's done. I have an idea of how to find out," he was saying as a rising tide of voices in the street drowned out his voice.

A man leaped into the vestibule, the frosted-glass door held open behind him with one hand, his hat in the other. His face was radiant.

"Sherman's coming, boys!" he cried, then grinned. "Again! Got it on the word of Henry Grady hisself. Be in the paper tomorrow! Just you watch that stock go now!"

Then he was gone, the door swinging shut on the space where he'd stood a second before.

The Bonanza was instantly in a fury of motion. Men leaped from their seats and grabbed for hats and coats, tossed bills on the tabletops. The bishop, too, was rising, and Wellingrath had begun to struggle upward from his chair.

"Gentlemen, I should be getting back to the cathedral," Bishop Drew said.

"Take care you don't stop by the exposition office on your

way," Vernon said, and winked. "There's a stampede in progress." To Canby, he said, "Wonder how much stock Grady
bought up before he let the news out?"

"As much as the son of a bitch could afford, I'll bet."

"Watch yourself," Wellingrath said to Canby, then he was
gone.

"He will," Vernon answered through a cloud of smoke. His
eyes were on the front door. Canby followed them to see Lee
Smith himself there, in the vestibule, apparently having come
out from his office to try to stop the throngs of men before
they ran out on their unpaid tabs. Someone pushed him aside
and he remained pinned against a fresco until the last few had
gotten through.

Canby looked out the flung-open door and saw that a hard
rain had begun to fall. Men rushed out into it unheeding,
hustling for the I.C.E. office before the news of Sherman got
widespread enough to raise the value of the exposition's stock
to its saturation point. Some going to buy, some to sell, he
figured. They seemed to be both coming and going. As he
watched and as Lee Smith shook his head and brushed at his
rumpled clothes, a pair of men counting their money collided
in the street and fell to the mud, one grasping at coins half
sunk in the muck of Decatur Street and the other rising, wiping a grimy bill on his jacket sleeve.

Vernon rattled the ice in his drink and turned away from the
door. "Atlanta," he said with a sigh to the now-empty saloon.
"Madness, you say?"

He tossed back the dregs of his drink and wiped his mouth
with his napkin. "Standard fare."

October 8

Nearly a week of sullen rain, unrelenting, cold. Canby and Underwood had been at this work of watching four nights now, paired silent as creepers for most of it, in the shadows of Negro Atlanta's most prosperous quarters— haunting its saloons and dry goods stores, cobblers, outfitters, smitheries, milliners. In that span of time Canby had been vouchsafed by Underwood throughout what the men on the force probably still called Darktown, past quizzical stares and terse exchanges and into back rooms and alleys—had in fact dined several times with the younger man, watching in bemused silence as Underwood bent his head in prayer before each meal of collards or fatback pork.

For most of the time Canby had been the only white man in sight. And the killings had, for the moment at least, ceased.

They sat now dry under the eaves of Atlanta University's South Hall, watching as the university's chaplain—also a lesser bishop of Atlanta's First African Methodist Episcopal Church—bolted the front door of his campus parsonage and snuffed the lights of its lower story in preparation for bed. The day before, the chaplain had been featured on the second page of the *Constitution*, quoted in one of Henry Grady's newfangled "interviews" as he voiced his support for the I.C.E. and urged Atlanta's Negro population to swell its attendance numbers. He had spent most of this evening, however, behind a locked door at Mamie O'Donnell's bordello in the company of a mulatto girl called Misty. Now, with the chaplain presumably ascending the stairs to join his sleeping wife, Canby and Underwood crouched under their eave, each shaking his head almost in time with the dripping rain.

"I thought surely our man would show himself tonight," Canby said. He glanced at his pocket watch and noted ruefully that the hour had slipped past midnight.

"Ain't right," Underwood muttered for perhaps the dozenth time in the past few hours. "Not for a preacher."

"What do you know of preachers and their private hours?"

"Enough to know they ain't supposed to lie with whores," Underwood said quickly, then added, "sir."

Canby tried to gauge the level of anger in Underwood's voice, the intensity of his disdain—whether it was of a measure with the controlled fury that had been loosed in Alonzo Lewis's shop or L. J. Dempsey's office. If it held any of the sadistic rage he had seen vented in Mamie O'Donnell's rooms the last week. He could not be sure. Casually, Canby said, "'For some are false apostles, deceitful workers masquerading as apostles of Christ.'"

Underwood stared at Canby as though the cistern beside him had spoken. After a moment he said, "'Yet no wonder, for even Satan himself masquerades as an angel of light.'"

"The words of Saint Paul himself."

"Yes," Underwood said. "Corinthians. Didn't take you for a religious man, Mister Canby."

"I'm not. I think of Paul as a holy fool. But my father did not. And so we read the epistles together. And both testaments, old and new. He was a minister. Methodist, in fact."

"Didn't mean no offense by what I said . . ."

"None taken. My father was a good man."

"But you didn't cotton to his faith."

"His faith did not save him." He looked at Underwood, saw the intensity with which the black man was looking at him. "Underwood, you believe what you like. It's not my place to tell you otherwise. But I saw no angels in the war, no devils, either. I think it's a bygone way of looking at the world, reading signs and portents all around. For me, this," he said, rapping his knuckles on the ground beneath him, "is enough."

"You lost your faith."

Canby looked out over the campus as the rain redoubled its intensity. The creek behind the privies and the stables was beginning to flow out of its banks.

"Yes. July seventeenth, 1864."

Why tell the younger man this? Canby thought. If indeed Vernon's suspicions of Underwood were valid, what good would it do to tell of his father? Or, looked at another way, how could it worsen things?

"You've heard of the great famine, perhaps? An Gorta Mór, it was called. After my mother died my father resigned his parsonage and we took the boat over. He settled at Emory College. Have you seen it? No? You should ride down to Oxford sometime. Beautiful setting, like this. Peaceful. He taught Latin and Greek there. But it did not last long. They hoisted the Confederate flag over the campus right after Fort Sumter, in April. My father's lectures took a turn away from the classics after that and his students did not care for it.

"My father could not believe he had traded tens of thousands of starving Irish for tens of thousands of enslaved Africans. Worse still that tens of thousands more were willing to die to keep those chains in place. I suppose the students tired of his perspective."

Canby told of how he had come home from one morning at the grammar school shortly after and seen that someone had slung black paint across their porch and painted NIGGUR LOVER in dripping black letters across the front of the faculty house. He and his schoolmates had lingered out front of the cottage, nervously shooting marbles in the dust of the yard, until Angus had come home from the day's lectures. His father had stared at the vandalism for a long moment, then begun to laugh until he dropped his books in the dust and had need to dab at his watering eyes with his handkerchief.

"My days here are done, lads," Angus had said, clutching the handkerchief in a trembling hand. "Perhaps I could not teach these Georgia boys to love their brothers, but by God, I should have taught them at least how to spell 'nigger' correctly. What kind of southern gentleman cannot spell *nigger*? *Nigger!*"

Angus's brogue had drawled out the final syllable of the word in an awful way. A word the son had never heard from the father's lips now repeated three times, like a portent that made Canby suddenly and quite consciously aware that the works of his outsized father were in the end earthbound and frail, and that someday he would indeed be alone in the world.

"We came to Atlanta as soon as he ended that term at the college," Canby said. "He opened a little grammar school on Whitehall Street. Said the war was going to make widows and orphans aplenty, especially the latter. He set up a kind of combined school and chapel for them."

"And that's what killed your faith?" Underwood asked.

Canby shook his head. He remembered the little building, rubble now, that had been on Whitehall, his father's table at the front of the long room that had served double duty as headmaster's desk and altar. The slate board behind it, and above that, set high in the wall so as to catch as much northern light as it could, the small stained-glass window his father had been able to glean from the Methodist Church, South, as part of the parcel of its beneficence for this bit of mission work. The blue and gold glass that was lit glorious every morning.

"No," Canby said, "that was four years later. When Sherman came. A longer story for another time."

Underwood was silent for a moment. Then he said, "Mind if I ask what was it happened between you and Mamie O'Donnell?"

"What've you heard?"

"That you went down on a bribe," he said in a low voice. "That you were taking protection money from her."

"I took money from her, Underwood. A loan, between friends." He looked up at the lowering clouds. "I had others I could have asked but I was too proud to go to them. I knew Mamie would not tell."

"But she did."

"She was approached by a detective, I'm not sure which one. Maybe Maddox. Whoever it was had the Ring behind him, I'm sure. I guess they didn't give her much choice.

"She and Vernon had their own interests to protect. And I had sided with the Republicans. Sticking up for me would have cost them. Dearly. But I did not believe Frances would have truckled. We go back, you know. But she did. By the time I believed it, it was too late."

Underwood nodded, staring down at the ground. "Mind if I ask what the loan was for?"

"You'll be a detective yet," Canby said. He made a sound he had intended to be a laugh. "That's the question you should ask. Something for a lady."

Canby rose and stretched his legs. "We'll work separately for a day or two. Get a few hours' sleep if you can. I want you to go to the Cotton Exposition, nine o'clock sharp." He took his wallet from his jacket and counted out fifteen dollars from it. He handed the bills to Underwood. "Spend this there, all of it. Conspicuously. I'll be about town. We will see what happens."

Underwood looked at the money in his hand as through it were dirty. "Conspicuously," he repeated. "Like a sitting duck."

"You'll be a moving duck," Canby said, "unless you refuse the assignment." His eyes locked on the black man's until Underwood folded the bills and tucked them into his breast pocket.

Canby looked out over the sodden campus, at the rain still falling. Dawn would be a muted affair, in this weather. Over by the stables the creek had now come out of its banks. The swollen water was lapping at the base of the privies, fresh rain and overflowing waste licking at the weathered clapboards. He remembered again his father's laugh at Emory those years ago, the sound more like a cough than one of mirth.

"Tonight's done for us, Underwood," he said. "It's all a bunch of shite."

ANSON BURKE stepped off the seven-thirty Western & Atlantic train with a large flowered carpetbag in one hand and his hat in the other, his big Colt revolver tucked under his chambray shirt but bulging enough beneath it to be clearly outlined against the cotton. He stared about him at the activity of Union Depot without noticing Canby's approach, the country mouse awash on the swelling tide of noise and movement that were Atlanta at this hour—at most hours. When Canby touched the big man's arm, Anse flinched and seemed to take a moment to focus on the one familiar face before him.

"Good God, Thomas. How many are there here?"

Canby smiled. "Not many with a grip as pretty as yours."

Anse blushed and looked down at the bright bag. "It was Mama's," he said slowly.

Half an hour later the carpetbag was safely ensconced with the porters of Kimball House and Anse, penthouse key of his own in his pocket, was following Canby through the streets of Atlanta as they made their way northward through town. Anse's pace seemed to quicken as the homes they passed grew smaller and more modest and the faces of their fellow pedestrians grew darker. Sprinkled among the residences here was industry of all types that could process whatever was brought in on the rail lines, from cotton and timber to mercantiles and ores. Every building that was not a house, it seemed, belched forth either smoke or steam into the Georgia sky.

"How'm I supposed to keep track of a single nigger in Atlanta, Thomas?"

"*Negro*, Anse. You're going to have to get that right."

"All right, then, Negro. How will I know him?"

For answer Canby pulled him into the shadows of a lumber kiln that sat radiating heat from its walls as it cured its contents on the west side of Marietta Street. He nodded toward a whitewashed two-story house across the road that had seen better days.

"He boards there. His name is Cyrus Underwood. I want you to follow him to the Cotton Exposition and keep track of him. If anybody asks, you're just in town for the fair. But don't let him out of your sight, not till he's back here. Follow him home this evening and keep south on Marietta. You'll see the top floor of Kimball House soon enough."

After a time the front door of the boardinghouse opened and Underwood strode out of it and down the front steps. He settled his hat on his head and set out south on Marietta Street toward the roundhouse and the depot, where the W&A was running trains out every fifteen minutes for the exposition.

"Note the suit and the hat, Anse. Don't lose him."

Anse nodded and tugged at his belt, whether to reposition the Colt or to adjust his prodigious belly, Canby could not tell.

He looked like a man readying himself for battle as he stepped out from the shadow of the kiln.

"And Anse?" Canby said, trying not to smile. "Try to blend in."

THE SMALLER BLADE of Canby's penknife fit the lock easily enough. With a jiggling turn of it he was inside Underwood's quarters, taking in the spartan room. An iron bed, neatly made, two spindle-backed rocking chairs with a side table between them, heaped with books. Night jar in the corner. He stepped to the bureau, which was missing one of its drawers, and on which sat the apparatus of Underwood's toilet, catching as he did a hazy reflection of himself in the smoked mirror pegged to the wall above it. Canby regarded the lather brush, the well-worn hone, and the razor itself. A folding straight-edge, cheap but sharp enough. The washbasin in which it lay was chipped but the blade was unmarred—no nicks or burrs to indicate rougher usage than that for which it was made.

The stack of books on the rockers was another matter. Canby recognized a name from several spines of the books. George Fitzhugh. One of his father's particular bêtes noire from the days of heated debate and then open rancor that led up to secession. He picked up *Sociology for the South* and read a passage that had been underlined: "We have fully and fairly tried the experiment of freeing the Negro . . . and it is now our right and our duty, to listen to the voice of reason and experience, and reconsign him to the only condition for which he is suited." Another of Fitzhugh's treatises, *Cannibals All! or, Slaves Without Masters*, had been similarly marked. "Free laborers have not a thousandth part of the rights and liberties of negro slaves," Fitzhugh argued, adding, "Where a few own the soil, they have unlimited power over the balance of society." Canby remembered how he had been startled from his lessons one evening by the report of *Cannibals All!* hitting the mantel above the fireplace, where it had struck after being thrown from Angus's hand.

That copy, he assumed, had been returned in damaged form to the Emory College library. The one he now held, he noted from a bookplate pasted inside its front cover, was checked out from the Young Men's Library Association. He set it with *Sociology for the South* on the bed for the moment, then took another look around the room and decided to pay a visit to the Y.M.L.A.'s quarters up from Pryor Street next. But his eye fell to the open pages of the book he had uncovered when he moved Fitzhugh's works. A worn Bible, left open on the rocking chair's seat, a passage from Revelations highlighted, in contrast to the other books, with a red ink: "But the fearful, and unbelieving, and the abominable, and murderers, and whoremongers, and sorcerers, and idolaters, and all liars, shall have their part in the lake which burneth with fire and brimstone: which is the second death."

"Underwood," he muttered, "goddamn you."

ANSE SETTLED HIMSELF into the leather seat and looked around balefully as the train began to pick up steam. His was the only white face in the car and, worse, this man Underwood was staring right at him on account of it. Forty years of living in the mountains and Anse had seen nary a black face in that time, save for his rare visits down to this capital city. Had also seen the famous sign at the Forsyth County line in north Georgia that read NIGGER DON'T LET THE SUN SET ON YOU HERE. Talk had circulated about putting up a similar signpost at Ringgold's corporate limits but Canby would have nothing of it, elections be damned. Now Anse felt the distance of every mile that separated him from home. And he was surrounded.

A hand settled on his shoulder and he jumped.

"First time in the big city?"

Anse looked up and saw that the voice, and the hand, belonged to a white man outfitted in the uniform of the Western & Atlantic. He also wore a conductor's cap.

"Naw," Anse said.

"Could have fooled me. You're in the colored car, Hiram. Move on up to the next one. I think you'll be more comfortable." He dismissed him with a shooing gesture and began taking up tickets from the black passengers. Anse made his way to the front of the car, turning his wide hips sideways to navigate the narrow aisle, and slid open the vestibule door to the rushing air outside. He balked at opening the door to the car ahead, although he could see it was filled with white people, the ladies seated and men standing with hands slung in the leather straps that hung from the brass rails above. Instead he stood on the steel platform and breathed in the whistling air. So many smells in it: coal smoke, wood smoke, creosote, people, every kind of food. God knows what else.

When the train pulled into the Oglethorpe Park station he was the first one off, climbing down the car's welded steps to the decking of the depot. When Underwood came down from the colored car Anse fell in a few yards behind him, hands in his pockets, trying his best to look like a man strolling through the exposition for the third or fourth time.

But it took an effort not to gawk. He followed the rail passengers making their way to the I.C.E. entrance and his gaze went up to its gate, which seemed to loom five or six stories high in wrought iron, with INTERNATIONAL COTTON EXPOSITION welded right into its arching metal. Next to it a fountain spewed water nearly as high. The fairgoers, white and black, formed a single line, there being too many of them, he guessed, to be segregated here. As he walked under the arch, he followed the lead of those in front of him and dropped a quarter into an iron box at the turnstiles. The usher smiled at him. The man wore a uniform of blue, buff, and green with brass buttons, all of it trimmed in gold braid. Dressed for the circus, Anse thought as the turnstile trundled behind him.

Whatever notion of pandemonium Anse still had from the Sunday school days of his youth was here confirmed. Pandemonium sped up, no less. He walked down a boulevard lined with stalls of vendors selling everything but livestock. A weird cacophony of music and noise, of pianos and organs playing in their stalls and the cries of vendors hawking wares—tobacconists, haberdashers, sellers of painted china, antique bronzes, iron novelties, jewelry and art. He paused for a second at a booth that had been set up to sell concertinas. The man in the booth a Chinaman, he guessed, with a long, braided ponytail hanging down his back, the hair as black and shiny as a crow's wing. He stood behind his display table playing one of the concertinas, the little accordion breathing melodies in and out in his small hands.

And apparently there was more yet to be built. Carpenters and bricklayers were working everywhere, trying to finish the construction that seemed to be running far behind schedule. Anse saw aproned and sawdusted men harangued by foremen who exhorted them with cries for haste. On the hillside west of the park he saw that a city of tents had sprung up, overlooking the racetrack that marked the park's boundary. He wondered how many of them housed these tradesmen.

Ahead of him Underwood had nearly reached the main building, a giant structure, cross-shaped, with windows high in each wall of it, flags from every state in the Union snapping on poles set at the edges of the building's roof. He saw from its signage that it was the model cotton factory and he hurried, lest he lose the black man in the crowd pouring in.

Inside was quiet. Though the factory was outfitted with all manner of outsized cotton gins, presses, looms, and sewing machines, all were silent, inert. A man atop a ladder, balance uncertain as though he had just climbed it, cleared his throat and spoke.

"Ladies and gentlemen, I give you the man the newspapers call a steam engine in breeches, the exposition's director general, Hannibal Kimball, ladies and gents."

The speaker climbed down and another man, with a sizable mustache and hair swept to one side of his head, took his place. A robust round of applause greeted him.

"Thank you, ladies. Thank you, gentlemen," he said. "I thank you all for joining us and welcome you to another day of Atlanta's exposition. We have gathered exhibitors from New England to the Middle West and from six foreign countries, eleven hundred exhibits in all. I believe you will see that it is a new kind of South we herald—one of energy and industry. It can't all be seen in a day. Perhaps you'll stay and spend a night at the new Southern Hotel here on the grounds. Or at the Kimball House downtown."

He nodded and smiled at the scattered laughter.

"I say a new kind of South, ladies and gentlemen, because the old one is dead. The old system is completely overturned. Sherman, in his rather flammable way, did us a kind of favor. As Henry Grady likes to say, the war also freed the slave*holder*— of the obligation of hungry mouths to feed. We were too much dependent on slavery, and too much dependent on growing cotton without milling or weaving it. For too long we have shipped our staple to the north to be processed. We are now bringing the mill to the cotton. Atlanta will lead the charge from the fields to the factory.

"Folks, I'm glad you're here. We're witnessing a birth, you see. The birth of the New South. Here and now."

"*Attends! Attends!*" someone cried from the back of the crowd. Anse followed the turning of heads and saw that a tall man had climbed up the side of a loom, where he clung with one hand and waved a handkerchief from the other. "One week, Monsieur Kimball, one week since opening day we have waited for the booths for the industrial pavilion!"

Kimball smiled. "My friend, the lumber that is to go into

that exhibit is not sawn yet. But I told you ten days, and we will make it."

The man wiped at his brow with his handkerchief. "But the money!" he said.

As if to answer in kind, Kimball pulled his own handkerchief from his breast pocket and waved it. All the cotton machinery sprang to life instantly and simultaneously, it seemed, gins and combs raking back and forth, sewing machines chattering into motion. The man on the loom sprang down from it just as the loom's arm swung into the place his hand had been a moment before. Still smiling, Kimball tucked the handkerchief back into his pocket, climbed down the ladder, and began shaking hands.

Underwood was moving again, scanning the crowd as he made his way through the factory. Anse dropped back a bit. After fifteen minutes of walking through the place like a patrolman on a beat, Underwood had made it to the factory's north door. He seemed to be looking at the black faces in the place most intently.

Just outside the factory he looked back in Anse's direction and Anse turned away and stepped a few yards to a steaming tin cart from which a black boy was selling boiled peanuts. Once the money had changed hands, Anse turned back with his soggy paper sack in hand and saw Underwood enter a wood-framed building designated as the Arts & Industrial Pavilion, though "PAVILION" was yet unfinished, a painter on a scaffold brushing the last letters into place.

He found him inside, in yet another line. This building housed the truly heavy equipment, machinery for lumber and manufacturing that ran so deafeningly loud that the floor vibrated beneath his feet. Hemp ropes had been strung in front of the exhibits to queue the fairgoers before each machine at the closest safe distance. He took his place between the ropes. While he waited, he picked peanuts from the bag, splitting the shells with a thumbnail and dropping them to the plank floor.

The machine ahead of him was turning a length of pine log before feeding it into a circular saw that screamed like a fury each time it bit into the wood. It was steam-powered and he could see from his place in line that it was operated by a man raising and lowering an iron lever at intervals. With each raising of the lever came a great pneumatic hissing of steam and with each lowering a softer exhalation. In between, the log jumped and danced in the carriage thunderously, bark chipping and flying. He could see Underwood now directly in front of the machine, holding up the line. Underwood's eyes moved from the machine itself to the little sign that had been erected in front of it to explain its function, this one being far too loud for the operator to talk over. He lingered on the sign itself the longest. His face bore a strange expression of curiosity and distaste, as though he suspected that the little plaque might spring into motion as well. After a long minute the white man behind him in line said something to him and he looked up, moved on.

Anse inched forward with the others. He could see now that the lever powered two metal cylinders: one that pushed the log over and the other out of which sprang a hooked metal arm that pulled it back. At each turn the carriage carried the log forward, into the saw, where the blade sheared off side boards.

After four turns and shuttles the log was rendered into a perfectly square length of pine, fit for a column or to be cut down smaller into boards for framing lumber. Anse had spent hours cutting each log to build his own house; here, one was planed in a minute. He had never in his life seen so many machines as he had this morning, and this one perhaps the granddaddy of them all. By the time he got to the prime place in the queue another huge log had been dropped onto the carriage and he was able to watch the process all the way through.

He looked down at the sign that had so interested Underwood. It was a metal plaque, finely cast from steel and glazed over with a glossy coat of black enamel. STEAM NIGGER, it read, and in smaller letters beneath, WM. H. HILL & CO., KALAMAZOO, MICH.

"Be damned," Anse said. When he looked up to locate Underwood again he could not find him. The black man in the sage suit and hat had disappeared in the mass of men and women, melted back into the crowd of his fellow Atlantans.

THE YOUNG LIBRARIAN had been sheepish about Canby's inquiry as to the Y.M.L.A.'s pro-slavery holdings. "Most of those books have been cleared out. Our subscribers lost interest in the topic some years ago," he had said, carefully logging in the Fitzhugh books Canby had set on his desk. "I was surprised to find Chief Thompson had any interest in the slavery argument at all."

"Thompson? Vernon checked out these books?"

"His boy did, sir. On his orders, I'm sure."

Canby nodded. "And these Fitzhugh titles are all you have left? No others by McDuffie? James Henry Hammond?"

The young man set *Cannibals All!* aside with both of his slender hands and looked up at Canby, blushing. "You might check with Robert Billingsley, sir. The holdings at his house alone are nearly double the volumes we have here."

And so Canby found himself on the front porch of the grand Billingsley manor on Saint Paul Avenue. While he waited for the bell to be answered he gazed down the street at Lemuel P. Grant's mansion and at the park named for Grant across the street from it, where the trees were just beginning to turn with autumn. The Billingsley place was even newer and grander than Grant's, a two-story edifice of red Georgia brick and white-painted columns and shutters, four chimneys jutting above the roof at each of the house's corners. When Billingsley had moved into the city he had done so in earnest, one of the few of the old planter class who managed not only to weather the war but also to build from its ashes an empire. And his house was said to be wired throughout for the electric lights Billingsley's Dixie Light hoped to bring to the city grid. Billingsley's was the kind of story Henry Grady evangelized, every chance his editorials gave him. Canby imagined that could Grady afford it, he would be erecting his own place next door.

The black face that peered out from behind the great cypress door was already bobbing and nodding before Canby spoke a greeting. Clad in white tails, the butler led Canby back to "the libry" down a dim hallway lined with a thick carpet runner. The black man pushed open the door to Billingsley's study. Billingsley was at his desk, dozing, head down on an open book splayed across the desk's surface. The butler cleared his throat and Billingsley sat up and shut the book on which his face had been resting. He fitted a pair of wire spectacles on his face and regarded Canby for a moment, then smiled.

"Detective Canby," he said, rising, "please come in." He nodded toward one of the wingback chairs that faced the desk, while the butler, unbidden, moved to a sideboard and poured two drinks from a crystal decanter.

"I'm sorry to have disturbed your constitutional."

"Constitutional? Mister Canby, my friend, keeping regular hours is the hope of a bygone time for one my age. One takes a constitutional whenever one can." He waved a hand, lassitude in the gesture, at the butler, who set the drinks before them and moved about the room pulling lamp chains. Each pull was followed by a barely audible hiss as the electric bulbs in them caught the current, and the room was filled with a light of such steady whiteness that Canby could not help but marvel.

Canby looked up to see that Billingsley was regarding him with amusement. "A vast improvement on gaslight, is it not?"

"It barely flickers."

"Indeed. Electric is the light of the future. If my engineers can complete the project in time, we will have the entire city center lit with it before the Cotton Exposition is over. Perhaps even the exposition itself."

Billingsley nodded at the glass before Canby. Canby picked it up and took a long sip. Irish whiskey, certainly, but not Jameson. His eyes watered as its mellow warmth burned down his throat and settled in his stomach. "That is fine whiskey," he managed.

Billingsley smiled. "Aged. I am pleased you have a taste for it."

Canby took in the room again, bathed in the electric light. On every wall and stacked floor to ceiling were shelves of books—bindings of every description, leather to humble cloth; oversized books of maps, he supposed; folios; small bound pamphlets. He understood now why the librarian had blushed; this room alone surpassed the Y.M.L.A.'s entire collection.

"My father would have loved a room such as this, sir."

Billingsley's eyes crinkled before he spoke. "Indeed?"

"To the bottom of his soul. He loved books. All manner of wisdom, is probably how he would have put it."

"He was a man of the cloth, was he not?"

"Yes. And a scholar, as well. A good man."

Billingsley nodded. "There are good friends on each of these shelves," he said, setting his drink on the table beside his chair. "Though not all of them are. One would be a fool to embrace every idea."

Canby found himself leaning forward in his chair. "I had not thought of it that way, but of course that's how it is. Some to keep . . ."

"And some to be cast aside."

"I always thought it wise to consider every vantage."

Billingsley clapped his hands together over his knees almost soundlessly. "Every vantage, of course!" he said. "But then comes selection." The older man rubbed at his eyes under his spectacles. "I wonder what brings you here to me."

Canby drained his whiskey, head shaking involuntarily as the flame of Irish spirits jarred his throat. He set the empty glass on the desk. "I'm sorry to intrude business, sir, but . . ." He watched a moment as the electric lamp on Billingsley's desk burned, the arc current dancing across the filament. "You, sir, are one of the Confederates who never sought pardon after the war. If I understand rightly, you were not allowed to vote in the last national election because of it. I do not mean to offend, but do you, perhaps, have holdings in your library of some sort that might espouse a similar kind of . . . should I say, unrepentance?"

Billingsley's gaze had gone uncommonly cold. "A gentleman, sir, has no need to ask pardon if he has not given offense. Contrary to what the United States government may claim, I committed no crime. I merely defended what was mine." But after a moment his expression softened. "I suspect you would disagree with that assessment."

"In some particulars, sir."

"This inquiry, does it involve the business of our recent killings?"

"It does. I apologize for having brought it here. It seems that our man might have some notion of a mission about his work. The killings, you see, seem to target Negroes in a particular way. There seems to be some race hatred involved. I suspect he has been reading some of the slavery apologists, Fitzhugh and the like. I was hasty in assuming you might have some such holdings."

"In my measured opinion," Billingsley said, "Fitzhugh was a buffoon."

"My father thought so. And I share the opinion. But I believe our man is less enlightened."

"Perhaps he is." Billingsley waved his hand, languidly, at one of the walls of books. "Please take a look for yourself. I do not collect the likes of George Fitzhugh, but you may find something of use."

Embarrassed, Canby stood and stepped over to the nearest bookcase. The books were arranged in some system of order he could not quite decipher, but their number and variety were staggering. "My God," he said, "the languages!"

"I was educated in Latin and Greek, of course. The rest are just a dalliance. *Badinage avec les belles-lettres*," the older man said.

"My father taught me a fair bit of Latin. He said I was hopeless as a scholar of Greek." Canby glanced at titles on theology and history, quickly, then surveyed a shelf that seemed to be devoted to the sciences: Darwin's *The Origin of Species*, Jean-Baptiste Lamarck's *Philosophie Zoologique*.

"I have some lines here sent by a friend in France," Billingsley was saying. He had moved to his desk and resumed his seat there. In his hand were several loose sheets of stationery on which measured lines had been written by what seemed, from Canby's vantage, a flamboyant hand. "I trust you know of Victor Hugo?"

Canby smiled. "Of course I read the *Hunchback*. And *Les Misérables*. I found it moving."

"Did you read it in the French?"

Canby felt his cheeks coloring. "No, sir. In translation. You know Hugo personally?"

Billingsley nodded. "I should say, casually. Hugo's politics have long been vulgar but I have admired his poetry for many years. His greatest work, I believe, remains unfinished. I have urged him to revisit it." Billingsley put the spectacles back on his nose, held a sheet aloft, and read: "'And thus the wise man dreams in the deep of the night, his face illumined by glints of the abyss.' That notion seems particularly apt for a man in your line of work, Detective."

"It is, in fact. But one has to remember that the world is not the abyss."

A trace of a smile played across Billingsley's face. "But the abyss is definitely a part of the world, is it not? How many have been murdered now? Four?"

"Three."

"Three. You mentioned race hatred. Have you not considered the notion—the old notion, I should say—of simple evil in this case?"

This time, Canby smiled slightly. "*Evil* is not a word I use much, sir. It's more fit for newspapers, sensational journalism. Most crimes, in my experience, come down to your baser motivations. Greed. Anger. Envy—all the way back to Cain and Abel. But evil? More like the result of ignorance. I think what I am trying to say is that the impetus behind all the bad acts I have seen is not so much evil as it is simply human. Although hatred should not be underestimated. I see it in this case."

Billingsley was studying him like a curio. "I wonder that the war did not temper that view."

"It tempered it, absolutely. But as you said yourself, sir, you were fighting for what was yours. Even the poorest private thought the same. Month in and month out, I saw a conflict between two powers—over power."

"And the circumstances under which you left the police force before: you see no evil in that nasty business?"

Canby smiled. "In Henry Grady? In the men of the old force reclaiming their status? No, sir. Again—envy, ignorance. Certainly ignorance in the case of Grady. He thinks of himself as infallible. That's why he misrepresented my connection to Mamie O'Donnell. I took a loan from her; he called it a bribe. His pride is his weakness. He misconstrued the facts of my case."

"And cost you your job and reputation."

"I intend to reclaim both."

"Yet in the meantime you suffer under charges of graft and commerce with prostitutes."

"I'll grant you, sir, that I harbor anger. But I know the truth of the matter. And my anger is not so great as to spur me to murder, or to despair of the truth coming out in time." Canby sighed. It seemed that all the accumulated weariness of the past days settled on him at this moment. "I suppose you could say I am cautiously optimistic, Colonel. Despite it all, I hope for better days."

"Sounds like an Emersonian notion."

"I have read Emerson."

"Indeed. Take a look at that high shelf there. A complete set of works, signed by the Sage of Concord himself."

Billingsley rose and reached for a pewter bell on his desk, rang it twice. "I believe you are something new, Mister Canby. I will be interested to see how Atlanta treats you this time."

He came from behind the desk and reached for Canby's hand as the study door swung open, the butler waiting just beyond it in the hall. "Mister Canby," Billingsley said, smiling again, "Godspeed with your investigation."

The butler bowed and gestured down the long hallway. Canby was nearly to the front door when he realized he would be leaving empty-handed.

THE DAYS WERE beginning to shorten as October progressed, Canby noted as he walked through town. He'd had a tolerable shepherd's pie at a pub new to him on Mitchell Street for supper, with two neat Jamesons on the side. He had thought ruefully that the Jameson paled in comparison to the whiskey Billingsley had poured for him, had given a thought to querying the older man about the brand, but dismissed it in an instant. What point? God knew from whence it came and at what expense.

He turned up Whitehall Street with a heavy feeling in his chest. A chimneyville, as they called it, it had been, after the war. This part of the city so thoroughly scorched by Sherman that only the river-rock and brick chimneys, fireproof, had survived. For a time after the siege they alone rose above the leveled ash, like the bones of the corpse that the city had become.

No longer. Whitehall had been entirely rebuilt. He stopped in front of a two-story building midway up the block, stared through its plate-glass windows at headless mannequins adorned with men's and ladies' clothing. Gas chandeliers burned inside and he saw painted on the glass above the store's double doors, in gold letters, M. RICH AND BROTHERS. So this was the new Rich's store, relocated and twice the size of the last one. He watched as the clerks shuttered the windows, maneuvering around the mannequins as they closed the louvered panels. Seven p.m.

He looked again at the lettering above the door: 54–56 WHITEHALL STREET. He'd never known the proper address for Angus's little school but as he looked up Whitehall to Alabama Street he gauged the distance to be about right. Not even a chimney left for a marker.

He stood and listened to the last of the clerks latch the front doors. The flames of the chandeliers dimmed. As he had done so many times on his night watches as a patrolman, he wondered if he was the only one to sense Atlanta's peculiar hauntedness. There was an understanding that it was not to be spoken of. The consensus seemed to be that industry and speed would replace the city's grief, if she moved fast enough. As if her bustling energy could banish the ghosts that lingered on every corner. He walked on.

THE LIFT SHUDDERED to a stop on the sixth floor and Canby stepped into the hallway of penthouse suites, bidding good night to the operator as the man slid the grate shut. He was fishing the room key from his pocket when he noticed the door to his suite was slightly ajar. Anse, who seldom even latched his screen door in Ringgold, was going to have to learn Atlanta rules.

But as he stepped into the rooms he knew something was wrong. He could hear the steady drip of water and before he was halfway to the bathroom his boots began to make squelching sounds with every step, the sodden carpet beneath his feet becoming softer as he neared the bathroom door. He threw open the door and as a cloud of steam billowed and cleared he could see that the man in the claw-foot bathtub was Anse.

Anse's back was to the door but his eyes were fixed, it seemed, on the doorway and on Canby framed in its opening, his body wrought into the peculiar contortion by the cut in his neck, which ran through ligament and tendon and down to the spine. Canby saw that the trachea was severed and gaped open like a pipe. Anse's head, thus so nearly separated from his body, lolled over the lip of the tub, all but upside down, as if to survey the exit his killer had made.

And carved above the glazed eyes, neatly as a surgeon's work, was the letter *T*.

Canby crossed the distance and pressed his fingers to Anse's neck, vainly, for sign of a pulse. Then, as gently as he could, pulled the eyelids shut. He put a hand on Anse's shoulder and felt that the body was still warm. He reached for the tap and shut off the valve, then stood over the tub as the sound of water gradually subsided to a series of erratic drips. The big man's naked bulk was mostly submerged in the water with which his lifeblood had mingled and Canby felt within himself too much dread to reach into the water and pull the plug from the drain. He stared at one of Anse's arms, draped languidly over the edge of the tub, a runner of blood still dripping slowly down the length of it to where his fingertips touched the floor. There the blood and water mingled in pinkish clouds on the white tiles.

Before this day had dawned he had talked with Underwood about faith; this afternoon he had bandied good and evil with Robert Billingsley. He knew what he had to do next, and that haste was paramount. Why, then, did he find himself first pausing to bow his head?

HANNIBAL KIMBALL was not pleased. With his hotel locked down and his staff being rounded up for questioning, he had placated his captive customers in the hotel bar with a free round of cocktails, but the evening was wearing on and his patience wearing thin.

"This is the opposite of the kind of discretion for which you were hired," he hissed at Canby. "Another murder, and in my own place of business!"

"That was my friend who died upstairs."

"And two fifth-floor rooms flooded, to boot."

Canby was considering putting his hands on the man when the lobby's front door began to rattle. He looked up to see Vernon Thompson pounding the glass door with the heel of his fist. Kimball nodded to the doorman and Vernon was soon striding across the lobby. Underwood followed him.

"Where the devil have you been all day?"

Canby ignored the question. He stepped up to Underwood

and grabbed a lapel of Underwood's suit coat in each hand. He drew Underwood's face up to his own until their eyes were inches apart.

"Whites-only, my ass," Canby said. "How'd you get in? In a bellboy's uniform?"

"Thomas!" Vernon said.

"I think you've been right, Vernon. I think this black son of a bitch killed my deputy."

Underwood's gaze did not waver. Canby could not gauge which was the more prominent in his eyes, denial or defiance. "I did not," he said.

Canby flung the black man to the marble floor. When Underwood made to rise, Canby put his boot on his chest and pushed, hard enough to throw himself off balance. Underwood did not try to stand again. He scuttled across the floor on hands and heels, backward, until he reached the reception desk. He sat there against it, dusting off his shirtfront and glaring at Canby.

"Good God, Thomas!" Vernon said, stepping between the two men. "What has happened? What deputy?"

"Anson Burke. From Ringgold. I had him come down on the train. He was tailing Underwood all day. And now he's dead, up in the room. You made a mess of him, you bastard."

Vernon looked bewildered. "When?"

"Late. An hour ago, at the most."

"Thomas," Vernon said slowly, "Underwood has been with me since suppertime."

Canby felt a cold prickling in his spine.

Vernon stepped closer. "We've had a girl go missing. A white girl."

"Gentlemen!" Kimball cried, sotto voce and with a placating smile toward the gawkers at the bar. "This will not do. Not here."

"Where can we talk quietly?" Vernon asked.

Kimball shot a glance at Canby, at Underwood still down on the marble floor. "Perhaps the livery would be best."

"Fine, then. Have one of your boys bring us out a bottle."

Vernon gestured for Underwood to rise, then led him and Canby out through the service door at the back of the lobby. "Quietly, indeed," he said as they emerged into the gaslit busyness of the livery stable, where horses shied in their stalls and Negro hands moved about, independently of one another, currying the animals or pitching hay into their troughs, hanging saddles and reins on wooden pegs fixed into the stanchions between the numbered stalls. In one corner a bootblack sat on his box, furiously shining a pair of riding boots with an oiled rag; in another corner the blacksmith's anvil stood mutely, silenced for the late hour though with a half-formed horseshoe left draped on its horn, the furnace behind it still glowing dully from the embers within. Each of the Negroes glanced up through half-lidded eyes to register the newcomers' appearance and then, a half second later, turned back to the work before him and conspicuously redoubled his efforts on it. Vernon leaned against the door of an unoccupied stall, wiped his forehead with a handkerchief, and sighed.

"I am sorry about your deputy, Thomas," he said.

"He was a good man."

"I've no doubt about that. I'll see to it that he is treated well."

Canby nodded.

"You are fairly certain of the time of his demise?"

"The water in the bathtub was still warm. It can't have been long."

"Was he . . . marked, like the others?"

"A *T* this time."

"Goddamn it," Vernon said, wiping his face again. "Well, there's one bit of progress, bitter as it may be. If you're right about the hour of the murder, Underwood did not do it. I have no choice but to vouch for him in that regard."

Canby looked at Underwood, who seemed to have settled himself into a kind of sullen resolve. He was about to speak when one of the bartender's boys emerged from the hotel carrying a whiskey bottle with a shot glass capped upside down atop the bottle's neck. Vernon took it from the boy without a word, inspected it, then lifted ruefully the single glass.

"Rye," he said. "Cheap son of a bitch." He poured the shot glass full and gave it to Underwood, then handed the bottle over to Canby. Pulling a flask from within his breast pocket, Vernon raised it. "To your man."

"Anson Burke."

"To Burke."

The three men drank in silence for a moment. Vernon took another draw from his flask, then capped it and tucked it away.

"Underwood has a theory of his own."

"Does he? From the Book of Revelation? Whoremongers and the lake of fire?"

"As a matter of fact, he has regaled me with his version of the End Times."

"You're a pragmatic man, Vernon. Surely he hasn't led you down some hoodoo path to another dead end."

"You were raised with religion yourself, Thomas."

"I was, and the war swept that all away. Do you know, Vernon, there were men in my regiment who honestly thought of us as the veritable Second Coming? The long, blue arm of God? The Negroes who followed us through South Carolina certainly believed it. They were physically starving on that belief. And where did that get them? Or us?"

Underwood raised a hand, tilted his head deferentially. "Study on it a minute, Mister Canby. That's all I ask. Look who this man been after. Usurers. Whores."

"Negroes."

"People who been profiting from wrong. Certain kinds of wrong."

"That would cast a wide net in Atlanta."

"Would indeed. But that Deputy Burke up in the penthouse, he wouldn't be a Negro, would he? Not from up in the mountain country?"

"Anse was a good man," Canby said again, wearily.

"And this missing girl, Thomas," Vernon said. "White as you or me."

"I read all the Fitzhugh I could stand, Mister Canby. Guess you know that from the books you took from out of my place. This case was looking to shape up that way, it was. But what I saw of that girl in Mamie O'Donnell's place has just got one name. That was evil."

Canby stared at Vernon, who cleared his throat before he spoke. "It's true, Thomas, that we've never seen killings like this before."

"Vernon, if he wants to contort this thing to fit his theology, he'll surely find a way to do it."

"As you said, I'm a pragmatist, Thomas. I want to follow every lead."

Canby took a long pull on the bottle of rye, then corked it and set it down on the dirt floor of the stable. "Underwood," he said, "I hope your ambition and your faith don't collide."

But as he was rising, he felt himself listing to his left and in a moment Vernon was at his side, an arm around him, steadying him.

"You've had a rough go these last few days," Vernon said. He pressed a key into Thomas's palm. "You remember the house. Still on Butler Street. Still a bottle of good bonded in the cupboard. Go rest yourself. I promise your friend will be properly seen to."

Canby nodded and without a word to Underwood made his way out of the livery, past the outer fringes of Kimball House's gaslight, and into the semidarkness of Decatur Street, heading south. Thinking as he did so of Anse's body and of those of dead soldiers he'd seen, how he had seen them handled, even in the winding-down days of the war, like cordwood, stacked on wagon beds, on the flats of freight cars.

Not a clash of good and evil, he had come to believe. He knew too many good men—on both sides, gray and blue—

who had made a demarcation that clear untenable. To reduce it to so simple an equation was an insult either to their memory or to their sacrifice.

Not simple good and evil, he had told himself. It was the only way he had been able to bear it all.

October 10

THEY STOOD ON THE NORTH SIDE OF FORSYTH Street looking at it, the Georgia Pencil Company, light from the rising sun gleaming on the façade of the four-story edifice, the top floors shouldering proudly above the rest of the buildings on the block. The eastern light shone brightly on its signage, and beneath that, upon an advertisement for patent medicine that spanned the top two stories, painted black into the bricks and framed in white:

THE WORLD'S GREATEST MEDICINE
S.S.S.
FOR THE BLOOD.

The whole structure a bold incarnation of the Atlanta Spirit, dedicated to the latest in manufacturing technology, industry, and commerce, and on the second floor of which awaited, if the report proved accurate, the violated body of a fourteen-year-old girl who had died within its walls two days previous.

But for now Canby and Vernon could only wait across the street from the factory, hats pressed against their chests, halted by the procession winding its way past them down Forsyth Street. At its head had been Henry Grady and Bishop Drew, Grady solemnly bearing the state flag of Georgia on a gilt staff and the bishop trailed by an acolyte swinging a censer, from which issued dusky tendrils of incensed smoke. The bishop's murmurings were barely audible over the tinny clanging of the links in the censer's chains; Grady had been, for once, silent. And now behind them came the war widows, many of them mutely weeping and some with their children in tow, carrying miniature versions of the Georgia flag or the Confederate Stars and Bars on little sticks. All of the processional quiet enough that Canby and Vernon could hear the creaking of axles before the wagons bearing the coffins hove into view.

The caskets—six of them, each on a wagon of its own— were draped in six Confederate battle flags, the flags' edges tucked neatly under the corners of the new wood. The coffins newly carved, Vernon explained under his breath, though the remains inside them dated back possibly to the first of Sherman's cannonades, the bodies presumed to be those of Confederate artillerymen fallen early in the siege and buried in haste. Such shallow and provisional graves had been unearthed in every year since the war, as Atlanta's expansion strained far enough to reclaim the outlying network of breastworks and trenches that Joe Johnston's Grays had thrown up to defend the city. The entrenchments ran up through Buckhead and all the way up to the base of Vinings Mountain, upon which Sherman had reconnoitered his siege. These men had been found not far from the base of the mountain, Vernon said, and were now on their way to their reinterment in Oakland Cemetery, Atlanta gathering her lost Confederate dead, one by one, back to the city's center.

Canby and Vernon stood by as the last of the procession passed them, veterans bringing up the column in motley gray, some limping from old war wounds and others lamed by the march of time. As the last of them filed by, Canby could scent on the air, as it settled in the wake of the wagons and the waving flags and as the last of the incense dissipated, the sepulchral odor trailing the pine boxes.

They crossed the street to the factory's loading dock. Vernon, with the agility Canby still found remarkable for his age, climbed up the dock first, then offered down a hand to Canby.

"Likely you should brace yourself, from what Underwood said," Vernon told him. "Unnatural things were done to the girl."

Canby nodded wearily and dusted off his pants legs and looked out over the shipping bay. Crates were stacked against the walls, their slatted sides stenciled with G.P.C. and the dates of their packing. Elsewhere on the dock stood stacks of cedar planks, bundled into eight-foot lengths. Deep in the shadows of the bay, next to the double doors that led into the factory proper, stood Leon Greenberg, his brows knitted as he worked over figures on a clipboard with a pencil tied with string to its eye. His face bore the same look of worried concern that Canby had seen when the man spoke at the Decatur Inn, only redoubled now. Vernon hailed him and he hung the clipboard on a nail driven into the doorframe, shook their hands, and beckoned them inside. The pencil swung on its string tether as they passed.

"Awful, awful," Greenberg was saying as they entered, though his voice was drowned out by the churning of the machinery within. Canby saw to their right a giant drum, big as a boiler, being turned by a Negro on each of its ends. They worked in a contrapuntal rhythm, one turning a crank upward while the other carried the motion through its cycle on the bottom.

"Graphite drum," Greenberg barked in Canby's ear. "Mixes graphite and clay for the pencil leads."

"Why so much noise?"

"River rocks inside it to help the mixing. Chattahoochee rocks and water."

Canby listened to the groaning of those elements mixing, falling, separating, coming together again. A slurried, stuttered chattering. Watched the men working the rolling drum to see how closely they watched him, looking for the evasive glance, for tension or guilt in the eyes. He saw none.

They climbed an open staircase to the second floor and the noise of the drum faded below them. They entered a tall-ceilinged room where the work was quieter. Canby saw, in the morning light falling through the high windows, that the workers on this floor were all girls. Each of them busied herself at a cubicle of her own, joining erasers to the wood shafts of the pencils one at a time, then bundling the finished pencils with twine. Save for the small clatter of the pencils being handled, the girls worked in silence, though their eyes darted toward the men watching them. The tang of cedar shavings hung heavy in the air.

"Mary Flanagan was the best stamper I had," Greenberg said. "A bit older than the others. Very efficient."

"I wonder that you employ white girls in this work," Vernon said.

"Small hands are best suited to small work," Greenberg replied, never taking his eyes off the girls as they worked. "See the clamp they use to attach the ferrule to the shaft? I designed it myself. A patent is pending in Washington."

Greenberg resumed his walk, leading them through the cubicles, and as they passed, Canby noted that their hands and the rims of their nostrils were grimed with graphite dust. On one of the smaller girls' faces, he saw that a tear had coursed through the gray dust on her cheek.

"Do they know?" Canby asked.

"Mary was a kind of leader to them. She will be missed," Greenberg said, his voice losing some of its Brooklyn edge, "by more than me alone."

Greenberg threw a bolt on a door sized big enough for a barn and slid it aside on runners set into the floor. He nodded for Canby and Vernon to step through, then followed them and trundled the door shut, cutting off most of the light from the stamping room. He leaned against the door for a moment before he spoke.

"You'll find your colored officer in the back corner by the chimney. I'll go no farther."

In the dim light Canby could make out two patches of white and as they approached he saw that one of them was a handkerchief that Underwood held pressed against his mouth and nose. Underwood sat on a stool with his elbows on his knees, head down.

The other patch of white, Canby saw as they neared it, protruded from a metal-cased opening in the chimney. And he saw, as his eyes adjusted to the dark, that it was a pair of bloomers.

"She died like that," Underwood said. "I pulled her partway out to be sure there weren't no life left in her, then put her back like they found her."

Canby saw that the upper half of Mary Flanagan's body had been stuffed into the chimney grate. The bloomers, he now saw, had been pulled down in the assault. What had been done to her was unspeakable, unbelievable.

He looked away as best he could while he tugged the underwear back up to cover the damage, then gently pulled the body from the chimney. Her arms had been flung out before her, down into the dark of the chimney shaft. Around her neck, biting into the flesh, was a leather thong. Into her forehead had been carved an *H*, as neatly as the others. He laid her body out on the floor and Vernon closed her eyes.

"God Almighty," Vernon said.

"You wonder," Underwood said, kneading the handkerchief in his dark fist. "Did he rape her first, then strangle her? Or did he do both at once?"

Probably, Canby thought, they were the concerted parts of a single act. He figured the *H* had been carved postmortem. He hoped it had not been done until the girl had passed. And that the other carving had taken place only after Mary Flanagan was long, long gone.

"WHY IN HELL is he here, Vernon?"

The question was out of Canby's mouth before Henry Grady could even settle himself into his chair in a corner of the station's interrogation room. Grady smiled. The smile seemed to Canby, in this dingy room and in the greasy light dropping from the station's dirty windows, unseemly.

"Grady has an interest in seeing this thing through. Better him here than one of his cub reporters. Grady will work with us. As my daddy used to say, we'd rather have him inside the tent pissing out, than outside pissing in."

Canby turned his back squarely to Grady's corner, facing Greenberg again. The note Underwood had found in the factory lay on the battered table between them.

"Mister Greenberg, we'd like to make sure we have the sequence of events correct. You came in Saturday morning at seven, your usual time?"

"Yes."

"And Mary Flanagan came in when?"

"On towards one in the afternoon, as I recall."

"She was late for work?"

"No. The metal room was shut down on Thursday for the week. Our shipment of tin was delayed so she and the other girls were laid off."

"Until this morning."

"Correct."

"Then why was she in on Saturday?"

"Saturday noon is pay time. She had wages due her."

"Do you often work on your Sabbath?" Vernon asked.

Greenberg shrugged. "One works when one has to."

"And how much was she paid?"

"A dollar twenty. Hers was the last pay envelope I handed out Saturday."

"That was the last time you saw her?"

"Yes. She left the office with her pay; I closed up a short time after."

"You never saw her alive again after that?"

"I said I did not."

"And the factory is usually vacant from Saturday afternoon to Monday morning?"

"Except for the janitor, yes. His work week starts Sunday morning, to get ready for the manufactures resuming Monday."

"So you weren't in on Sunday?"

"Not until I let your men in to search the place."

"Would it surprise you to know that we found the pay envelope in a pocket of her dress?"

"I would have no reaction to that, Mister Canby."

"The full amount of her pay was still in it."

Greenberg only stared across the table at the men.

"No response to that, either?" Canby took the note from the table, uncreased it, and handed to Greenberg. "Would you read this aloud for us?"

Greenberg stared at the rough handwriting on the paper for a moment and frowned.

"I would rather not."

"Read it," Vernon said.

"May I have an attorney, please?"

"We'll send for one of your choice here directly," Vernon said. "In the meantime, we talk a little longer. Read it."

His face slack, Greenberg read, "'Mom that negro down here did this when i went to make water he said he would love me and push me down lay down and play like the night-witch did it he said, but that long tall black boy did it hisself.'" Greenberg set the note back on the tabletop quickly.

"Is that Mary Flanagan's hand?"

"I would not know."

"Does it sound like her to you?"

"It sounds like gibberish. I have no idea what it means."

"Do you not find the message troubling?"

"Of course I do. I find all of this affair something beyond troubling." Greenberg glanced down at the note and nodded. "You should talk to Campbell as well."

"Campbell?" Vernon asked.

Greenberg's exasperation was nearly palpable. "Yes, Fortus Campbell! The janitor!"

Canby let the silence hang in the room a full minute before he spoke. "Detective Underwood is interviewing him now in the colored section downstairs."

"There's your Negro," Greenberg said. "There's your tall black boy, like the note says."

"Yes," Canby said, tapping the table with his finger. "But so much of this does not add up. Campbell did not find the body until this morning. Where was the body before? And Underwood found this note downstairs, by the furnace."

"I tell you, Campbell is shiftless. I've written him up several times."

"And Mary Flanagan was not seen at home after Saturday morning," Vernon said. "Which makes you the last person to have seen her alive."

"So much of this does not add up," Canby said.

Greenberg was shaking his head. "These mauthers often come from troubled backgrounds. Their families don't know their whereabouts much of the time. Perhaps she was somewhere, and seen, on Sunday."

"Wait a minute," Grady said from the corner. He was flipping the pages of his notebook.

"Mauthers?" Vernon said.

Canby felt his pulse quicken. He tried to catch Greenberg's eyes.

"Spell that out?" Grady asked.

"Greenberg . . ." Canby said.

"Pardon me. British slang. I suppose I picked it up while I was in Leeds. A mauther is a factory girl."

"M-A-U?" Grady asked.

"T-H-E-R," Greenberg finished. "Why?"

Canby was rising, hooking Vernon's elbow as he stood. "No more," he said. "No more for now."

He hustled Vernon out the door and into the hallway. He was grateful for the general din of the station outside the questioning room, for the bustle of cops coming and going and the muttering of the most recently apprehended where they sat shackled to the bench by the booking counter.

"This man needs a lawyer, Vernon," Canby said as they leaned against the wall.

"For whatever good it'll do him. Hot damn, Thomas, that's as good as a confession." Vernon was grinning. "We've got this thing wrapped up."

"I think Greenberg is not our man."

"You heard him in there, Thomas. What more do you need?"

"Greenberg is a company man, Vernon. A factotum, an office man. Can you really conceive of him being capable of what's been done?"

"I've been around long enough to know I don't know it all. Stranger things have happened, Thomas. And that man just handed himself over to justice."

"Vernon—" Canby began, but Vernon cut him off with a wave of his hand. He leaned close to Canby's face.

"Must I remind you that I'm under a great deal of pressure to wrap this thing up?"

The door to the interrogation room swung open. For a moment Grady's small stature seemed to fill the doorframe, then the door was shutting behind him as he pushed past them in the hallway, his face aglow. He was halfway to the station's exit before Canby spoke.

"Grady!" he called, but Grady did not turn and they watched him move down the front steps at a clip. Within an hour his presses had begun to roll.

October 20

On his couch in the new and less opulent rooms he'd been given on the fifth floor of Kimball House, Canby stirred. His dreams were a wash of swirling figures, faces in mist. And behind the images, sounds: door hinges and footsteps, the clinking of glass. He strained toward waking, reached beneath his pillow for the pocket revolver he'd put there. A hand settled firmly on his forearm.

"Now, now, Thomas, it wouldn't do to draw down on a friend, would it?"

Canby cracked open an eye. It felt swollen nearly to a slit. "Vernon."

"In the flesh," Vernon said. He cleared a space on the coffee table and sat, selecting from the detritus scattered there Canby's nearly empty bottle of Jameson and an Atlanta *Constitution*.

"This paper is three days old," he said.

"I couldn't stand to read any more."

"I don't understand you, Thomas. How often have we had a case so neatly wrapped up as this one? You should be pleased."

"You saw Greenberg at the preliminary hearing. Was that the demeanor of a guilty man?"

"They all plead not guilty, Thomas. And they all act like they never dreamed of finding themselves there."

"I need to tell you something."

Vernon raised a hand and turned his head to the side. "Not me. Tell it to the judge. You're due in court at nine."

Vernon studied the label on the Jameson bottle for a moment. "Rest your mind, Thomas. The case is closed." He turned the bottle up and drank, then held the bottle out to Canby. "Here. A dram to get you going."

Canby drank, his throat clenching. His parched mouth, which had a minute before been cottony and coppery at once, burned and then was numbed. He settled back on the couch.

"I can't do it."

"Of course you can."

"I know Greenberg is an innocent man, Vernon."

"That is for the court to decide. Your job is to get on that stand and tell them what you have seen. The rest is the court's bailiwick."

Vernon tapped the *Constitution* against his knee. "You've missed some fine testimony, lying up in here. One of the factory girls came forward and said Greenberg made advances toward her. His landlady says he's been asking about another set of rooms, to bring in one or two of 'his girls.' That's sworn testimony."

Canby looked at him blankly.

"You could have been reading about it," Vernon said, and tossed the newspaper onto the table. He rose and walked across the room. Canby heard him drop the plug into the bathtub and turn the water on full-bore. After a moment he reappeared in the doorway and leaned against the jamb. He studied Canby for a long moment until the younger man rose from the couch and began unbuttoning his shirt.

"And I don't need to tell you a good showing today will ensure you a place on the force again."

Canby nodded. Behind Vernon, wisps of steam had begun to issue from the tub and to cloud the doorway. The carpet beneath Canby's bare feet was sumptuous—rich, dark, and new like all of Kimball House, save for the wrecked room upstairs.

Vernon stood aside for Canby to enter the bathroom. Canby shrugged out of his nightshirt and eased into the steaming tub.

"You'll make me proud," Vernon said.

"One time I didn't."

"It still pains me to think about that shitty mess."

"Not your fault."

"Tell me, Thomas, was the greater good served by you taking the fall for that whore? Was Mamie O'Donnell worth it?"

"No," Canby said as he settled into the steam and water. "Turns out she wasn't."

HE'D HAD SOME WARNING, of course, from the editions of the *Constitution* he had read recounting the opening days of the trial, from the breathless accounts of Grady and his stringers; he should have known to expect a circus. But what he and Vernon found as they descended from the hansom was beyond the scale of any trial he'd yet seen: a pandemonium of crackers, carpetbaggers, goober-grabbers, sharps, and dandies moiled and hustled across the lawn of the Fulton County Courthouse hawking wares and bartering for seats inside. There was even a redheaded boy of ten or eleven selling sandwiches so that those lined up for the best positions in the gallery would not have to give up a coveted seat for noontime recess. As if all of them had come here to celebrate, collectively, their own private hatreds. Early in the week the papers had begun calling it the trial of the century, but now the crowd and the energy seemed to have doubled themselves. All gathered this morning for the double bill of testimony from Fortus Campbell and Thomas Canby.

Canby and Vernon had not walked a dozen paces from the hansom when a rawboned man detached himself from the crowd and pressed his red face close to Canby's.

"You gone put that jewboy away today, ain't you?"

Vernon stepped between the two men. "Back away from my deputy," he said.

The man raised his callused hand and backed up a half step. "Don't mean no harm, Chief," he said. "But it was my sister-in-law's cousin that Jew raped and murdered."

"I know your kin, Malcolm. Thomas is going to do the right thing."

"I hope so. I surely do." The man shuffled away, the heels of his brogans dragging, and took a seat on a wagon bed pulled to the courthouse square's curb. A half dozen men who shared his raw features made way for him to sit, the gaggle of them perched all over the wagon. None spoke when he rejoined them, but a stream of tobacco juice shot into the dust near one wagon wheel.

Inside, they had just taken their seats when the gavel began to rap to commence the day's proceedings, and in short order Fortus Campbell had been sworn in and seated in the witness box. As though relishing his position higher than all but the judge, he scanned the crowd of white faces below him haughtily. Canby watched him a moment, then turned to get a better view of Leon Greenberg where he sat at the defense table. The man's bespectacled eyes seemed to be trying to bore through Campbell.

The prosecutor rose with a sheaf of papers in his hand. He wore French cuffs and a silk bow tie and his hair was slicked back against his skull, his face as clean-shaven as Canby's. Vernon leaned in close to Canby's ear. "Solicitor General Franklin Denton," he said. "I hear he has ambitions for the mayor's office."

"Will he have the *Constitution*'s endorsement?"

"If he can close this case before the exposition is over, no doubt he will."

"And Judge Reinhardt, is he still active with the Ring?"

Vernon only stared straight ahead. His eyes narrowed as he watched Denton walk to the witness stand, studying the papers in his hand.

"Fortus Campbell, you work in what capacity at the Georgia Pencil Company?"

"As janitor."

"Is it typical for you to be in the factory on a Saturday afternoon?"

"Saturday and Sunday are my busiest days."

"Doing what, exactly?"

"Sweeping up shavings, oiling machinery. Getting things ready for Monday start of work."

"And what was unusual about Saturday, the eighth of October?"

"Greenberg was acting funny."

"*Mister* Greenberg," the judge said.

Campbell nodded slowly. "Mister Greenberg was acting funny."

"Funny in what way?"

"Nervous-like. From the time we both come in about seven till he went upstairs to his office. Told me he'd stomp on the floor if he needed me. He ain't never done that before."

"And you were working on the ground floor?"

"Right. Sweeping up, burning trash in the furnace."

"And you told the police you saw Mary Flanagan enter the factory and go upstairs at what time?"

"'Bout noon."

"And after that?"

"Heard a scream."

"And you did what?"

"Well, I dozed off. I'd just had my lunch. That furnace room gets warm. I took my break."

Denton shuffled his papers. "And sometime later you were awakened?"

"Heard Mister Greenberg stomping on the floor. Went upstairs and saw Mary on the floor of his office, kind of crumpled-up, like. He was acting funny for sure, then. Gave me a hundred dollars out of the cashbox and had me set down and write that note they found."

"He dictated the note to you?"

"That's right—dictated it."

"Let's be certain we have these events straight for the record," Denton said. He turned to face the jury. "Mister Greenberg was the only person on the second floor of the factory that Saturday. You saw Mary Flanagan go up the stairs alive, then later that day saw her dead in Mister Greenberg's office. At his feet."

"That's right."

"Nothing further, Your Honor."

As Denton sat down, Greenberg's lawyer rose from behind the defense table. He was a thin, pallid man who moved with the bearing of one aggrieved.

"Proceed, Mister Loehman."

Loehman let a long moment of silence play out, staring at Campbell, before he spoke. "Is it common to hear screams in the pencil factory?"

"Not unless someone get something caught in the machines."

"Let me specify: Is it common on a Saturday, when the machines are down, to hear a scream?"

"Nope."

"No, *sir*," the judge corrected.

"Nossir."

"And yet on this Saturday, you heard a scream and did what?"

"Dozed off, like I said."

"In a nearly empty factory, near midday on a Saturday, you heard a girl scream and then drifted off to sleep?"

"Like I said."

"So you said. Unbelievable." Loehman looked at the men in the jury box for a long moment. Then he walked back to his table, studied the papers there, and selected one. "Mister Campbell, you are well acquainted with the Atlanta Police Department, are you not?"

Campbell shifted in his seat.

"I will help you with your recollection. In the past eight years, four indictments on petty larceny, three convictions. One conviction for assault. You have been in and out of the chain gang several times. As has your father, no less. It seems crime runs in the family. If Mister Greenberg has committed any wrong in what we are discussing today, I submit it was in taking you into his employ from the first."

Campbell sat silent.

"And yet you expect the jury to take you at your word above that of an honest businessman?"

"Wasn't honest what he done to Mary. I seen it."

"Your Honor?" Loehman asked.

"Only answer the questions put to you, boy. Nothing extra."

"Yessir."

"Mister Campbell, no money was discovered missing from the cashbox. The factory's ledgers balance perfectly. The Atlanta police will confirm this. And you admit the note was written by you, in your own hand. Further, it was you who found Miss Flanagan's body. Why is it, Mister Campbell, that it is not you on trial for your life here?"

"Objection. The defense is grandstanding."

"Sustained. Save that for your summation, Mister Loehman."

"I will do that, Your Honor. Most certainly, I will. Just one more question, Mister Campbell. Why in God's name would a man like Leon Greenberg do something like this?"

"I do not know, Mister Loehman," Campbell said. "But I don't understand none of you peoples."

The silence that followed was so entire that Canby could hear Loehman sigh.

"The defense believes Mister Campbell's character and credibility render his testimony entirely suspect, Your Honor. We have no further questions for this witness."

"Rebuttal?"

Denton looked over to the jury box, surveyed the men seated there, and nodded to himself as though satisfied with what he saw. "None, Your Honor."

"Thirty-minute recess, then. When we resume, the next witness will take the stand. Mister Campbell," the judge said, "I am relieved to excuse you."

"I TELL YOU, Greenberg is not the man." Canby was entering his second hour on the stand, beginning to understand how the suspects must feel being sweated down at the station: it seemed that with every ebb in his energy, Denton gained the more resolve.

"Are you, sir, attempting to testify for the defense?"

"I'd like to get at the truth."

"Your Honor," Denton said, "the prosecution requests permission to treat Detective Canby as an adverse witness."

The judge raised an eyebrow. "To what end?"

"That I might impeach him, Your Honor."

The judge leaned back in his chair, his brow furrowed. "On what grounds?"

"I believe that Mister Canby, for whatever reasons of his own, intends to subvert the reasonable prosecution of this case."

"Objection!" Loehman cried, rising. Judge Reinhardt held out a hand to him and Loehman slowly sat back in his chair. The judge's heavy-lidded eyes left him and moved to study Denton, then Canby. Slowly, he lowered his hand and nodded at the prosecutor.

"Proceed, Mister Denton."

"Thank you, Your Honor. Mister Canby, Chief Thompson has confided to me that you were brought back to Atlanta for your expertise, is that correct?"

"And at the request of the Ring."

Denton seemed to subdue his smirk with some effort. "Surely you know the Ring has not been extant for years. Again I ask: You were engaged for your expertise, correct?"

"Yes."

"Then let us enumerate the progress that was made with that expertise. No killer was apprehended on your watch. Two additional victims were claimed—one your own deputy from Ringgold, and the other a child of tender years whose innocence was ripped savagely from her and upon whom depravities were performed of such a nature they cannot be discussed in open court. This, Detective, is the résumé you present before this court."

"Regardless of what I've done or haven't, Greenberg is not the murderer."

For answer Denton turned his back to the witness stand and

walked swiftly to the prosecutor's table, held a hand out to an assistant, who placed a file on his outstretched palm. He flipped through the pages, glancing up now and again at Canby.

"When did you first begin in the employ of the city of Atlanta, Mister Canby—originally, I mean?"

"January 1866."

"After you mustered out of the army?"

"That is correct."

"Which army was that?"

"The Union army, Second Division, Seventeenth Corps," Canby said. He could hear, in the jury box, a chair leg grate against the floorboards.

Denton seemed surprised at the answer. "You fought for the Union?"

"I enlisted when the siege ended."

"The Second Division? Was that not General Sherman's own command?"

"It was."

"Hardly the action of a patriotic Atlantan."

Canby took a deep breath. "My father died during the siege. He was killed during the shelling. I had a score to settle."

"With General William Tecumseh Sherman?"

"The shelling killed my father. Sherman ordered it done. I intended to take an eye for an eye."

Denton waved the pages of the file in the air, the long arc of his arm pantomiming exasperation. "You intended to *kill* General Sherman?"

"If I could, yes. I was fourteen years old. He'd killed my father. I still see a kind of sense to it."

Again Denton rattled his papers, but Canby saw that two of the jurors were nodding. The shadow of a grin was visible on one of the men's faces, beneath his beard. Perhaps one whose house had been razed by Sherman. Canby looked out over the spectators and saw that Robert Billingsley had slipped in among those standing at the back of the courtroom. Saw that on the older man's face, too, was the trace of a smile.

The judge lifted his gavel, then, seeming to think better of using it, leaned forward and gave Denton a baleful glance. "May we, Mister Denton," he said in a careful cadence, "expedite this process?"

"Of course, Your Honor. For the record, Mister Canby, you were appointed in 1866 by the Reconstruction government of the United States to a newly constituted police force of the city of Atlanta. You served as patrolman, then night inspector, and finally rose to the rank of detective in 1875. Correct?"

"Yes."

Denton flipped a page in his file. "And the record states that in March 1877 you were dismissed from the force on charges of embezzlement, graft, and improper commerce with a woman known to the city of Atlanta as a prostitute."

Canby had to wait as the gavel pounded, and the grumbling from the gallery abated, before he could answer.

"That's what the record says. But it's not true. I've known Mamie O'Donnell since we were children. It was a loan."

"A loan? No doubt that is what I'd call it if I found myself in such a compromised position." He cut his eyes to the jury box and added, "Which of course I would not."

"Vernon Thompson can tell you it's not true."

"Really? Because the papers I have before me bear Chief Thompson's signature. All of them do."

"Vernon had no choice. They finally managed to run off the Reconstruction appointees in '77 when the new constitution was ratified. I was lucky to have stayed on that long."

"Who are *they*, Mister Canby?"

"The Ring."

"The Ring again! Would that we all had a nebulous Ring on which to pin our misfortunes and moral failures!" Denton dropped the file on the prosecutor's table. "Your Honor, I believe I can indeed expedite this process. Mister Canby, in short, you are a disgrace to the men of Atlanta's police force."

Denton moved up close to the witness stand, leaning toward Canby. He was close enough that Canby could smell the brilliantine in his slicked-back hair.

"Whatever I am, Greenberg is not your killer."

"Even further you descend! Based on your highly circumspect expertise and this sullied record of prior employment with the city, you advocate on behalf of this man. You would vouch for a child of the slums of Europe, risen to some prominence of late, yes, but no Atlantan. Hardly even an American."

Canby looked out over the courtroom, wishing sorely he could steal a sip of whiskey from the flask in his breast pocket. Henry Grady sat in the front row with an open notepad propped on the knee of his crossed legs, pressing the point of a pencil to his damp lower lip. In the back, Billingsley still stood among the others, his eyes hawklike with scrutiny. Canby looked over to Greenberg, slumped wretched-looking in his chair behind the defendant's table. Canby struggled to swallow before he spoke.

"*Mauther* is not the word the murderer intended."

"Is it not? By your demonstrably deficient methods of deduction, what word would you have put forward as this madman's message?"

"I do not know."

Denton nodded curtly, cocking one eyebrow. "No idea?"

"Not *mauther*, certainly. That much I'm certain of." Canby heard a murmur beginning among the spectators. Again, he swallowed with effort. "Because I carved the *U*. Originally it was an *L*." With his finger stretched out in front of him, Canby described the gesture in the air.

Later Canby would not be able to recall the exact sequence of events as he registered them from his vantage on the witness stand—whether first he saw Vernon's head drooping toward his chest or noted the declamatory outrage of Denton's turning toward the jury box or Underwood starting from his chair in the colored section and straining to be heard over the burst of noise from the gallery or the nearly athletic fervor with which Grady began to scribble notes on his pad. Or the sad resignation he thought he saw in Billingsley's eyes, or Greenberg's face falling into the palms of his rising hands.

"Your Honor," Denton cried, with a sigh audible over the tumult and a gesture toward Canby of inexpressible disdain, "the prosecution rests."

Canby hung his head, thinking how sorely he wished that the rest were indeed silence. No such merciful oblivion for him.

Though he shut his eyes he could not shut out the roar of the spectators' outbursts and the hammering of the judge's gavel on the sounding block, quickening, but sure as the sounding of a knell. The whole of this din filling his ears, the announcement of and accompaniment to his utter and final disgrace.

CANBY SAT ALONE AT A BACK BOOTH OF LOVEJOY'S Saloon with the *Constitution* spread out before him and the nearly empty bottle of Jameson at his elbow, his tattered copy of Emerson's *Essays* beside it. Here at Lovejoy's for a second night because the Big Bonanza was now strictly off-limits and the Shamrock, over on Pryor, had proven to be another old haunt too full of ghosts. Killing time. He was reading with half-drunk bemusement the latest installment of a series called "Negro Atlanta" by an ambitious young reporter named M. C. McMillin, who had announced that he planned to tour as much of black Atlanta as he could discover. Canby took a swallow of whiskey as he read.

"Few people in Atlanta ever stop to consider how the colored people of the city live. We see them every day; they are about us and work for us, and at night go to their homes; but what these homes are and where they are, and the little picture that each hearthstone presents, we never think of," this McMillin reported, indulging in what Angus Canby would have called a too-pronounced fondness for the semicolon. "But by far the largest proportion of Negroes are never really known to us; they drift off to themselves, and are almost as far from the white people, as if the two races never met."

The story ended with a list of sites the reporter planned to explore in the following weeks: Pig Alley, the Anthole, Beaver Slide, Hell's Half Acre, Snake Nation. All of them regular stops on the police beat. Places that Canby remembered well as highly inhospitable to the likes of M. C. McMillin. He wondered how the young man's zeal would fare in those most sullen and volatile corners of the city.

He closed the newspaper and looked once more at its front page. This special afternoon edition of the *Constitution* that had run, for the first time in its short history, a double-bill feature of "Atlanta and Her Enemies" at the bottom of page one. Canby studied his likeness sketched in newsprint next to Greenberg's, whose Semitic features had been sharpened and darkened, some shadings of charcoal, perhaps, employed to heighten the shadows of his face, giving it a sinister aspect. Canby himself looked the worse for the portraiture: nose a bit bulbous, bags beneath his eyes.

And above the crease, "GUILTY" spread over all four columns in outsized letters. He scanned the article again. The jury had, at least by appearances, deliberated overnight before reaching its verdict. But it was the *Constitution*'s presses that had really delivered the verdict, and would deliver the sentence as well, Canby thought. Greenberg's defense had filed an appeal immediately, the article said. Word of mob justice for Greenberg had been circulating among the lower classes of whites. For his safety Greenberg was being kept in Fulton Tower instead of the city jail, moved now to the infamous cell for the condemned that the guards called Spot 12, in the front of the tower, near the door and the watch desk. There he would be under the supervision of two guards at all times save the third shift, when the guards retired for the night and the jailer took the wee hours alone, "save for the company of Mary Flanagan's murderer, kept under lock and key but scarce a half-dozen strides away."

Canby folded the paper and looked out over the saloon. Nearly all of the patrons had gone. Even Joel Chandler Harris had left at some point without Canby's noticing. There'd been an awkward moment between them when Canby came in: Harris looking up from his notebook to give Canby a short nod, then back to his work. No reporting at this hour, in Lovejoy's, Canby figured. Most likely more Remus tales of Brer Rabbit or Brer Fox. Harris mixing his pleasure and business these days, with seven mouths to feed at home, maybe eight now. It had not been Harris's byline under the stories about Canby and Greenberg. Canby pushed the paper across the tabletop, away from him.

A black boy of grammar school age was wiping down the empty tables and booths. Lovejoy was behind the bar rinsing glasses in the zinc.

"What time have you got, E.B.?" Canby asked.

"Closing time, Thomas."

"That's not a proper time, E.B."

"Proper time is 'late.'"

Canby refilled his glass and pressed the cork into the bottle with the heel of his hand. He sipped the whiskey and watched the black boy as he worked his way toward this last booth.

"You can take those," Canby said when the boy finally got to him. He nodded at the newspaper and the bottle of Jameson. The boy rolled the paper and stuck it in his back pocket. He put the bottle on the bench across from Canby and began cleaning the table. Canby set his glass on the book of Emerson and moved both out of the reach of the boy's dishcloth, pressed against the pine beadboard that lined Lovejoy's walls.

"It's a weeknight."

"Yessir," the boy said, dragging the wet cloth in circles over the table.

"That means school tomorrow."

The boy looked up, a trace of a smile in his eyes. Canby imagined he was used to the drunks funning him and that he wanted to let him know he was in on the joke.

"I'm not kidding. School. Tomorrow."

"Yessir." The eyes dropped back to the table and the cloth resumed its circuit.

Canby reached into his jacket for his wallet, fat now with what Vernon had diplomatically called his 'muster pay,' and took out a dollar.

"Make you a deal. I give you this, you go to school in the morning."

After a moment's consideration the boy nodded and Canby gave him the bill.

"How far is home for you?"

"Nine blocks out to Shermantown, sir."

"Be careful getting there. You shouldn't stop to talk to anyone."

"Yessir."

"I'm serious, now."

"Yessir." The boy folded the dollar up. He took off his left shoe and stuffed the bill into its toe, then put the shoe back on and carried the bottle behind the bar.

Canby picked up his glass and the battered *Essays* and rose. He took a pull from the glass, then another, longer one, and set it on the bar as he said good night to E.B. Lovejoy.

Outside he stood under Lovejoy's shingle and weighed his options for a moment before he admitted to himself that he had none, other than to spend another night sheltering at Vernon's. He set out down Peachtree Street toward Butler. The hour was nearing midnight now but the streetlights were still lit, gaslight glowing for the safety of those travelers who continued to arrive in the city at all hours for the Cotton Exposition. He looked up in the night sky for some constellation but the city's light was too bright to see past it. He supposed that boded well for Lovejoy's boy on his way home, though he knew the gas grid had never extended out as far as Shermantown, likely never would.

He marveled at the rarity of being the only pedestrian on Peachtree. Late indeed, he thought. The wee hours. The late wee hours. He knew he'd had too much to drink. Was that the word the *Constitution* reporter had used, *wee*?

He stopped and looked around him at the stores shuttered for the night on the other side of Peachtree, the three-storied white mass of First Methodist South behind him, its slate steeple reaching up past the light of the lamps. Wee hours, the story had said. And the reporter had pointed out that the jailer took the last shift alone.

Then he was moving again, heading southward now to Porter Street, his footfalls sounding off the macadam of Peachtree as he stepped up his pace toward Butler and then Fair Street, toward the tower.

Midway there he heard the clatter of wagon wheels on the pavement and then he was running, cutting across a short block of Butler Street toward the lighted hansom racing up Hunter, shouting to hail it.

THERE HAD BEEN no torchlight to herald their coming. No snorting of horses; no creaking of wagon wheels. Not even the sound of the jail door's lock being jimmied. As the jailer told it, there was only the settling of a noose around his neck by hands unseen, the swift draping of a pillowcase over his head by figures behind him and out of sight. He was lashed to the bars of Spot 12 himself while Greenberg groaned inside the cage and they worked their way through the jailer's pilfered key chain. They talked of Buckhead, the jailer said, where most of Mary Flanagan's kin still were. And of the big oak out front of Henry Irby's store, there at the crossroads.

So Vernon told it after nearly running Canby down in the middle of Fair Street with the police hansom. Vernon had been whipping the reins across the horses' necks, speeding them northward to the rail yard and the Western & Atlantic depot, when a dark figure had stepped into the middle of the street waving his arms. Vernon said he'd had half a mind to mow down the fool, another drunk peckerwood the likes of which he was trying to intercept. But he had recognized Canby at the last moment and slowed the hansom just enough for Canby to jump into it. And now, pulling into the rail yard, he said that their likeliest chance of beating the mob to the tree in Buckhead was the W&A's Number Nine Line. How much time had elapsed before the jailer had worked loose the knots and sent for Vernon was anyone's guess. Right now their best hope was speed.

"Likely the bastard was asleep," Canby said, climbing up behind Vernon into the smoking locomotive.

"Likely. But he also was scared. He'd soiled himself. That was quite evident." Vernon leaned from the locomotive cab, half his body out of the engine and in the night air, hanging by the handrail, adroit as a yard hand himself. "Ho, there! Got those cars uncoupled?"

"That's my job," the engineer said sourly. He cocked an ear toward the rear of the train and, satisfied by what the clanking song of metal told him, nodded to Vernon. "We're ready."

"North, then. With speed."

Vernon clapped the fireman on his shoulder, where he was shoveling coal into the firebox at a pace too slow to suit him. "Feed that box, you dirty Irish son of a bitch," he yelled. "Stoke it up!"

The engineer tugged on the whistle and pushed forward the handle that unlocked the brake. Like a slumbering beast awakened, the engine began to churn and the locomotive to move, its wheels slowly gaining purchase on the slick rails.

They pulled out from the shadows of the Western & Atlantic depot and northward through town, the steel wheels beginning to keen on the rails.

"And thus the Number Nine departs up the Marietta Line, hours ahead of the schedule," Vernon said.

"And short of its freight," the engineer added.

But Vernon seemed not to have heard. As he measured the progress of dark buildings against the pace the train was picking up, he seemed satisfied, or at least eased. He pulled a cigar from his vest and lit it, tossed the match over the rail. "There is yet time."

"If they are on horseback."

"Which they surely are. And one of them with Greenberg in the saddle afore him to slow the group down."

"How long was the guard tied?"

"He figures an hour before he worked himself free."

Canby smiled bitterly. "*Figures?* Then he surely was asleep when they broke in. We will have to do better. Are you well armed?"

"Quite. Yourself?"

Canby patted his jacket, where under the cloth and snug against his chest hung his .32 Bulldog. The pocket revolver tucked into his boot. Anse's big Colt, he regretted, was still under the couch in Vernon's front room where he had slept last night. And the rest of his arms still at the Kimball House, in the empty room there. He knew that whatever force they met at Buckhead would surely outmatch these meager munitions.

"We are a small posse, Vernon."

"A small posse in search of a large one. How fucked is that?"

Because he had had the same thought himself, Canby did not bother to answer. Instead, as the city lights faded behind them, he watched the ember of Vernon's cigar flare and ebb in the darkness, smelled its rich smoke fill the small cab of the locomotive with each exhalation before it was snatched away by the night wind. Once, they lumbered over a trestle, the wood planks popping like shots and the Chattahoochee roiling below. At regular intervals the fireman would feed the firebox, and each heave of coal into the box brought forth a shower of sparks before he shut the door. And at some point between the openings and closings of the firebox door Canby became aware of a muted glow on the horizon ahead.

The light grew. While the sleepers clacked beneath the engine it seemed to be burning with a rhythm of its own. As they drew nearer Canby could see that it was the flickering pulse of dozens of torches held aloft by the men in the mob and that some of them, off to a corner of the crossroads, had started a bonfire. The engineer threw the brake on the train and the wheels began to grind against the steel of the tracks, fighting the momentum the engine had built up in the miles since Atlanta, and before it had slowed to a jog Canby and Vernon were leaping out of the engine and running.

Most of the men circled around the tree had turned at the sound of the train; those who hadn't now glanced over their shoulders at the sound of bootheels on the hard-packed clay of the road. They parted for Canby and Vernon, stepping back with torches in hand to make way. Canby's sprint had carried him nearly to the trunk of the tree when he brought himself up short before it, looking up at what hung there.

"Goddamn," Vernon said.

Leon Greenberg's wrists and ankles were still shackled. His rent clothing hung on him like rags. They had covered his face with a white handkerchief but the noose's knot under his chin exposed the throat's elongation, the brutal realignment of skull and body that the rope and his broken spine had created. The body still twisted in a slight pendulous swaying against the rope. Canby thought he could hear, under the snickering of the flames, the hemp fibers creaking. He reached up a hand and put it against Greenberg's shin to still the dead weight.

"How long?" he asked.

"You just missed his last kicking," one of them said. "Pulled that wagon bed out from under him and he commenced to jumping like a cat in a skillet."

Canby lowered his hand and turned around, looking at the men and boys in the crowd. Their faces seemed dazed and Canby knew the look: bloodthirst slaked, and after it, a kind of guilty wonder turning in the minds of each of them at what they had unleashed. He reached into his jacket and pulled out the Bulldog.

"Bring the wagon back around."

"Now, just you wait a minute." One of the men, older, took a step forward. Canby recognized him from the courthouse yard. Not even bothering with a hood for this work. "This ain't your deal here."

"Oh, indeed it is, Malcolm," Vernon said. "Shall I even begin to list the felonies you've committed tonight?"

The man's sunburnt face cracked into a crooked smile. "You aim to take me in? For hanging that wicked son of a bitch?"

"I've a mind to."

The smile dimmed. "Boys, y'all cut that jewboy down and get your souvenirs. Mary's got her justice. Let's wrap this up."

Canby felt his hand rising, the revolver's weight steadying his arm. "Cut him down, yes. But the first one to maim him is a dead man."

"You ain't got bullets enough for all of us."

Canby looked at the pistol's barrel, then at the man. "You're right," he said, cocking the pistol. "But the first one is yours, Malcolm."

Canby kept his eyes on the man's face until he saw the peckerwood cunning leave his eyes. Light flickering on his face, he nodded to the men closest to him and three of them broke off from the group, one mounting to the wagon's bench and the others climbing in back. The driver snapped the reins and the horse came around, snorting as it passed Greenberg's earthward-pointing feet. The wagon stopped and one of them wrapped his arms around Greenberg's waist and lifted while the tallest man sawed at the rope with a Barlow knife. They lowered him first to the wagon bed and then, almost gently, to the dust at the foot of the oak.

Wordlessly, they began to depart, the circle dispersing. Men tossed their torches into the bonfire as they left, the fire itself beginning to dwindle now, and untied their horses and mounted. Soon the last sounds of hoofbeats had faded into the distance. Vernon sat down wearily and leaned himself against the oak tree.

"Well, that's the end of it, Thomas. I hate to see it done outside the law, but that is an end to it."

"An innocent man, Vernon."

Vernon did not answer. Canby stood regarding the locomotive, still and dark now where it had come to a stop on the tracks. His chest felt hollowed out. "Think we could take him back on the engine?"

"No room. Go on over to Irby's and ask him to wire Atlanta for an undertaker."

Canby looked over to Irby's store. Its windows were resolutely dark. Irby too good a man to have sought or taken any kind of profit from this affair. Straining, Canby could nearly make out the profile of the buck's head hung over the door. Still too dark to see how much it had weathered since he'd last passed through. He started across the road.

"And Thomas," Vernon said, "see if he has a horse to spare."

Canby stopped and turned around. "What for?"

"Solomon Pace is still taking lodgers at his place," Vernon said, lighting another cigar. "Vinings is only five or six miles."

"Vernon—"

"Go on up to Vinings, see Julia. Uncle Solomon will put you up. I'll see if anything can be done in Atlanta to save your job. And mine."

"Vernon," Canby said, waving a hand at the hanging tree, Greenberg's body, "this is not over."

Vernon shook out the match, exhaled a plume of smoke, and leveled his eyes on Canby. "I'm not speaking as a friend, Thomas. That's an order."

Canby's footsteps sounded leaden to him as he crossed the empty road. He knocked on a window, called out, "Police," and watched as a point of candlelight appeared and made its way to the front of the store. Soon there were sounds of the door being unlatched from within.

He emerged from the store fifteen minutes later with the telegraph receipt. He had asked the telegraph office to send a courier out to the undertaker's home immediately, Bond's or Roth's, whichever was closest to the telegraph office. Just before the transmission went out, he appended, DID WHAT WE COULD TO STOP IT.

As he walked back to the tree he saw that Vernon was standing over the dying bonfire. As Canby watched, he pitched a length of rope into the flames. Canby knelt by Greenberg's body and lifted the handkerchief from his face. His glasses were gone—a trophy, he imagined, taken by one of his executioners before they strung him up. Canby saw that, above the handsome but bloodied mustache, Greenberg's nose had been broken. Gone, too, was the noose from around his neck. It had left only its mottled imprint in the flesh.

He looked over to the fire again. Vernon was walking toward him. He lowered the handkerchief over Greenberg's face.

"Irby's saddling the horse."

"Good. You are overtired. Get away for a while. That's at least some good to come from this."

"This is not over. Innocent blood, Vernon."

"I told you, it is an order."

"I should be in Atlanta."

"Atlanta will still be there when you get back. Let me see what can be done in town. I'll wire you. Meantime, get yourself rested. Give my best to Julia."

Vernon put a hand on Canby's shoulder and they stood in

that filial pose for a few minutes, nothing spoken. Above them, dangling from a broad limb of the old oak, the severed length of rope swayed in the predawn breeze. Canby fingered the folded telegraph receipt in his pocket. The response from the undertakers had come back quickly. He imagined he could feel the words of their reply on the paper in his pocket, as though etched on the paper with the finality of chisel on stone: WOULD THAT IT HAD BEEN ENOUGH.

After a few minutes, Canby saw Irby emerging from the back of his store, leading a horse by its bridle toward them. Saw, too, that to the east, beyond the rim of the dark horizon, the sun was struggling to rise.

October 28

◆━━━━━━━━━━━━━━━━━━━━━━━━━━━━━━━━━━

AND YET THE KILLINGS HAD STOPPED. THE ROUTINE
of days in Vinings with Julia, awaiting word from Vernon that
did not come and did not come. A telegraph from Underwood
nearly every day. But no progress. The overwhelming numb-
ness of his guilt hanging on Canby like a pall, refusing to lift
despite the mountain air, despite Julia's presence. Every afternoon he scanned the *Constitution* for news of another murder,
report of the killer who surely was not Greenberg resuming
his dark work. He had read that the expenses for Greenberg's
funeral had been paid by Morris Rich, the department store
man, and that the viewing of his body had been attended by
hundreds. Burial, the paper reported, was to be in his native
Brooklyn. Just as well, the writer editorialized; he never
belonged down here anyway.

But the news of Greenberg had run on page three, pushed
to the back of the paper by coverage of the International
Cotton Exposition. Columns of glowing words on the city-
within-a-city, praise for its technological marvels, its brilliant

electric lights, its swelling attendance numbers. News of the impending arrival of William Tecumseh Sherman, the general descending on the city to confirm the reconciliation of this New South the I.C.E. celebrated, to toss a garland for this phoenix arisen from its own ashes.

Canby folded the paper and set it aside. The breeze here on the mountain moved through the trees and scattered the gold and auburn leaves that had begun to drop from the oaks, the hickories, the sycamores. There was a hint of winter in it. The fallen leaves had begun to pool against the headstones of the little cemetery at the mountain's summit, where the early settlers of Vinings' first families—Paces, Randalls—had been laid to rest. He looked away from the stones. Far to the south, near the end of his vision's range, Atlanta teemed in the valley, the railroad roundhouse smoking at its center. He knew his business there was not yet finished.

He heard the clap of wood down below him and figured it to be the door of the Vinings school slapping against the front of the schoolhouse. He looked down and picked out the school from the other buildings of the village, all of them green-shingled, whitewashed clapboard, save for the Negro settlement that sat at a short distance on the northernmost part of the mountain, where the buildings were all spare parts, tumbledown and ramshackle. Surely enough, the dirt lot out front of the school had filled with Julia's scholars, noisily dispersing as though they had flung themselves off its porch in their eagerness for room to move, for fresh air, the precious stretch of an afternoon's freedom in these shortening days of autumn. He smiled. If there had been no truants or idlers today to be held after, Julia would soon be on her way up the mountainside to meet him.

For a few minutes he drowsed with his back pressed to the rocky soil of the mountain. It was, by Appalachian standards, a modest summit, but an elevation fair enough. The air here was cleaner even than down in the little town, and a far cry from the smoking gully of downtown Atlanta. It had seemed at times, in this week of afternoon meetings, that the breezes up here blew not only into his lungs, but through him, with Canby ever hoping that this elevation, given time, might cleanse him of the worm that had been turning in his gut since they'd cut Greenberg down.

"'Does the road wind uphill all the way? Will the day's journey take the whole long day?'" her voice called.

Canby sat up and looked down the slope. Julia had climbed to nearly a stone's throw of him while he dozed. He smiled as he watched her coming up the trace of a path, holding her skirts up over the rockiest parts.

"I'll guess. Longfellow today?"

Julia settled down next to him, light as a bird, and tucked a wisp of bang behind an ear. "Rossetti," she said.

"Haven't read him."

"*Christina* Rossetti, you lout. Do you read at all anymore?" Julia sighed. "No reason a country school can't be as au courant as any other." She touched his hand and cocked her head so that he could brush her cheek with his lips. She paused a moment to catch her breath. "Though your method of courting is going to wear me down to nothing."

"I'd be happy to call on your house. If you'd let me farther than the porch."

"We're not *that* au courant up here. Not yet. I need to maintain appearances on my way to spinsterhood."

"You're no spinster. Nor will you be."

She studied his face in the uncomfortable silence. After a time, she said, "Anyway, it's better up here."

He reached into the basket beside him and pulled out the bottle of Riesling and the glasses. The wine was still cool from where he had stored it, wedged between two rocks in Stillhouse Creek at the base of the mountain. He poured for both of them and she raised her glass. Canby shook his head.

"No toast today."

Julia touched his face, her fingers tracing the scar down his left cheek.

"What about to new beginnings?"

He laughed mirthlessly. "I'm out of fresh starts, Julia." He touched his glass to hers. They drank and looked out over the valley. Canby studied the sunlight where it gleamed in the bends of the Chattahoochee, let his eyes wander down the stitching of railroad tracks that ran like seams across the valley. The sun was behind the clouds above them and it cast cloud-shadows on the valley floor, pools of shade that coasted and paused over the topography with the wind.

"The chautauqua is tonight in the pavilion," Julia said. "See the train coming up from town? There, on the Marietta line?"

"What's the topic?"

"No topic this week. A performance. Something of Handel's with a string quartet. How wonderful it would be if I had an escort."

Canby raised his glass. "My honor and pleasure. That, I'll drink to."

Julia leaned on his shoulder, her head under his chin. They sat and watched the train pull into Vinings Station and the smoke from its stack diminish as it sat idle while the day trippers from Atlanta disembarked. They emerged from beneath the green roof of the station in pairs and groups and mounted into wagons to carry them the short distance to the pavilion. The musicians came last, toting their instrument cases and climbing into the wagons with the black cases in their hands, clutched close as children might be held.

After a time, Canby stretched his arm behind him, slowly, and emptied his glass of the sweet wine onto the ground. And some time later he rose and lifted the basket in one hand and reached for her hand with the other. And they began to make their way, slowly, down the slope.

HE WATCHED and listened at once. Watched the departing sun light up the wall of the mountain above the pavilion in a band of gold that mingled with the turning leaves, creeping higher on the mountain with every movement of the string music and drawing behind it a swath of shade that heralded nightfall. And listened to the music, Handel indeed from what the quartet's first violinist had announced. He would not have known it from any other, but it was fine to his ears. Listening, he forgot himself and forgot time as well, forgot all the

bright young set of Atlanta crowded into the pavilion on folding chairs around him, only a few gray heads in their midst,
Robert Billingsley's among them. He watched as the players
bent to their instruments, coaxing the wood and catgut, the
notes springing from the bent bows rising to the eaves of the
pavilion as if to find their way back to some higher source.
Canby's cheeks burned in the presence of it. The players leaned
in toward one another as the music rose to its crescendo, as
they held the minor chord, then resolved into the tonic major,
faces rapt, then relaxing as the strings shuddered over the last
drawn note. In the silence that followed, Canby imagined that
they had, for a few measures, bent time itself.

The applause was earnest but diminutive by comparison, little clapping echoes coming back off the mountain as the players nodded over their instruments. The audience began to rise
and the scraping of the chairs on the boards of the pavilion
brought him fully back. He realized that Julia's hand was still
held tight in his own.

"Grand, wasn't it?"

Canby looked up to see Robert Billingsley standing above
him, a smile on his face and a hand extended. He pried his
fingers away from Julia's and took the hand offered, pressed
the cool flesh.

"It certainly was."

"Ma'am?" Billingsley said. "I don't believe we've met."

"Of course," Canby said. "My friend Julia Preston."

Billingsley bent his head as he took her hand. Canby wondered if he intended to kiss it. Instead, he straightened from
his half bow and returned his eyes to Canby.

"I have something of yours, Mister Canby. Given over to me by Vernon Thompson, and to him by one of Hannibal Kimball's men. A rather weighty knapsack that clanks when it is moved, apparently heavy with small arms."

Canby blushed under his smile. "I did not know when I left Kimball House I wouldn't be returning."

"No need to explain."

"I suppose Kimball wants his key back."

"It's my understanding that he has had the lock changed," Billingsley said, his face clouding. "But that is neither here nor now. I have your bag on the back of my surrey. I ask only a small fee in exchange for my courier services."

Billingsley nodded to Julia and placed an arm over Canby's shoulders, guiding him down the pavilion steps. He lowered his voice as they passed a group at the base of the steps and walked toward the edge of the lamplight that shrouded the pavilion.

"I would like for you to be my guest out at my country place hard by Mableton. The quail are in fine fettle this time of year. My hands have harvested the corn but left the back acres cut over. Every fall, the quail feed there by the score. Please be my guest for a hunt. You could bring your lady friend back a few braces of birds—and it would also ease my conscience over the unpleasantness in Atlanta. I offer it by way of apology, Mister Canby."

"I don't see how I could decline."

"Excellent. My driver and I will pick you up at Pace's Inn in, say, half an hour?"

"How did you know—?"

But Billingsley was already stepping away. Canby walked back to the pavilion. The musicians were packing up their instruments, strapping down latches on their cases, but the platform was otherwise empty. He scanned the sphere of light around the pavilion, strained his eyes to see past it into the night. But Julia was gone.

October 31

UNDERWOOD COULD NOT SAY, EXACTLY, WHAT IT was that had drawn him to this mountain, miles outside of town, or what had compelled him to beg the loan of a horse from Vernon Thompson to get here. Could not say why two telegrams to Canby gone unanswered had raised in him a sense of foreboding. Or rather, would not have said. He trusted it was something beyond his knowing mind that set in when he left the telegraph office on Decatur Street and commenced on this errand.

He sat his borrowed horse outside the little schoolhouse Canby had told him about. Its door was shut. The lady's voice came from inside, running down a list of conjugations that the scholars repeated after her, point and counterpoint. She spoke in that half accent that was the voice of white Atlanta— quicker than the drawl of the other Georgians, but still far south of Yankee diction. Her voice was clear as she and her pupils worked through the verbs he guessed to be Latin. His own schooling, of course, lacked any such exotica and was truncated at the sixth grade, when the slate board and chalk stick were replaced with shovel, hoe, broom. Better than what his slave parents got, though, forbidden to learn to read. Progress, he supposed. He hoped the New South would do better. Here it seemed to be on its way, but he doubted if any of Miss Julia's students had a face as dark as his own.

He looked around at the little village. All the clapboard buildings whitewashed, all the roofs shingled in green. He looked up the mountain and saw a group of houses set apart from the village proper. These did not match the white and green buildings of the village but were made, he could tell even at a distance, of surplus materials too poor and motley to be worth painting. They dotted the north face of the mountain, most seeming ready to fall in and some looking as though they were barely still clinging to the steep slope. Above a few of the tarpaper roofs, leaning chimneys smoked in the October air. Inside the schoolhouse, the sounds of Latin continued. He tugged at the horse's reins and set off north on the Pace's Ferry Road.

As he neared the settlement he saw little movement outside the houses. He figured that most of the inhabitants were inside, away from the chill and likely preparing their noontime dinner. Or at work elsewhere. On one of the porches an old man sat with a quilt on his lap, a shotgun resting atop it. His garden out front was coming up abundant in beets, peas, mustard greens. Underwood paused in the road and lifted his hat. He had begun to speak when the old man shook his head and raised the shotgun to port arms. Underwood moved on.

The northernmost house in the settlement sat off on its own,

surrounded by a rickety picket fence and its dirt yard adorned
with a variety of flotsam such as he'd never seen. He had seen
bottle trees, of course, but the yard of this house had a half
dozen of them, and the biggest tree, a sycamore, had been fes-
tooned with shards of mirror hung from twine. From nearly
every limb they glinted in the sunlight, and as they twisted
in the breeze threw off hundreds of brilliant flashes. Beneath
them, the yard was filled with all manner of artwork fashioned from unlikely sources, around which chickens pecked
and strutted. He saw a wagon wheel painted scarlet and half
embedded in the dirt, a torn umbrella with its handle stuck in
the earth and its canopy scrawled over with drawings, a dented
milk can likewise half sunk and sprouting a burst of pansies
from its mouth. All of these objects painted with the kinds of
bold colors Underwood had read about in Melville's Polyne-
sian novel, or in Robert Louis Stevenson's tales. As if everything broken and cast off had made its way to this place and
got itself a new life here.

An old woman sat on the porch, singing low to herself and
working on something in her lap. The house behind her was
as strange as her yard: its front wall was covered with images
painted right onto the boards—crudely drawn cats and crows,
giant butterflies pinwheeling across azure patches of sky. Like
her neighbor, she had pulled a quilt over her knees. He could
see, below the quilt, the hem of a flowered dress, two spindly
brown shins, and a broken-down pair of men's brogans. She
rocked gently as she worked, and after a moment Underwood
realized she was singing *to* the thing in her hands. He pulled
up his horse at her gate and bade her a good morning.

"You the police?" she asked. She squinted down at him from the porch. Her eyes were milky white with cataracts. After a moment's surprised silence he told her that he was.

"Come on up to the porch. Horse got to stay in the yard, though."

He tried to hide his grin as he tied the horse to her fence. Before he had shut the gate behind him a flurry of chickens had gathered around his legs and he walked mincingly up to the house lest he trample one of them.

"You ride down from the Smyrna constable's?"

"No, ma'am," he said, every one of the porch steps creaking beneath him. "Out of Atlanta."

The woman leaned forward in her chair, focused the milky eyes on his face. "You *black*," she said.

"Yes, ma'am. May I sit down?"

"What kind of foolishness you bringing up in here? A black *po*lice man out of Atlanta? That'll be the day."

He showed her his badge, though he doubted she could read its numerals and lettering. As she took it from him, he saw that what she had been working on was a doll. She was making it by stuffing raw cotton into a length of woman's hosiery. She'd fashioned a head and arms, but cotton trailed out of the doll's unformed bottom end. He saw that one of its hands had six fingers.

"Thought you were here about the chickens," she said.

Underwood tucked the badge back into his jacket, thinking he was wasting good time on this crazy woman.

"Old Titus down the hill's been shooting every one of them that hops the fence. Say they're eating up his garden." She had picked up the doll and was stuffing the rest of the cotton into it. She pulled and twisted and knotted the hose until she had tied off legs.

"Shoots them and throws them back over the fence." She shrugged her bony shoulders. "But I can't eat them fast as he been shooting them."

"No, ma'am, I rode up to see Julia Preston. I'm looking for a friend of hers."

"You got ties to Vinings? One your people worked the railroad crews?"

"No, ma'am. My mother brought me up here to service at New Salem a few times. Saw a baptism here when I was twelve or thirteen."

"Whereabouts?"

"Down in that creek on the other side of the village."

"Stillhouse Creek," she said with a chuckle high in her throat. "Bet the 'shiners wasn't running the still that day."

Underwood thought of what Canby had told him about white moonshiners, here and farther north, up to Ringgold and beyond. He couldn't recall having seen a white face that morning; he remembered only the joyous shouting and the coldness of the water. Perhaps they were farther up the creek, deep in the trees. The real mountain men, Canby said, were Scots-Irish who never came out of the hills except to sell what they'd distilled up in them. Mountain crackers, tough characters who would either kill you or kill for you, Canby said. There was no middle ground with them.

"No, ma'am, didn't see any 'shiners that day. But I think I'd have remembered this place."

The old woman smiled. "You would have, if it looked like this then. My husband didn't cotton to art. Said it was foolishness. Too much work to do to fool with pretty." She pulled a threaded needle from a pocket of her dress and went to work on the doll with it. Underwood looked around the porch again, from the half dozen dolls scattered around her chair to the bright figures she had painted on the side of her house. Some were tracings of her hand, outlined and magnified. Some were scenes interpreted from Bible verses. He saw one that he recognized as the Good Samaritan. Her Samaritan was black. Grace born out of poverty, Underwood thought.

"Did your husband pass on?"

"Mmmhmm," she said. "Him and the one before him. Only man I live with now is Jesus. Suits me fine. One day I quit making supper and got busy making my playhouse." She looked up quickly and saw that Underwood was staring at a golden sun painted on her house's door. It had several other suns radiating out from it.

"That ain't no voodoo, if you're wondering. Or heard stray talk down in the village. No hoodoo, no voodoo, no juju. Just Jesus."

She held out the finished doll to him. Its eyes were mismatched buttons, but it held a kind of humble beauty in its sewn-in smile. "That's one of my playbabies." She looked at it lovingly for a moment, then set it down next to her rocker.

"And I'm Lettie Lee." She held out a hand and he took it, shaking gently. Her hand was all angles, twisted arthritic bones.

"Cyrus Underwood," he said. "I'm looking for Miss Julia's beau."

"Then why you asking me? You ride straight past the schoolhouse?"

"She was teaching. Thought I'd wait until dinnertime."

The woman looked out over her yard, past the fence, at the dirt road that led from Pace's ferry to points north. She stared as though she could see the ruts in the road, the dust furrowed by wagon wheels.

"I was out here couple nights ago, trying to listen to that pretty music down in the village. You don't think they'd let me set up on that fine pavilion, do you? Sometimes you can just hear a bit of it if the wind ain't high. Was still out here when something went by down there in the road."

"Something?"

"Two white men in a wagon, black man driving."

"You could see that? In the dark?" He looked from the old woman to the road, looked back at her, into the white-filmed eyes.

"Course it was dark. Said it was nighttime. They making fools into detectives down in Atlanta now?"

"Beg your pardon, ma'am."

"Some things don't need sight to see. Shouldn't have to tell you that."

"No, ma'am."

"Not if you've been to New Salem."

"Yes, ma'am."

"You could feel it going by, straining up the hill. Something left out of here that shouldn't have."

"White men, you say?"

She looked at him a moment, then began to slowly shake

her head again. She pulled the quilt tighter in her lap. "You make sure Julia Preston knows whereabouts your friend is. You don't want no part of that wagon."

Underwood pulled out his pocket watch and saw that it was not quite noon. Lettie Lee asked him if he would say something to Titus about the chickens and he told her, absently, that he would. As he put the watch back into his vest pocket he decided that he was going to have to interrupt Miss Julia's lesson after all.

November 1

THE DOGS LIT OUT AHEAD OF THEM, TWO SPANIELS, eager to bound across the cut-over fields but constrained at intervals by the dog man's sharp whistles. The dog man walked ahead of Canby and Billingsley, swinging a knotty snake stick alongside his calf, though Canby doubted that given the morning's autumn chill he would have much use for it. Like Canby, he was dressed in Billingsley's worn hunt clothing from a few seasons prior. On Canby, the cotton duck fit snugly at chest and thigh, but on the old black man the sleeves were rolled up against excess length and the cuffs of the pants pooled at his ankles.

The borrowed shotgun, however, was another matter. It was a Purdey, of English manufacture, a 20-gauge side-by-side, the finest gun Canby had ever held. He had already dropped three quail with it, meeting the birds bursting from cover with the shotgun's perfect alignment of shoulder and bead, eye and target. The birds rode now in the game pocket of his vest, their light weight there early assurance of a good day.

Up ahead the dogs stopped, went rigid, their necks elongated and tails out straight behind them, their trembling bodies forming a level line from point of snout to tip of tail. Quietly, the dog man stepped aside for Canby and Billingsley to move ahead to the point. The brush they had come through had now given way to the cut-over cornfield. Canby felt one of the dropped cobs underneath his boot. Around them now were a scattering of the ears, gold and white kernels loosed from them by the pecking of the birds.

"Bird!" Billingsley called as just in front of them the stalks and brush erupted in high-pitched bird cries and a panicked fury of wings lifting into the air. The quail shot straight upward and then canted left. Billingsley's gun barked twice and the quail dropped, each of them leaving a quivering nimbus of feathers in the air behind it. The dog man whistled and the spaniels ran forward, noses to the ground, looking for the downed birds. Billingsley broke his shotgun and plucked the spent shells from the barrels and dropped them, reached into a vest pocket for fresh ones and pressed them into place and snapped the barrels shut again.

"Nice shooting," Canby said. Billingsley smiled and reached into the vest again and produced a silver flask covered with filigree. He handed it to Canby and squatted on his heels, shotgun across his knees, to wait on the dogs. Canby took a pull from the flask—the same Irish whiskey as before, smooth beyond belief—and sat himself down beside Billingsley. He took another sip and gave the flask back to Billingsley, looked over to the dog man. He was watching the brush where the dogs had disappeared. He seemed to be listening to their rustling there for some confirmation.

"I know you, don't I?" Canby asked.

The dog man smiled faintly and looked down at the ground. He nudged one of the fallen ears of corn with the gnarled end of the snake stick. "Nossir, don't believe so."

"I have a good memory for faces."

The black man whistled, apparently having heard what he'd been listening for from the dogs, and the spaniels trotted out of the stalks, each of them with a bird held gingerly in its mouth. They brought them to him and he reached out a hand to each dog, his hands more gray than brown, workworn, and rung the birds' necks. Billingsley nodded toward Canby and the man brought the birds to him and held them out. Still beautiful even in death, from the ringed faces above the sedge-colored wings to the speckled feathers of their breasts. One of them white-necked—a male—and the other with plumage the same shade of amber as good honey. Canby took them, the female still trembling, and reached behind him to drop them into his vest pocket. The black man never met his eyes.

"You should have seen this place in its prime, Mister Canby," Billingsley said. He was still nodding, but his eyes looked back out, over the land they had covered since starting just before dawn, at the big house. Canby saw that they had come to a slight rise on the place and that the distance they had traversed in the past hour made a great bowl between the white-columned house and the ridge on which they now rested.

Billingsley's eyes narrowed as he looked out over the fields. "A thousand acres of white cotton swaying in the wind, two hundred black faces in the rows, picking. We had our own blacksmith shop, commissary, slave quarters, and overseer lodgings. A place for everything, and everything in its place."

"It must have been grand."

"The war changed it all. That house yonder is a pale shadow of what once was. I came home to smoking ashes and fallow fields. All of my hands went away with Sherman, you see, then came back when they saw he had nothing for them.

"We rebuilt it from the foundations as best we could. But in time I found myself negotiating with my own Negroes. A tenth share one year, a sixth the next. The bottom rail was on top.

"We are experimenting with the 'progressive' agriculture now, building it back up with a variety of crops. The old cotton kingdom is gone. But if you could have seen it, Mister Canby!"

Billingsley shook his head and rose, brushing off his pants. The dog man whistled and the spaniels took off in front again and the party resumed their walk, Canby and Billingsley spaced a half dozen yards to either side of the Negro.

"You miss it."

"Very much. There was an order to it we're not likely to achieve again. Bird!"

The dogs, without Canby's noticing, had frozen in their point stance. The stalks ahead of them seemed to explode with an upward burst of feathers. Canby quickly counted six, seven, as the quail darted and wheeled and he picked his birds and fired. He dropped one and winged another, which spun in narrowing circles until it hit the earth. Billingsley shot twice and his birds plummeted. The rest of the covey winged out over the field, out of range now, while the men reloaded.

Canby felt a quickening to his pulse that the shooting could not account for. He breathed slowly, deeply, before he spoke again.

"But you've done all right in Atlanta, if I may say so, haven't you?"

"With certain adjustments. One adapts. I suppose I will survive if I've made it this far."

The dogs returned with the first pair of birds, dropped them, and disappeared back into the stalks.

"But what about you, Mister Canby? Are you on the lookout for other employ? Or will you go back to Ringgold?"

"I think I have to go back. To Atlanta, I mean. Cyrus Underwood is still beating the bushes down in town."

"For whatever reason?"

"He thinks Leon Greenberg was not the man."

"Underwood, the Negro detective?" Billingsley smiled. "Another first for Atlanta. Atlanta is all chaos. As it ever was."

"But doesn't it trouble you, Colonel, about Greenberg?"

"Why would it trouble me?"

The spaniels trotted out of the brush with the second pair of quail and set them down. The bird Canby had winged made flailing motions in the dirt and the dog man shooed away the spaniel that was nipping at it and picked it up by the head and spun it in his hand. He bent and gathered up the other three and handed them to Canby. The dogs moved down the corn rows, tails wagging, noses down, and the men followed.

"Why chaos, sir?"

"Her growth is uncontrolled, Mister Canby."

"Then how, sir, would you control it?"

Billingsley's eyes seemed to be seeking the horizon's limit as they walked across the field. He stopped and looked at Canby, his eyes lit with a kind of quicksilver appraisal.

"The old system held everything in its proper place."

"Checks and measures."

"Correct."

Canby walked several paces before he spoke again. "Such as Thomas Malthus postulated?" he asked, careful to keep the tone of his voice conversational. "Do you know his essay on population? My father had me read it when I asked about the Irish famine."

As they walked, Canby stepped over one of the mounded rows away from Billingsley. With every other forward step, he crossed another furrow, drawing out the distance. He stepped up his pace toward the dogs' tails bobbing ahead of him, as they worked the field out front.

"I have read Malthus," Billingsley said.

After a moment he heard the sound of Billingsley's boots resume walking, rasping in the cut stalks. Then they stopped.

"Bird," Billingsley cried. Canby raised his shotgun, though the dogs were still trotting ahead of them. His eyes darted for a gray silhouette against the sky. It was empty.

"I suppose I regret this," Billingsley said.

Canby began to sprint, to put more distance between himself and the shotgun's barrels, but he heard the shotgun boom and felt the ripping of birdshot across his back, a rash of puckering burns, each of them a hot pinprick of pain. The second blast knocked him down on his face. Then he heard the sound of Billingsley's boots coming toward him.

Canby tried to turn onto his back, but the searing pain, against the jagged rubbing of the stalks, stopped him. He lay on his side, trying to get his shotgun out from beneath him as Billingsley advanced, reaching into his vest for more shells. And then, like a shadow, the dog man was coming up behind Billingsley with the snake stick in his hand. He raised it and brought it down on Billingsley's head so swiftly it was a blur in Canby's vision.

Then Canby's sight was fading as he felt the blood leaking out of him from what felt like hundreds of holes in his back. There was only the hearing, then, for what seemed to be minutes, of the sound of the stick falling as methodically as a scythe in wheat, a machete chopping sugarcane.

With a heave, Canby turned himself over, his back on fire and singed by the dry stalks that scraped his wounds. He opened his eyes.

The dog man stood with the stick hanging by his side. Its knotty end was clotted and dripping with blood. Billingsley lay at his feet, his head a pulp of tissue through which Canby could see patches of skull. At intervals his legs moved, writhing like a snake that has been struck.

The dog man picked up Billingsley's shotgun, broke the action open. He pulled a fresh shell from his pants pocket and fitted it into the top barrel, snapped the action shut again.

"Tell me, Mister Canby," the dog man said, "you take that bribe from Mamie O'Donnell?"

"No."

The black man nodded. "Didn't think so. You a good man, Mister Canby. You gone heal up all right. Yes, you'll be all right."

Canby seemed to have to fight his way through the pain to speak again. "I know you. You're Tunis Campbell, aren't you? How many years gone now?"

"Three years on the chain gang and two down here on the Billingsley place. Yessir, Tunis Campbell, that's me. And Fortus is my boy," he said. He fitted the double barrels into his mouth.

"God!" Canby shouted, trying again to rise. "Don't!"

Campbell pulled the barrels out of his mouth far enough to speak again. "Ain't no use, sir. I'm dead and gone and long ago bound to hell."

He put the barrels back into his mouth and, reaching down with his right hand, worked the trigger with his thumb. Canby thought he saw the damage before he heard the shotgun's blast, watching the red mist flying upward into the perfect cobalt of the autumn sky before the finality of the gun's report confirmed it. He lay back against the rustling stalks then and watched the sky diffract to a blue pinprick. He felt the darkness coming to take him and allowed himself to go.

DESCENT

November 3

HIS EXISTENCE WAVERED BETWEEN SHEETS OF flame and leaden weight. His face still pressed earthward, gravity upon him like a burden nearly too great to bear, but at some point the dry earth of the Billingsley plantation had been replaced with a cotton sheet, smooth and cool against his cheek. His back, however, glowed like a bright plain of burning pain. At times when it flared brightest he went away, into the darkness again. He dreamed that he lay in a gulch and that his back writhed and undulated with the glistening black of the feathers of vultures that had roosted on it. He felt their scarlet beaks, dripping with offal, pecking at his flesh. They fought over the choicest perch upon him and he woke screaming to bursts of white light, hospital smells, the sweet wisp of ether that took him away again.

And, once, he dreamed of Robert Billingsley. Standing over the buzzards with his arms raised as though to conduct their feasting. Grown taller, thinner, clad in a suit of sheening black himself, lips moving, forming words Canby could not understand, whether chanting or cheering the buzzards, the dreamer could not determine. Only the last word came clear above the singsong chant and the rustling of the buzzards' shuffling wings: *Canby*.

"Easy there, boy. Thomas, you're safe."

Canby felt the dream withdraw from him like a foul tide receding. The hospital smells returned. "Vernon?" he said.

"Yes. Open your eyes, for Christ's sake. I'm here."

Through a cracked eyelid, he saw that Vernon sat on a chair beside the bed, his hat set on his lap. Vernon smiled.

"Goddamn. Will I ever get out of Atlanta?"

"Glad to see you've still got some of the old salt left in you. I don't know if you'll ever get out of Atlanta, but I'm surely glad you made it out of Mableton."

"It was him."

Vernon nodded.

"The whole time. Right in front of us."

Vernon nodded again and pulled a cigar from his vest. He kept nodding as he lit it and puffed the ember to life. "I'd not have believed it," he said.

Canby rested his face against the cool sheet. "How bad is my back?"

"You'll need another little while to heal up. We're all just glad you didn't bleed out. You know, it was Underwood found you. He's a sight better policeman than I'd have predicted. He took himself off to Vinings and then to Mableton after he'd talked with Julia. It was him who put you facedown in a wagon bed and damned near ran the horses to death to get you here."

"Last thing I remember is the sky."

"Yesterday I sat here and watched Doctor Johnston pick all those pieces of shot out of you. *Pick* with the tweezers; *plink* into the pan, over a hundred times. That's one patient man. He weighed the shot, after. Right at two ounces of lead. I'm proud of you."

Canby flexed his shoulder muscles tentatively. They worked. The burn was still there, bright on the surface, then fading to a dull ache beneath the skin.

"I'd advise you to keep your shirt on next time you go courting Miss Julia, but she's already seen it. Came down from Vinings. She's lucky she missed that first part of it, though."

"Where is she now?"

"Either at the grocer's or at my house, I imagine. She'll be glad to hear you've come around. I'm hopeful she's cooking something at my place."

Canby nodded, felt a wave of fatigue come over him. He willed his eyes to stay open and lay in silence for a few moments watching Vernon smoke.

"Billingsley," he said at last. "Goddamned Billingsley."

"I did not believe it. Till I heard it from the man himself."

"What?"

"He told me so."

"That can't be. I watched him die."

"Oh, no, Thomas, he did not die. Underwood left him in the field. But he didn't die. When they brought him in, his head looked nearly as bad as his bird dogger's, I'm told. They stitched it back together as best they could. I told them to make a quick job of it and I don't think Doctor Johnston liked that. I told them, 'Just fix him up good enough for us to hang him.'"

"They brought him here?"

"Yes."

The hospital room's door opened behind Canby and he worked his hands underneath him as quickly as he could, trying to rise. Vernon reached out a hand toward him but seemed unsure of where to touch his peppered back, his shoulders.

"Don't get excited," he said. "They treated him here, but he's in the tower now. Spot Twelve, as a matter of fact." Vernon's eyes rose as Canby heard the door shut. "Good evening, Doctor," he said.

Canby heard the man's measured footsteps on the floorboards before he stepped around and into his vision. The doctor had kindly eyes, bespectacled, and he wore a neatly trimmed beard flecked with gray. He waved at the thick smoke in the air as though it aggrieved him before extending the hand to Canby.

"Frederick Augustus Johnston," he said. "I'm pleased you've made it. For a time there a positive outcome was not at all assured."

Johnston bent close to Canby's back, touched him lightly on his shoulder, the small of his back. His hands were cool.

"I would have liked to have cupped you, Mister Canby, as a safeguard against infection, but your wounds were too extensive. How is the pain now?"

"Tolerable."

"We'll continue the morphine a day or two longer, then."

"How soon until he's discharged, Doctor?"

"Two or three days at the earliest."

"We have pressing police business. There's a hanging he's needed for."

"Of that I wash my hands, gentlemen," the doctor said, and patted Canby, gently, above his spotted shoulder. "Good evening."

Vernon watched until the doctor had shut the door behind himself. "He's a good doctor, whatever the gossips say."

"What do the gossips say?"

"Some ugly business about bad debts in Carolina. That's the way of it, isn't it? A man gets ruined in the East and heads west to start fresh with a new slate."

"Grady should write him up in a story. What happened back East?"

"Negro trouble," Vernon said, and stared at the cigar in his hand for a moment. "Anyway, Billingsley came around enough yesterday to make a confession."

"What did he say?"

"No details. He said he did it, that's all."

"That's not much of a confession, is it?"

"It was enough to haul a judge in for him to plead."

"Did you get a sentence?"

"Right then and there. He's to be hanged by the neck until dead as soon as he's able to stand up on his own. Meantime, Billingsley's said he'll make a full confession when he's ready."

Canby snorted. "When will that be?"

"When you come to take it."

Vernon fingered his hat and looked around the room as though seeking a place to douse his cigar. Canby breathed deeply for a moment, trying to quiet his thoughts.

"All right," he said at length.

"Good," Vernon said. He set his hat on his head and began to rise from the chair.

"Just a minute, Vernon."

Vernon settled back into the chair but did not remove his hat.

"I need for you to get a book to me. They may have it at the Young Men's Library Association. I'm sure there's a copy in Billingsley's library if you have men there."

"Oh, rest assured I have men there." Vernon reached into his jacket and pulled out his pocket notebook, fished a pencil from another pocket. "What's the title?"

"*Essay on the Principle of Population*," Canby said. "Author is T. R. Malthus."

"Malthus, huh?" Vernon said, his pencil pausing. "*Malthus*. I should have no trouble remembering that, goddamn me." He folded the notebook and tucked it and the pencil away. "I'll send Underwood and have him bring it around."

"And Vernon? You might as well tell Underwood to bring his Bible with him."

"All right, then. I will. Good night, Thomas."

Malthus, Canby thought as he heard the door shut again. The very book had sat on Angus's shelves throughout his childhood. When he closed his eyes he could even remember the printing Angus had owned, the slim leather-bound volume in its place among the other works. Red binding, it was.

He kept his eyes shut for a long time. The weight on his back had returned, heavier now by a measure of bitter remorse.

November 4

SHE LOOKED NEITHER RIGHT NOR LEFT AS SHE
walked toward the heavy-looking door at the center of Fulton
Tower, only kept her eyes straight out front of her, her package
held in two trembling hands before her at her waist. Off to
either side of the walkway, men in stripes were bent hoeing
and weeding in the prison garden, and though they worked
steadily under the watch of a mounted guard with what she
thought was a shotgun laid across his saddle, their eyes had
fixed on her the moment she stepped down from the carriage
and had not yet left. She heard a murmured word once, and
as she neared the great door a low whistle sang out over the
garden. The guard spoke harshly and the whistle cut off and as
she knocked on the big door she could hear only the sound of
the hoes working, blades hacking the earth.

The face that greeted her when the door swung open had
no welcome in it. She started to speak her introduction but the
man behind the door shook his head and began to shut it. She
shifted her package into one hand and unsnapped her purse

and brought forth the badge she had slipped out of Thomas's coat. The man studied it quizzically for a moment, then swung the door fully open and stood beside it for her to pass. All without a word spoken on his part.

She had read about Spot 12 in the papers and knew to expect a place of squalor and despair. Still, she was nearly overwhelmed by the oppressive air of the place, the silent gloom that had descended when the jailer shut the door behind her. He leaned against it now, watching her with the same suspicious glare with which he'd greeted her.

The man lay on a cot bolted to a wall of brick, on which had been written all manner of names and dates and foul language to accompany them. The man on the cot was in a state just as motley, resembling a scarecrow more than a man. He lay on his stomach with his face toward the brick, and she was grateful for this because the back of his head was a horror the likes of which she'd never seen, a mess of sutures and scabs from which patches of white hair sporadically sprang. They had not even bothered to bandage the wounds. It put her in mind of Mary Shelley's monster, or the damned in Dante or one of Poe's revenants. She steeled herself before she spoke.

"I am a friend of Thomas Canby's," she said. "I've come to bring you something."

She watched for a sign of movement in the man but did not see any. The scabbed head was still.

"Thomas will live, Doctor Johnston is sure of it. He will live to see you hang. Can you hear me? You did not murder him. He is on the mend. He will see you into the ground for what you've done."

She thought of poor Mary Flanagan and shivered. She resolved to conclude this visit.

"I've brought something to you. Or back to you."

She held out the Mason jar she had brought with her, then lifted it. "Can you hear this?" She shook the jar and the lead pellets inside it rattled against the glass. "This is what you tried to kill him with.

"I've brought this back for you to study. You can think about the meanness and futility of your life. A handful of lead that did not stop a good man. You see, it all comes back, the good and the bad."

She moved to set the Mason jar on the stone floor, just past the point where he might have reached through the bars to it. The pellets shifted in the jar as she leaned over, making a tinkling sound against the glass.

She stopped midway, took another glance at the unmoving wraith on the bed, at the rude jailer. Stood upright again.

"Perhaps you haven't heard me," she said, and turned the Mason jar upside down. The pellets hit the floor and scattered, the misshapen pieces of lead bouncing and rolling erratically, each pellet that had impacted Thomas's back charting its own course across the floor.

Then she turned and walked out. The mute jailer looked outraged, but he held the door open for her exit.

She would tell Thomas about this visit after all, she resolved. Even though she had taken the badge without asking and had not been able to summon the temerity to tell him about her plans beforehand. She would tell him how insensate was the man who had shot him, how wrecked and ruined. How the pellets that had been in Thomas's back sounded as she shook them in the Mason jar, how they sounded scattering across the floor, so that they would echo through the murderer's conscience.

What she would not tell him, because she did not know— had turned her back and could not see—was that in the silence after the last of the pellets had fallen, the scarred and scabbed head had begun to tremble.

"THOSE WERE GRAND DAYS, LONG BEFORE THE WAR and everything that led up to it," Billingsley said. "I came and went as I pleased, not only in the house and outbuildings but in the slave quarters as well. I was left alone to *become*.

"I took a special pleasure in watching Banks, our overseer, discipline the hands. Banks was not a cruel man but in those days the whip was as much a part of a plantation as was the plow. He was efficient with it when it had to be put to use. The whipping post was out behind the barn, where Mother would not have to see it, and I prevailed upon Banks against his better judgment to allow me the privilege of watching. At first I kept a distance, but every lashing drew me closer. In time I was tying their hands to the iron ring myself.

"Banks left the untying to me—after he had coiled and hung the whip in the barn and gone back to the fields. Some of them had taken lashes so deep I could lay my finger inside the cuts. I remember the colors in such detail. The shade of their dark skin and the shine of blood on it. The acres of white rows around us, swaying in every breeze. The color of the ground by the post, where the dirt had been stained. Quite beautiful. Their backs were scarred in much the same way I imagine yours is, Detective."

For the first time since Canby and Underwood had entered the cell, Billingsley opened his eyes. He lay on the cot that was bolted into the black brick wall on the opposite side of Spot 12. Billingsley's head had been shaved, unevenly and apparently in haste, and his scalp was a variegated mess of stubble and bare skin, through which ran black sutures in a convoluted network of patches where the doctors had knitted his head back together. The skull beneath was knotty and ridged, either from his beating or from the bones working to mend. The eye that Billingsley turned to them was red from its pupil to its lid, shot through with blood. If Canby had seen a man worse damaged in the war, he could not remember. It pleased him to see it.

"My back is nearly healed. I'd predict a worse prognosis for that face of yours. Though we'll cover it with a sack soon enough."

"I'll settle with Campbell by and by."

"Which Campbell do you mean—the father or the son? Did no one tell you that Tunis Campbell is dead? By his own hand."

The red eye closed. "By and by."

"We did not come for the auld lang syne. Just your statement of the murders. I have Underwood here as a scribe and witness." He saw that Underwood's gaze had fixed on Billingsley and that his jaw was rigid. He held the pencil in his hand tightly enough to snap it.

"Will my old friend Vernon Thompson not deign to visit?"

"He sends his regards and says he'll see you at the hanging. Meantime, I'm to get your full confession."

"I had hoped for a jury trial. I wished to proclaim my guilt to the world."

"Then why plead as you did?"

Billingsley raised a hand to his head, felt along one of the ridges there gingerly. "My time draws nigh. I likely would not survive to the end of a jury trial. The spirit is willing but the flesh is weak."

"That's Scripture," Underwood said.

"It is, nigger-boy. I have found another avenue. The two of you will be the vehicle for my message."

"Let's stick to present business," Canby said, watching the set of Underwood's jaw. "Start with Alonzo Lewis."

"In due time, Detective. A confession is only part of the last testament I mean to give to you."

"There'll be no thousand and one nights. We'll hang you without it if needs be."

"I will not be rushed, Canby."

"*Detective* Canby," Underwood said.

"It is not your place to correct me, boy," Billingsley said. He struggled to raise himself to a sitting position against the brick wall behind him, the names of the former condemned scratched and carved into the bricks. He leaned against them, his head drooping from the exertion. His breath came raggedly. "You are a child of Atlanta, Canby, and Atlanta will never have a proper regard for history. But to understand the *now*, you must know the *then*. In time that will be clear to you.

"You have your black friend here, and I had one of my

own back then. Older, though. The other darkies called him a conjure-doctor. Saul was his name. Father bought him off another planter over the state line in Alabama. But Saul was never much for Alabama. In fact, he was not really of any time or place, although his bloodline ran back to Haiti. Saul introduced me to mysteries from that part of the world—voodoo, Santeria. And darker mysteries of his own contriving. Crude stuff, but wondrous to a child. We spent many late nights together and I was an ardent pupil. He marked my progress until I outstripped him, and then he kept a fair distance from me.

"It was Saul, you see, who introduced me to my destiny.

"Before long, I had developed a kind of contempt for Saul. When Banks took ill and died, Father assumed one of the hands had poisoned his food. There was no shortage of fingers pointed at Saul. He fled; Father rounded up a contingent of the local white trash, and Saul met his end."

Billingsley raised his head and took an appraising look at Canby, at Underwood.

"I assumed Banks's duties, over Father's mortified objections. But I loved the work. I grew more subtle with it, more refined in my methods. The wenches seldom showed a mark. I moved among them enough to spread my work around. The cotton grew, the corn grew; Father was happy, the plantation prospered."

"And then the war," Canby said.

"The war ruined everything. In spite of a heroic effort on our part. We made a splendid start of it. We harried that Yankee rabble all over Virginia at the outset. How I loved to see those blue bodies stack up like firewood. But in time . . ."

"You lost everything."

Billingsley's battered face assumed a nearly wistful look. "A person as common as yourself can barely imagine what I lost. Absolute power. Total order. We drew it from the blacks and from the land itself."

"Hell on earth," Underwood said. Billingsley smiled at him.

"I begin to see your motivations now," Canby said. "The old order broke down, didn't it? And you've hated seeing anyone who would have been a field hand or house slave back then do better for themselves. Where did that leave you?"

"You have a primitive mind, Detective. I suppose it's what suits you to your profession—that you break work such as mine down to crude particulars. But yes, to descend from such sovereignty on one's own land to slinking around this cesspool of a city like a pickpurse or a cat burglar—I confess I resented it. I raged."

"And Malthus. I should have seen it. By your lights, the plantation held perfect balance intact. Malthus wrote that the only histories we have of mankind are histories of the higher classes. Your era was over."

"Oh, Malthus is an old name."

"Like Legion?" Underwood asked.

"You may be on to something there, boy."

"And you feel, like Malthus, that equality among all would only lead to misery. The Cotton Exposition fairly celebrates that."

"A very old name."

"But why did you kill Anse? How did he fit your desiderata?"

Billingsley was reclining, in increments, back to his supine position on the bunk.

"You tire me, Detective. Your pedestrian thinking. You stutter and stumble along your way and still you do not see. I expected better of you.

"If you dream tonight, Detective, ask your father about his last view of this world. Did he see blue and gold? Or only blood-red?" Billingsley sighed hoarsely. "No more tonight."

His eyes closed and a rattling breath came from his chest. It sounded enough like a dying breath that Canby held his own until he saw the chest rise again.

"Should we wake him?" Underwood asked.

Canby was slow to answer. "No," he said.

"I can wake him. I'd be glad to."

"Leave him be," Canby said, getting to his feet. "I need a drink."

"You know I can't serve colored, Thomas," Lee Smith said.

"It's police business," Canby said. "Make an exception tonight. It's been a hell of a day." He showed him Vernon's badge.

"You think you're the only gent in here with a badge?"

Canby set Anse's Colt revolver on the mahogany bar, its long barrel not quite pointed at the apron wrapped around Lee Smith's waist, and tapped the trigger guard with his finger.

And so the Jameson was on the house this evening and they found themselves at the darkest table in the quietest corner of the Big Bonanza with the bottle and two glasses and the Colt set between them, talking of Malthus the English parson and philosopher and of magic and madness and how soon they could noose the bastard that had brought them all together in Atlanta.

"I know nothing about this voodoo business," Canby said. "What is it, some kind of black magic?"

Underwood shook his head. "No. But it can lead to all kinds of wickedness."

"Used the wrong way."

"Yeah. Can open up the wrong kinds of doors. Specially if you go looking for the wrong door."

"Spirits and such? Spells?"

"You making fun?"

"No. Just thinking about the so-called spirit world."

"Well, that's some progress there."

Canby sat for a while, looking at his glass set on the table, half filled with amber whiskey. The movement of the other drinkers in the bar, the tramping on the floorboards, made the whiskey move in the glass, the surface of it tilting slightly, forward and back.

"In the old country," Canby said, "they talk about thin places. Ever heard of those?"

"No."

"It's a natural place—maybe a rock, or a waterfall, or a very old tree, or a grove of them—where they say the boundary between the physical world and the spiritual one is stretched thin. Where you can almost cross over. From one to the other."

"You wanting me to call that superstitious?"

Canby shrugged.

"You believe in thin places?"

"No," Canby said. He shook his head and sat up and took the glass and drained it. "Not at all. Just old Celtic superstition."

"Felt like some kind of thin place up in Spot Twelve to me. The wrong kind of thin place."

"I've not seen one like Billingsley in my time, I'll grant you."

"Pure evil."

"More madness than evil, Underwood."

"I'd have thought he was testing your notions."

"He is—of madness."

"Up till here lately he's done pretty well for a crazy man."

"He's done well because he enjoyed the privileges of his position. The Ring and their like, they protected him without knowing it, people looking the other way in the name of discretion. Southern manners, you know. There's your old order, still with us, at least a little."

Canby refilled his glass.

"Do you know what this man Malthus actually wrote, Underwood? There wasn't anything sinister to it, just common sense. Common sense from an Anglican parson. Maybe I should say refined common sense. He looked around in Europe in his day and saw that the people were outgrowing the food supply. He'd been moved by the Irish famine. He pointed out the need to control population."

"That's what Billingsley was doing. One nigger at a time."

Canby looked up. "You think I'm making light of it?"

"Only it wasn't all Negroes, was it? Wasn't Thomas Malthus he was about by the time he got to your friend. It was a new Malthus, *him*. That's the only coherence I see. Just evil."

Canby refilled their glasses, cocking an eyebrow at Underwood.

"There you go sliding off into superstition again." He slid the Colt across the table to Underwood. "Put your faith in this. It's the best answer for the likes of Billingsley."

Underwood glanced around the bar before he touched the pistol. Quickly, he slipped it into his jacket. Then he looked again at Canby as though the forbidden transaction were already off his mind. "Couldn't you *feel* it up there in Spot Twelve?"

"Hocus-pocus, Underwood."

"How do you want to explain the hold he's had over them Campbells? Fortus up there in Fulton Tower for perjury and abetting, and the old man's head blowed clean off?"

Canby thought of Tunis Campbell's last words. Dead and gone and bound to hell, had the old man said? He shook his head. "More superstition."

"You heard him back there. Conjuring and such? I tell you, he ain't entirely of this world."

Canby let out a long breath and leaned back in his seat. "Underwood . . ."

"Study on it, you'll see it adds up. Tell me. What was it he said to you about your father?"

But Canby was suddenly rising to go. He tossed back the last of his drink and set the glass on the table. "Good night, Underwood," was all he said by way of an answer.

AGAINST HIS WILL, he dreamed that night. He was back on Whitehall Street, July '64, and the hot streets were exploding under Sherman's cannonade. Great clouds of sulfur smoke scurried over downtown in between the belches of the big guns, and the sun's efforts to penetrate the haze did no better than to render the sky a sheet of shimmering bronze, an impenetrable hot fog. Men and women—among them a father and his daughter—had died in their beds, asleep, or at clotheslines hanging wash, at kitchen tables eating. Still the shells rained down as though Sherman would never run out of ordnance. By then the city's better-off were spending their days huddled with their servants in bombproofs dug out beneath their homes or into the hillsides. Others, like Angus, still stubbornly maintained routine as though they could not hear the shells bouncing down the alleys, careening off the buildings. Or as if resolute that their faith would preserve them.

And so Canby, dreaming, found himself back in the little schoolhouse, of a Sunday in the siege, with his father and Julia and Frances O'Donnell. His dream-memory was ruthless in its accuracy: the hymnal lay spread open before Angus, though he knew the ritual by rote; he and Julia and Frances knelt on the raw-wood floor before the table and the meager loaf, the chalice half filled with sherry. Angus spoke the familiar words, his voice cadenced and rich, and Canby listened over and behind the voice to a cannonball bounding down Mitchell Street, heard the cracking of wood as it thwacked into clapboard siding, followed by the sound of brick crumbling.

It seemed that Angus had not heard it. He blessed the loaf and the wine, his hand hovering over each in turn. Together, the four of them recited the Lord's Prayer. Outside, a block away, a man's voice called out in pain.

Angus turned with the loaf in his hands. He raised it toward the stained-glass window set high in the north wall and broke it.

He had begun to turn back to the makeshift altar and the children when the shell struck the schoolhouse. The wall came apart, in the slowed sequence of Canby's dream, in stages: the dust first issuing forth from between the clapboards as though in a sharp exhalation, the boards splintering just after, and the stained glass shattering, bursting and flying inward in a shower of blue and gold fragments.

Angus turned back to the children before he fell. His face was transfigured. Shards of the glass protruded from his cheeks and forehead and his eyes were embedded with colored slivers. Beneath the girls' screams and the falling of boards and timbers Canby heard the glass cracking underfoot as he rushed to his father. He knelt beside him and watched, helpless, as Angus's hands sought the wounds in his face, winced back from the pain when his fingers touched the glass in his eyes. Angus shook his head from side to side and his hands went out over the floor, patting at the boards, reaching for what he could not see.

"I dropped it, boy!"

"Stop talking, Father," Canby said.

He saw blood seeping with Angus's pulse from a shard that had caught in his neck and Canby began to pull it out, carefully as he could. But the blood pumped faster. Angus was murmuring and Canby saw that his ruined eyes were leaking tears as well as blood.

At some point he was aware that Julia and Frances were

beside him and that his father had gone on. Frances reached out a hand to Canby's cheek and turned his head and gently pulled a blue fragment, a shard the size of a penknife blade, from his face. He looked at Frances and Julia, at his father's body and the halved loaf where it lay on the floor. He looked up at the ragged gash rent in the schoolhouse wall and that coppery half-light out beyond it.

That had been the end of it, in life. But in the dream, Canby walked out of the schoolhouse, down the front steps, and saw in the lone oak of the schoolhouse yard Billingsley perched on a thick limb in his suit of glistening black.

"Died blind!" Billingsley crowed. "Died blind!"

"You early," Szabó said through the wicket.

"I am a detective. There is no early or late for me."

The wicket shut and Canby stood listening to the flags atop Fulton Tower snap and flutter in the dawn breeze while the jailer worked the lock. The heavy door swung inward.

"A bad night he had," Szabó said, locking the door behind them.

"What the hell do you care?"

The jailer shrugged. "Colonel is gentleman."

Canby leaned close to the man, studied his furtive gray-green eyes beneath the brows, the hair nearly white where it grew out of his pale flesh. "Colonel is a murderer. Of the vilest kind. Do not forget it."

The jailer turned and walked to the cage that was Spot 12 and unlocked the door. His broad back to Canby the entire time, dumb as an ox. Once they had breached the front door, Malcolm Harrigan and his mob must have had the run of the place. Greenberg never had a chance.

This man Szabó was new since Canby's time on the force. And from what Vernon had told him, there had been plenty of grumbling not only when local men were passed over for the job, but when it went to a Hungarian immigrant, a protégé of Hannibal Kimball's. To men of a certain hardened stripe, the jailer's job was a sinecure—a sure livelihood from the county in exchange for making sure the inmates were kept fed and quiet. Any complaints could be fixed either with solitary confinement or a discreet beating. And since Reconstruction, at least, a paycheck from Fulton County never bounced. This man, though, had hardly worked his way up to it.

Szabó opened the cage door for Canby and began to shuffle his way down the hall to his living quarters. Canby pulled the door shut behind him until it latched. Billingsley sat up on his bunk and Canby saw that he was dressed in a suit and shined shoes, all of it, except for the boiled-white shirt with its high collar, entirely black.

"Where are this man's prison togs?" Canby called down the hall. But although he could hear Szabó whistling a foreign tune as he moved down the long hallway, the jailer gave no sign of having heard him.

"You and Vernon Thompson may deny me my due process, Canby, but I intend to go to the gallows as a gentleman." Billingsley whisked dust from his black trousers leg.

"You'll die a criminal's death regardless. Suit yourself. That jailer's days are numbered here, too."

"Szabó was raised in an old country. He has a proper respect for a man of station."

"Servile. What have you offered him?"

"He knows his place. He will have his reward. I had hoped that you, too, would come around to a right way of seeing things."

"But I didn't, did I?"

"That's regrettable. But in time you will. In time you will be convinced to your very marrow."

"You are insane, Billingsley."

"Malthus is my name now."

"But you didn't finish scribing your name, did you?"

"I am not yet finished."

"You know, you talk as though you actually believe this shite."

Billingsley was on his feet in an instant, a far measure more spry than he had been the day before. "Do not mock me, boy!" he thundered. "Bog Irish nigger-lover—you are everything that is wrong with Atlanta, with the world. And your arrogance!

"I'd have thought my work would have taught you something about that. Think of it, Canby—my work changed after you visited me in my home. Your asinine talk of crime, progress. Oh, you goaded me. You'd goaded me once, altering my work. That I could abide, could bide my time to correct. But to so . . . *belittle* what I was proving out, with every dead piece of trash. My work is *not* inspired by base motivations, Canby." He said Canby's name as though it were the pure expression of derision.

"As if evil could be dismissed from the world by the likes of you! As if an order of things as old as the world could be changed by common trash with presumptions! Think on it, Canby. My work changed with that visit. You redirected its course."

Billingsley sat back down on the bunk, a sudden calm seeming to come over him. He pulled a leather-bound ledger from under his pillow and opened it to a place marked by a pencil that Canby saw with a sinking feeling bore the stamp of the Georgia Pencil Company on its shaft.

"Mary Flanagan was never in my sights until you interfered with my work. You made her necessary, made Greenberg necessary. But I see now the way to get back on the track. I will not be delayed again.

"You would not believe the dreams I've dreamed since they brought me here. I see the shape of the rest of what's given to me to do. It will be sublime.

"You look a bit pale, Canby. Not feeling so clever now? I hid myself in plain sight, Detective. Do you know that the lift operator at Kimball House greeted me by name as he carried me up to the penthouses? Not a soul suspected. I hid from you, even—this ledger here, do you recognize it? It was on my desk when you visited my home. I was even then writing the names of the dead in it. And you, fool that you are, *stumbled* as you looked over my shelves. You stopped at Lamarck, with good Malthus scant inches away. How close you came! You could have saved poor Mary Flanagan, and your man from Ringgold.

"But their names were not yet in my book, not yet that day. As I said, you goaded me. You damned them. Their innocent blood is on your hands. Poor Mary, there was no one there for her at the end. She died screaming down into darkness. And your man the great, fat peckerwood. He died like a pig at skinning-time."

Yellow wick-light from the gas lamp outside the cell danced on the black bricks behind Billingsley. He smiled.

"And Greenberg. You damned him worst of them all, by altering my work. Look where that led. Another Jew on a tree! Priceless! Your doing, Canby—the trial, that mob of trash! All I did was set it in motion. Like swatting a hornet's nest with a stick, it was."

Without realizing it, Canby had risen to his feet. He held his hands, balled into fists, by his sides, felt his fingernails biting into his palms.

"Give me the book."

Billingsley clutched it to his breast like a babe, shook his head side to side over the high collar of his starched shirt.

"Nononononono," he said. "Not yet. You will have it before I go, I promise. But we still have my last testament to complete together."

Canby was reaching for the ledger with one hand, his other hand going into his pocket for the Case knife, when he heard the jail's door opening. He stepped back from Billingsley and glanced over his shoulder.

"Look," Billingsley said. "Here comes your sable amanuensis. Good morning, nigger-boy!"

Underwood came through the door, with Vernon behind him. Vernon's face was clouded with rage.

"I think I know why these men come," Billingsley said.

Vernon drew close to the bars and motioned for Canby to lean toward him. He whispered, "Another. The bishop's son's gone missing."

"Oh, yes," Billingsley cried. "Johnny Drew, are you just now realizing it? He is mine now."

"How does he know?" Vernon said. Canby only looked at him. Vernon nodded to Underwood, who started down the hall.

"Where is he off to?" Canby whispered.

"To check that Campbell's still in his cell."

"Why wouldn't he be?"

"No reason. I just want to be certain."

In a moment they could hear Szabó's voice, then the men's footsteps ascending the winding stairwell of the tower.

"You will get nothing out of Fortus Campbell." Billingsley had shut his eyes and the ledger had been put back under his bedding. He was leaning against the blackened bricks.

"What's this about Campbell, Billingsley?"

"You will be convinced, in time, Canby, that you have set the mark far too low in your appraisal of me. Fortus Campbell is dead."

"Did you kill him?"

"In a manner of speaking. He was a useful tool for a time, like his father was. Vernon, do tell Canby here how the senior Campbell came to be in my employ."

Vernon's cheeks colored.

"You did not recognize the old nigger down at my place, Detective, because he was quite broken by his time on the chain gang. When the chief paroled him to my farm he was enormously grateful. An arrangement was struck."

"I never should have done it," Vernon said, fairly spitting the words.

"Nor should you have allowed him to be arrested on such scant evidence back in '76. Tunis Campbell, like you, Canby, was a low man of ambition. Though of color, he had aspirations. He had a notion that Reconstruction could help him secure an office in the legislature—as though he would move from sweeping the floors of the Capitol to occupying a desk in it. He might have, too, if the Ring hadn't stepped in. Graft, I believe the charge was. His decline was even more precipitous than yours, Canby."

Canby looked at Vernon. Vernon hung his head.

"And look which side of the bars you are on now, Canby," Billingsley said with a low chuckle. "Best you watch your step around the good chief."

Vernon seemed relieved to hear the sound of steps coming down the stairs. But Underwood came up the hallway shaking his head. Szabó followed him, slowly.

"Was it the bedsheet, boy?" Billingsley asked.

Underwood stared at the prisoner with a barely concealed look of horror on his face. "It was," he said.

"Good boy," Billingsley said. He closed his eyes and began the slow reclining back to his bunk that Canby had seen the day before.

"Where is the bishop's son, Billingsley?"

"Billingsley!"

Billingsley's eyes remained shut and he did not move.

"Midnight, tonight, Billingsley, that rope goes around your neck," Vernon said between clenched teeth. He motioned for Szabó to unlock the cage and let Canby out, then leaned in to the bars as if to get closer in Billingsley's hearing. "You know, Robert, a hanging can go a couple of different ways. I've seen it.

"The humane notion of the gallows is that the drop breaks the condemned's neck. Less suffering. But if the drop's not hard enough, the man dies of strangulation. By degrees."

But the prisoner did not acknowledge him. He appeared to be fast asleep.

"Tell us where the Drew boy is and you'll go quick. Don't, and I'll tell them to drop you easy. It'll be a slow process, with plenty of pain."

Canby stepped out of Spot 12 and it was then, as the cell door's latch snapped shut, that Billingsley opened one of his bloodshot eyes and fixed it on Vernon.

"I know how it works, Vernon," Billingsley said. "You can ask Mary Flanagan when you see her, by and by."

BISHOP DREW PACED the slate tiles of his rooms as though he meant to wear a groove in the floor of the rectory. Canby watched him, noted that the man's anxiety seemed genuine. The black fabric of his vestments hissed and whispered as he paced, left then right, right then left, in front of the bookshelves that covered one of the church office's walls.

"He has always been a willful boy," he said, as much to himself as to Vernon and Canby. Underwood he had asked to wait in the vestibule. "Prone to truancy—'prone to wander,' as the hymn says. He may yet be out on one of his larks."

"Has he been out to the Cotton Exposition?"

"Doubtless. He comes and goes."

"And the mother? Your wife?"

The bishop cut a sharp glance at Canby. "My wife had a nervous disposition. She did not survive the siege."

"I have a man circulating John's ferrotype among the vendors," Vernon said. "We'll find out if he's been seen there."

Canby thought about the image of the boy that he'd burned into his mind when Vernon showed him the ferrotype. Towheaded, as they said in the country, hair pale and fine as cornsilk. Smiling. Innocent. "Did John know Robert Billingsley?"

"Socially, of course, Mister Canby."

"There is something Billingsley said. He said—"

"Johnny may have been gone the better part of the week, Mister Canby," the bishop said. He had stopped pacing. "To be frank, I am not certain how long. My shortcomings as a parent are coming to light."

"But Thomas, surely Billingsley was raving," Vernon said. "We've had him in custody longer than that."

Canby looked out the rectory's tall windows, through the leaded glass in granite casements. In the courtyard outside, crepe myrtles nodded in a breeze. The limbs of one of them scratched against the glass from time to time. Across the courtyard the east wall of the cathedral rose like a Gothic monument of stone gables and arches.

"Perhaps if I go to him . . ." the bishop said.

"To Billingsley?" Vernon said. "To what end? To administer last rites?"

"Yes, yes, I could."

"I was making a poor jest, sir."

"I have been at many a dying man's bedside, Vernon. Truths come out at such times. Even a man as fallen as Robert may unburden himself."

Vernon looked at Canby as though hoping the younger man would confirm his incredulity. Canby shrugged.

"You're certain, Bishop? It's no easy thing to witness."

The bishop nodded quickly. Canby could see a thin film of sweat on his upper lip.

Vernon picked up his hat from his lap. "All right, then," he said, rising. "Eleven o'clock should be in plenty of time."

The bishop escorted them to the door and nodded again when they stepped into the vestibule. Underwood rose from his seat there and he and Canby followed Vernon down the slate steps. Canby looked back and saw that the oaken door of the rectory had closed behind them soundlessly.

Vernon stopped in the hallway. He turned to Canby and said, "Don't mention the bishop's wife again. She died in a bombproof, suffocated."

"I did not know."

"It was not widely circulated. The scene was ghastly."

Underwood whispered, "You know that man's lying. Could tell that even from out in the hall."

Canby nearly smiled. "Underwood," he said, "there may be hope for you yet."

"ALL OF IT of a piece. If one cannot turn back time, one can at least leave one's bloody mark on the present."

Billingsley leaned against the brick wall languidly. In his

madness, Canby thought, the man grew more relaxed as the hour of his execution neared. "Where is the boy, Billingsley?"

"Malthus is my name now."

"It is Robert Billingsley we will hang."

"And Malthus who will return."

"Will Malthus then tell us where to find John Drew?"

"Little Johnny is safe. Rest your mind on that count. Johnny, too, will return."

Billingsley raised his chin as he spoke, the trace of the old aristocrat present in his bearing if not in his wrecked countenance.

"It'll be a shame to ruin that pretty collar."

"I am glad, Canby, that I selected you as the recorder of my last testament—you and your nigger-boy. Where the two of you were before—that was where you belonged. You will see in time that the old order of things was preferable to what this new system can offer you."

"The system is doing a good sight better for me these days," Underwood said.

"I have fucked your system."

Canby reached into his vest for his pocket watch. He flipped open its cover. "Not by my reckoning," he said, snapping the cover closed. "In an hour and a half, the system is going to fuck *you*."

"In time, everything will be made vile."

"Hear those sounds outside? That's your gallows they're testing. Listen close and you'll hear them dropping the trapdoor. That'll be an end to you. You'll be walked down to it from this cell like all the trash that's been locked up here before you."

"All in due time."

"Not after midnight."

"This business at midnight? Tonight is only a prelude to greater things."

"The gallows will have the final word on that."

"Nononononono," he said in a crazed singsong. "Remember this, Canby. I was never mortal. Not for a minute. And my last victim will be you. I will do things to your corpse that even the dead can feel."

As he spoke Billingsley's voice went deeper than Canby had ever heard it. Canby felt the hairs on his neck stiffen.

"Tell me something," Underwood said. "The letters on the foreheads, is that from Revelations?"

Billingsley turned away.

"Because Revelations says, 'His name will be on their foreheads.' Is that what you intended? Or is it just the mark of the Beast?"

"*Just?* Who taught you how to read?"

"Have you read Revelations?"

"It is chapter twenty-two you reference," Billingsley said. "Also seven, nine . . ." His voice trailed off and he looked at Underwood. The trace of a grin played across his face. "I forget the verses."

"But Revelations also says God's name will be on them. On the believers' foreheads."

"It's not God's name now, is it? It is mine. I say again, who taught you to read? Was it a white man?"

Canby looked at the two of them, their eyes locked. Underwood holding his own. Then the silence of the moment was broken by a knocking on the jail's door and the sound of Szabó coming, keys jangling.

"Where is it you come from?" Underwood said.

"You truly want to know, black boy?"

"Yes."

"Then I promise you, by and by, I will take you there."

Billingsley's eyes fixed on some point beyond Spot 12 and held there. He took another of his shuddering breaths as Szabó passed the cell, and looked at Canby with the same benign expression Canby had seen on his face in his study weeks before.

"There, I believe, is my old friend the bishop calling. So let us not end on a bad note," he said. "We should have some proper benediction."

He picked up the ledger and turned through its pages. "Yes, here it is. Mister Canby, I have finished my testament. All the names of the dead are in it. You can read it all for yourself at your leisure. Your name graces the last page. But now, before I take my leave, I would like for you to read this passage of reminiscence."

Billingsley leaned forward with the book outheld. Underwood tensed and reached inside his jacket.

"Where is the Drew boy?" Canby asked.

"All in due time," Billingsley clucked, and urged the book forward. "Please read. Aloud, if you will indulge me."

Canby took the book and began reading:

"'The hounds found Saul before sunset. By dusk he was swinging from one of the live oaks that shaded the barnyard. Father insisted that I be present to witness it. I watched in fascination, as only a boy of my sensibilities might, while Saul swung and his talismans dropped from his pockets and the tips of his old brogans stiffened and then drooped earthward. Father looked over at me and spoke harshly. He had seen that I was in the manly state and he tossed me his riding coat to cover myself. I still remember vividly the look on his face as he turned away.

"'That night, in my bed on the upper floor of my father's house, I took my manhood in hand for the first time. In the dark, as I held it and worked the flesh, I felt its tip fork, like a serpent's tongue, and I knew that I had been chosen.'"

Canby set the ledger down on the bench, holding it by the edges. He looked at Underwood, registered the revulsion on his face. He looked at Billingsley and Billingsley began to laugh.

Canby rose and struck him across the face with the flat palm of his hand. Still he laughed. Canby backhanded him, hard enough to hear the teeth coming together, but he laughed on. Behind him, he could hear Szabó shouting, the voices of the bishop and Vernon and his deputies joining the din. Canby balled his fist and began to land blows on Billingsley's face while Szabó rattled his keys, calling his name in that guttural accent, as he struggled to open the cell door. Underwood moved to block the cell door but the deputies pushed him aside and began to grab at Canby's flailing arms.

They hauled him off Billingsley and the laughter continued as they dragged Canby and Underwood down the hallway. "You've broke his teeth!" Szabó cried from the cell.

Canby looked back and saw that Billingsley was grinning, his mouth bloody and studded with cracked teeth. He spit out blood and Canby could hear the broken teeth clattering across the puncheon floor.

Then the laughter resumed, cascaded and pealed through Spot 12, and echoed through the entirety of the tower itself, it seemed.

"Mine, Canby!" Billingsley screamed. "Canby! You are *mine!*"

THE WALK from Spot 12 to the gallows in the prison court-yard was not a long one, but the procession made it at a funereal pace. Szabó led them, a lantern held aloft in one hand and the execution order in the other, reading it as they went. In his broken English he pronounced the court's sentence haltingly.

The bishop, ashen-faced, walked beside his old friend, speaking to him in a murmuring voice too low for Canby to hear the words. Whether he was administering the last rites or beseeching his friend for the whereabouts of his son, Canby could not determine. But he heard in the voice great sorrow.

Henry Grady stood by the gallows, his pencil and notebook held in hands that hung at his sides. For once, his bow tie was unknotted, hanging loose down the front of his shirt. His face was composed in an expression of public solemnity, but beneath it Canby thought he saw embarrassment, perhaps even a bit of shame.

Vernon watched Szabó and the deputies walk Billingsley up the gallows steps and loop the noose around his neck, then checked his pocket watch.

"Once more, Billingsley," he said. "Where is the boy?"

Billingsley smiled down at him with his broken teeth, but said nothing. Vernon pulled a cigar from his vest and cut it. Still Billingsley did not speak. Vernon put the cigar in his mouth and shrugged his shoulders.

"We're early, boys, but no cause to wait," he said as he lit his cigar. He nodded to the jailer and the deputy. "Just be sure you drop him gently."

They draped the pillowcase over Billingsley's head and asked for last words. "Ah, darkness," he said.

Then he dropped.

NIGHT

November 14

CANBY SAT IN THE WHITE ELECTRIC LIGHT OF
Billingsley's study with the calfskin-bound ledger spread open
before him. Next to it on the desk was the bottle of fine whiskey, the unknown vintage, from which he poured himself a
dram at intervals, when the reading required it of him. Most
of the day gone now and he had been over the bulk of the ledger twice, excepting the passages wherein Billingsley detailed
what he had done to the girl at Mamie O'Donnell's and,
worse, what had been done to Mary Flanagan. Though Canby
could weather the obscenities and blasphemies that riddled the
account as he combed through it again, he had only been able
to read about the outrages committed on the girls once.

He lingered several minutes over the page on which the
names of the victims had been written. *MALTHUS* was
spelled out in a descending line on the left-hand side of the
page, the victims' names or occupations listed in a correspond-
ing column on the right. Billingsley hadn't bothered with
Anse's name, or the prostitute's; they were listed as "pig" and

"whore." But Mary Flanagan's name seemed to Canby to be burned onto the paper like an indictment next to the *H*. Across the page from the *U*, Billingsley had written, *"Drew"*; across from the *S*, *"W. T. Sherman."* Canby smiled mirthlessly at the entry for General Sherman. *Too late for that, you son of a bitch,* he thought. But he could not dismiss the entry for the Drew boy. He felt a bone-deep certainty that in the coming days they would find the boy's mutilated body, in someone's well or a back alley. He could not gauge whether that conviction aroused in him more dread or more futility, could only be certain that the world was a far sight better off with Billingsley dispatched from it.

He turned one of the heavy pages and read:

The plantation was the apotheosis of the order the High Father had lost, restored here on earth. The peasants lackeys yankees trash envied it. Hated us for it and I reveled in their hatred until at last they won out. Improbably, impossibly, they won out. But for a long while there we had it. Had achieved it: the planter at the top the center the apex of it all. Judge and executioner to the rest, sovereign of all I surveyed. The big white house at the center. White! I wore white in the daytime and moved naked through darkness.

Hence Malthus, Canby thought, at least in Billingsley's version. The white man was ascendant, but there was no paternalism in it, no trace of noblesse oblige, not even feigned. What the philosopher Thomas Malthus saw as anarchy stayed by order, chaos held at bay, Billingsley saw as purely the exertion of power. He took another sip of the whiskey and turned the page.

That order was not to be recovered. Pissed shat vomited away by rabble. Unable even to rule themselves. The niggers bad enough but those yankee crusaders even worse. We had the carpetbaggers gone soon as we could. But then Grady and the others began to sound just like them. Not just capitulating to the new order but celebrating it! New men with no lineage all around us—one day stepping off the train and a year later stepping into the mayor's office. Grady's "editorials" singing the vapid minstrelry of his New South. A "new" South! There is nothing new under the sun.

They think money is the final currency. Not at all. Their cotton exposition set up like a debutante ball for this new South they laud. Intolerable. As if being forced not only to attend one's own funeral but to dance a jig on the grave.

Canby riffled the pages, scanning lines of Victor Hugo's that Billingsley had transcribed into his book. All of them from a poem about Satan that the Frenchman had apparently been working on over several years of correspondence with Billingsley. The devil Hugo described reminded Canby of his readings in Milton, yet this fallen angel was somehow both more sinister and beguiling than the character Milton had traced. Canby flipped the pages until they went to blank paper, then turned back to the last page on which Billingsley had written. Read:

Does it seem pedantic to quote my French friend once more, Canby? Victor catches the spirit of it precisely, I believe: "'So,' cried Satan, 'so be it! still I can see! He shall have the blue sky, the black sky is mine.'"

The black sky is mine, Canby. I will see you in it.

SSS—MALTHUS

Canby shut the book slowly, then drained the dregs of his glass. For a moment he studied the crystal decanter from which he had poured, from which the black butler had poured him and Billingsley drinks in this room, those bloodied weeks ago. Billingsley gone now—could Canby summon belief in its existence—to that very Hell whose praises he had sung. The black butler gone, too, no one knew where. When Vernon and the others had come to this house they had found the front door unlocked as though in anticipation of their arrival. And the back door still standing ajar, as though the black man had departed in such haste as to leave the door still swinging behind him.

Canby grabbed the decanter by its neck and was rising to leave with it when he heard a sound, furtive, beneath him. He paused stock-still and waited until he heard it again. The slightest of noises coming up through the floorboards, a faint grinding sound. Very slowly, he set the decanter on the desk and sat back down in the chair, mindful to ease his weight into it so as not to make the wood or the chair's heavy spring creak beneath him. One at a time, he pulled off his boots, then rose in stockinged feet and drew the .32 Bulldog from his chest holster as he crossed the room.

He found the cellar door at the end of a back hallway and eased it open. He studied the electric switch beside the doorframe for a long moment as he heard the sound come from below him again, trying to assess the risk of going down the stairs in full light, announced. He moved past the switch and began to descend the steps in a crouch, eyes wide to acclimate himself to the darkness.

It was no cellar, he saw as his ducked head came clear of the first story's flooring, but a full basement, bricked four-square along the house's foundation and eight feet down to the red Georgia clay. Spaced at intervals on the four walls were wrought-iron casements through which the afternoon's waning light drifted in. He saw that the household's food-stuffs were stored here, arrayed against the walls. As his eyes adjusted to the weak light, he saw sacks of coffee beans and canned fruits, a metal tin of raisins. All of it neatly ordered, down to the fifty-pound sacks of rice and shucked corn that were set atop wooden-staved barrels on the floor. Some of the barrels' sides marked with the stencil of Morris Rich's store, others branded from locales more exotic. Fish in brine from a San Francisco merchant, two barrels of chowder from Boston, five-gallon kegs of syrup from Vermont. Bricks and loaves of cheeses from abroad stored on high shelves.

He heard the sound again, scraping, and turned to its source at the base of the west wall. There a hogshead had burst open, the grain inside it spilling out through the split staves onto the floor. He saw movement in the grain, the whisking of a hairless tail and the working of a mottled black and gray rump. The rat had pressed its head into the gap, burrowing. As it dug for more purchase on the sifting grain its back and haunches rubbed against the lower of the two iron bands that encircled the barrel.

"Hanh!" Canby said.

The rat wagged its way out of the grain, making the rubbing sound again as its back pulled clear of the iron band. It raised its head, quizzical, for a second, until Canby grunted again. Then it darted off the little grain pile, claws scrabbling for purchase, and ran across the floor like a swift-moving shadow to a gap in the bricks through which Canby guessed he could not pass three fingers. It flattened itself against the ground as though boneless and squeezed its way through.

He holstered the Bulldog and climbed the steps far enough to reach the light switch and flicked it on. He took another look around the basement in the white light and saw the edge of something metal protruding from the grain. He crossed to the hogshead and took hold of it, found that he had to wrench it free from the gap in the barrel, while more of the grain sifted like sand down to the floor.

Canby held it in his hand and looked at it, thinking that the design of its function was as clearly evident as was the malevolence of its purpose. It was an iron band, three inches wide, hinged at one point of its circumference and with a hasp at the opposite point of the circle, through which a small padlock could be fitted. Its diameter, he noted as he turned it in his hands, crafted to fit a human neck. And stretching out from the band, as if the cardinal points of its compass, were four thin iron rods that tapered at their ends like grotesque parodies of a flower's stalk. Or rather three of them, for where the fourth would have attached to the collar was left only the bright spot of unrusted metal where that prong had broken cleanly away.

He studied it, the sinister curvature of the prongs. The weight of it. Thought of how it would feel when locked into place on the neck of the recovered runaway or the malingering slave. How the prongs would have made sleep a torture, the simple act of laying one's head down for rest a physical impossibility. Its design as purposeful as a horseshoe. The nadir of the blacksmith's art.

He set it down on top of the burst hogshead, glad to be rid of contact with it. Billingsley certainly was insane enough to keep it as a memento, but why such a strange site for storing it? Or the need to hide it? On his stockinged feet he made his way back to the stairs, eager to be gone from this house and outside in whatever daylight remained.

THEY KNELT in the falling light of the quickening dusk, waiting. The only sound above the flickering of the candles was the periodic scraping of the crepe myrtle limbs against the stained glass, the occasional clatter of dried leaves scuttling across brick pavers as the wind pushed them from one corner of the courtyard to the other. Then, the creaking of wood as, one by one, the older ones among the parishioners pushed up from their positions on the kneelers and settled themselves back into the pews, piety yielding to the exigencies of age.

One of them, the youngest of the ladies' guild, rose from her place near the back as quietly as she could and slipped out of the nave. The others sat or knelt as she had left them, listening to her footfalls fading as she went down the length of the vestibule, then coming louder as she ascended the stone steps. Faintly they heard her soft knock on the rectory door.

So they waited, ears cocked for some word on the postponement, of when this day's vespers would eventually begin.

They did not wait long. Though none of them heard the heavy door swing open on its oiled hinges, all of them heard the scream that came just afterward. And the screams that followed the first, one after another ringing off the granite, through the courtyard, and out into the gathering night.

THE LITTLE WOMAN in the vestibule was crouched down on herself, up against the wall like a frightened child or an animal gone to ground, shivering. She raised a bony finger and Canby and Underwood took the steps up to the rectory two at a time and threw open the timbered door.

The bishop was sprawled back in the chair behind his desk. A bloody *U* had been carved into his forehead but he was, so far as Canby could tell, otherwise unharmed. He and Underwood paused in their forward momentum, looking, watching the blood seep from the wan brow. Canby moved around the desk and put a hand on the man's neck.

The bishop groaned and slowly opened his pale eyes.

"I knew you'd come," he said.

"Shit," Canby said.

"He's alive?" Underwood said.

"For a while yet," the bishop said, nodding, the dripping letter made more grotesque by the gesture.

"Look around for the knife, Underwood. A letter opener, maybe, something with an edge or a point to it. He's done it himself. By his own hand."

"I have, have I?" the bishop said. He struggled to rise, stood, wavered, and tilted toward Canby. Canby put a hand out against his chest to steady him, pressing against the black fabric of the cassock the bishop wore. The man moaned and collapsed back into his chair. Canby heard the sound of something wet striking the floor. He looked at his palm. It was covered in blood.

Underwood made a choking sound and Canby looked down at his feet, at the space between them and the bishop. Gray and ropy coils of entrails lay there on the slate, one length of them trailing back underneath the bishop's robes.

"He wanted me to deliver a message, don't you see," the bishop said. "Leave him be. Let him finish his work and perhaps he'll have mercy on you."

"He was here?"

"Bullshit, Underwood. Of course he wasn't."

"Indeed he was."

"We saw the coffin go into the ground. We saw him dead on the rope."

"I saw him rise, Mister Canby."

"And how did he do that, Bishop? What sort of magic trick would that entail?"

"If you knew what he is, you would get yourself on his side."

"I'm not here to try God and the devil with you. Where is your son?"

"I do not know. In God's name, I swear it."

The bishop groaned again and Canby saw a gout of blood begin to spread on the slate floor.

"Good God, Mister Canby," Underwood said. "What more proof do you need that he ain't of this world?"

"All the proof I see is that madness is catching. See if you can find the blade he did this with."

"Poor boy," the bishop said, looking at Underwood with pity in his eyes. "Do you not miss your old station now? So much less was asked of you then. Now you will know true pain. There is no blade, Detective, because Malthus took it with him. The thousand years are over, and he is released from his prison."

"That's Revelations," Underwood said.

"It is. Prophecy. Return to your place, boy, and you may find clemency." The bishop was now straining to talk. "I tell you, Detective, if you knew what he is, you'd get yourself on his side."

Canby shook his head. "Do you know where your son is?"

"Only that he is safe. Robert has made provision for him."

"How do you know that?"

"I saw him. With Robert. With my own eyes. I doubt no more."

"You saw him here with Billingsley?"

"That was the arrangement."

"You *gave* him your son?"

"Yes, I did. As Abraham did Isaac. But he reneged on our agreement. He would not tell me where my Johnny is going."

Canby looked at Underwood. "At least the boy may still be alive."

The bishop's eyelids were drooping shut. "He would only tell me that Johnny will be safe," he said, "from me, from you."

Canby pulled a handkerchief from his coat pocket and wiped his bloody hand on it. He looked down at the bishop slumped in his chair and slowly ebbing toward the floor, his chest barely rising with breath. He tossed the handkerchief in the clergyman's bloody lap and turned toward the door.

"Underwood, we have another visit to pay this evening," he said.

Underwood lingered a moment in the room. "What about the bishop?"

"Him?" Canby said, beginning to shake his head. "Let him bleed."

SZABÓ'S WHIMPERING had risen in intensity until now it was nearly a squeal, porcine and desperate as an animal wounded and at bay. Canby stood back and regarded him. His mouth and nose were frothed with blood and mucus, hair matted with sweat. The nose, Canby thought as he rubbed the bleeding knuckles of his right hand, would likely never set right again.

"Take his keys and put him in the cell, Underwood. If he stays out here where I can get my hands on him, I'll surely kill him."

Underwood half helped, half dragged Szabó into Spot 12. Szabó seemed relieved to have the separation of the bars between himself and Canby. Underwood slammed the cell door and jangled the ring of keys in his hand. "Now search his living quarters?"

Canby nodded. "Lead the way."

At the door to Szabó's rooms, Underwood worked through the key ring until the fifth key fit and turned the lock's bolt. He pushed open the door, looked ahead for a moment, then slowly turned his head to Canby. He said, over his shoulder, "Think you're going to be revising that theory on evil here directly."

Underwood stepped aside so that Canby could see into the room. On its far side, over the head of Szabó's cot, the wall was covered with dark crosses. Crucifixes, all of them, some as simple as two crossed pieces of wood and others ornate, brought, Canby imagined, from Szabó's native land, crosses on which Christs in agony suffered in degrees depicted in a range from beatific to ghastly. Some shedding carved tears and others stoic, some with the build of athletes and others thin, tortured wraiths. But each and all of them arrayed on the wall above Szabó's bed had been hung, meticulously, upside down.

Underwood was moving back up the hallway, his footsteps gaining momentum. Canby listened to him go as he took in the rest of the room: the domestic items—a washbasin, a shirt and a pair of pants draped over a ladder-back chair—mixed in with the tools of the jailer's trade: manacles, leg irons. Atop a bureau he saw a half dozen of the foppish collars Billingsley had taken to wearing, resting there, perfect crescents of white. His eyes drifted back to the manacles. He thought how they covered such a broad swath of a man's wrists, how the leg irons could reach so far up from a man's ankles. An impenetrable band of iron. As he heard Underwood unlocking the cell door he picked up one of the manacles and set it inside one of the collars on the chipped and scarred top of the bureau. Studied the perfect circle of iron inside the broader circle of starched cotton.

Up the hallway Szabó's cries resumed, then ebbed into a series of low grunts, coming regularly. When Canby got back to the cell he saw that Underwood was working over Szabó's midsection methodically, like a seasoned cop would—like Canby should have—dealing out damage where it could not be seen in a courtroom by judge or jury. Underwood was acting more the professional than he had.

"Underwood," Canby said after a minute, "I think that's enough. Leave a little starch in him yet. He has some digging to do tonight."

THE BILLINGSLEY family plots in Oakland Cemetery were on a slight rise above the Confederate Section of the vast graveyard, so that as Canby and Underwood stood over the grave and watched Szabó dig his way down into it, they could look across Oakland to Atlanta. To the west, the International Cotton Exposition glowed with cheerful light at Oglethorpe Park, the fair's operating hours now extended late into the nights. Nearer were the lights of Atlanta, the beacon of Kimball House, and the smoldering glow of the railroad roundhouse, where the smiths and mechanics worked on the cars and engines through the night. The closest landmark otherwise was the Confederate Monument, which raised its stark marble obelisk above the tombs and mausoleums like a finger of bone. Surrounding it were row upon row of white-tablet markers, plain save for name and rank, of Georgia's Confederate dead. Their number, last Canby had heard, was nearly seven thousand—among them some three thousand unknowns who had fallen with their comrades, the lot of them, in Canby's estimation, dying in the stead of men like Robert Billingsley.

Szabó had dug himself down into the grave neck-deep, with Canby and Underwood standing above, when they heard the cock of a pistol's hammer behind them.

"Not a motion, you goddamn ghouls."

Canby spoke without turning. "Is that you, Mister Connelly?"

"Yep. Got the drop on you sonsabitches, didn't I? Which college you headed to with that dead man?"

"Imagine our lantern helped you spot us, sir," Underwood said.

"You getting smart with me, boy? You'd not be the first sack-'em-up man I've dropped in a hole of his own digging."

"He didn't mean any harm, Mister Connelly," Canby said. "We knocked at the gatehouse but didn't get an answer."

Connelly stepped up close, put a hand on Canby's shoulder, and turned him around. Canby could smell the sweet stink of bourbon on his breath. "I stepped out for a minute. But I stepped back in. Where's that leave you?" He gestured with the pistol, its enormous barrel pointing at Canby and Underwood in turn. Canby imagined the sidearm might have been standard issue for the Mexican War, if not earlier.

"I'm Thomas Canby, Mister Connelly."

"Angus's boy?"

"Yessir."

"Angus was a good man."

"Yessir."

"Well, it's a shitload of trouble you've got yourself into again, isn't it?"

"It is. Trying to get out of a bit of it here. Would you mind lowering that pistol?"

Connolly did not answer, only stepped around Canby to get a better look at Szabó in the grave. His eyes roved over Szabó's broken face and the blood- and clay-stained cotton of the blouse-like shirt he wore. He glowered at him until Szabó, doggedly, began to dig again. Connolly studied the ragged hole in the ground and the earth slung up to the side of the grave.

"Shoddy work, even the second time around," Connolly said. "Where the hell is he from, that he don't even know how to dig a square hole?" He nodded, as though to himself. "Trying to go shallow, he was. Had to ride his ass to get it six feet deep. But would he let me dig it? No. Just a bunch of that gobbledygook he talks."

"Was he alone?" Canby asked.

"He brought that bishop with him. They were friends, you know, him and the colonel. It was as small as a pauper's funeral, which I guess is fitting, knowing all the bad he done."

Underwood cleared his throat and spoke. "No one else with them?"

"Naw. Just the two of them, one on each end of the coffin when they lowered it."

"Doubtless it wasn't much weight," Canby said.

"How you figure?" Connelly asked as they heard the sound of wood being struck by the shovel.

"You think Johnny Drew's in it?" Underwood asked.

"I think it's empty," Canby said.

Underwood's eyes widened. "Think Malthus climbed out of it?"

"*Billingsley*, Underwood. In a manner of speaking. But not like you think. He was out of it soon as the wagon left the tower."

Szabó had nearly cleared the coffin lid of dirt. The shovel scraped on the wood and he moved from the foot of the casket to the head, tossing shovelfuls of earth upward indiscriminately, some of it landing on the boots of the men standing above. When Canby saw that the coffin had a split lid he called Szabó off the digging.

"Go ahead, open it."

"He's liable to be real ripe by now," Connelly warned.

Szabó shook his head. Canby reached a hand into his jacket and said again, "Open it."

Slowly, Szabó knelt down at the foot of the grave and reached for the latch that secured the casket's top half. "You don't know what you doing," he said over his shoulder.

"Just open it," Underwood said.

He loosed the latch and raised the coffin lid slowly, Canby and Underwood craning their necks to see over the lid and Connelly pressing a handkerchief to his nose. Connelly lowered the handkerchief as he and the others saw that the casket held no body. Upon the satin pillow of its lining rested, as though set there for viewing, an iron slave collar.

"Hand it up, Szabó," Canby said.

"Son of a bitch," Connelly said.

Canby took the collar from Szabó's outstretched hand. Its four prongs had been broken off, but not entirely. Four short nubs, filed round at their ends, remained attached to the ring of iron. Careful not to lock it in place, Canby fitted it around his neck, brought a splayed hand up from his sternum until his fingers caught against the nubs.

"That's how you survive a hanging, Underwood. Nothing supernatural to it." Then to Szabó he said, "You'll hang for this. Without a collar."

Szabó glared up at them defiantly. "He's loose, he's loose! Ain't nothing you can do now!"

The report of Connelly's pistol seemed as loud as a cannon. Its barrel barked flame and smoke and Szabó fell back against the far wall of the grave, then slumped down onto the closed half of the coffin. His head drooped, then rose, and looked down again. As Canby heard the last echoes of the report coming back from the headstones across the cemetery, his ears ringing, Szabó reached down into his lap and picked up the lead ball from where it had fallen. He pressed the fingers of his other hand against a spot on his chest, his eyes widening, and looked up from the grave.

"Goddamn," Connelly said, peering down the flintlock's barrel, then sniffing it. "Bad powder, I guess."

Szabó began to laugh, then to cackle. He sat up and held

the ball aloft like a trophy. "He did not lie! He lives! I live, too! What you say to that?"

Canby was reaching into his jacket again when Underwood began to fire. The Colt barked five times, as quickly as the revolver's action would allow, and with each shot a red blossom sprouted on the white cotton of Szabó's blouse. Szabó slumped again. The light that had kindled in his eyes a moment before ebbed just as quickly. He raised one arm, as if to bestow a curse, then his head and the arm dropped earthward together.

They stood staring down at Szabó's corpse as the gun smoke slowly cleared from over the open grave. Underwood, hand trembling, returned his pistol to his jacket pocket.

"Well, there's justice, I suppose," Canby said after a long moment. He remembered the line of Emerson's, *Your goodness must have some edge to it, else it is none.* Here was edge, indeed. "Though I'm not sure Vernon Thompson will appreciate the sentencing much."

"Piss on that," Connelly said. "Vernon's gone soft if he don't get it."

Unbidden by either of the policemen, Leonidas G. Connelly slipped down into the grave and began wrestling Szabó's body into the coffin. Once he had stuffed the corpse in, he stomped the lid shut and picked up the shovel and gestured for Canby to give him a hand up. Then he began to refill the grave, red clay piling up over the casket. After a few minutes he paused in his work, looked up at Canby and Underwood as if exasperated to see them still there.

"Well, go on with you, now," he said. "You've got your own work to do."

VERNON STARED AT the iron collar on the table before him and ran a hand through his graying hair while Canby gave him the report. Since letting them in through the front door on Butler Street he had said little, and now he seemed bereft of words. He sat in a cane-bottomed chair at his kitchen table clad only in his nightshirt and slippers, his eyes cutting from time to time between Canby and Underwood and the collar. Slowly, he picked it up and felt its heft, the nubs around its circumference.

"And I told them to drop him easy," he said at last.

"It might not have made a difference," Canby said. "The width of the thing could have kept his neck from breaking."

"Might have. Could have."

"He fooled all of us, Vernon."

"Twice," Vernon said. He set the collar down heavily. "Szabó fooled me, too."

"You don't have to worry about Szabó anymore, sir," Underwood said.

"No, only about Szabó's surviving relations, if there are any. Or the district attorney, or the county commissioners wondering why Fulton Tower suddenly has no jailer."

"Szabó is where he belongs," Canby said. "Procedure can get your neck wrung in Atlanta. You told me that yourself."

"Perhaps I shouldn't have, Thomas. I'm curious, which of you was it shot him?"

"We both did," Canby said. From the corner of his vision, he thought he saw Underwood's expression change.

"Both. Even better." Vernon sighed. He patted at his chest

absently and Canby realized that the older man was unconsciously reaching for a cigar.

Canby rose from his seat and opened the cupboard, found the bottle of bonded there, and set three glasses on the table. As he poured, he said, "Szabó is out of this picture. What remains is to find Billingsley, and John Drew if we are able. Remember, Sherman's name was in Billingsley's book."

"The last name, you say?"

"Mine was the last. Sherman's just before it."

"Ah, the *S* that will finish this thing. Sherman is to be on the morning's first train. Do you think he can pull this thing off?"

"Tell us about the bombproof where Mrs. Drew was found."

"Why in God's name would I want to revisit that scene?"

Canby set the bottle on the table. For answer, he leaned against the cold cookstove and sipped his glass of whiskey.

Vernon took a deep drink from his glass. "All right, Thomas. You have to understand, Lydia Drew was a strange woman. Half debutante and half hypochondriac, or all of both, you could say. Always either in high spirits or else sickly nigh unto death. When it got to be clear that Sherman meant to shell us all to hell, she had the bishop hire out a crew of Negroes to dig a bombproof on the south side of a hill over by Hunter Street. She was strange, I said, but not stupid. On the *south* side of the hill, safest from the artillery coming in from the north, where Sherman's front was. Closer to the roundhouse than it might ought to have been, but separated from the rail lines by two blocks of cotton warehouses. Sherman was not shelling cotton stores, you know.

"Those boys dug it out proper, then lined the inside with cedar planks and topped it with a double-timbered door on brass hinges. Where Drew got the materials for it by that stage of the war is your guess, not mine. They even replaced the sod on top of the door—nothing to be seen but a grassy hillside, unless you knew to look for it. She provisioned it full of stores and got down there with little Johnny before the first shell struck. And stayed. Even after the mayor carried out the white flag and the Federals themselves were walking the streets. Even after Drew took the boy back to the rectory with him, she wouldn't come up.

"Then Sherman set his engineers loose on the depot and the roundhouse. Tearing up everything related to the rail lines. Heating up the rails on fires made from the crossties and wrapping them around trees and light poles, 'Sherman neckties,' they called them. I imagine she resolved never to come up when she heard all that.

"The next night, the Federals set fire to everything. She'd survived the shelling but there was worse in store for her. What do you think burned the worst? Do you remember it? Those cotton warehouses were pillars of flame. The fire spread down the hillside, anywhere there was thatch or tinder. When it burned over and the Federals had left, we went down with Drew to check on her. Nothing left down Hunter Street but the gutted frames of the warehouses and a blackened hill.

"I was down in that bombproof that afternoon. You could not tell whether she'd asphyxiated or been roasted alive. But you could tell it had taken some time. She suffered more than a lady ought."

Vernon drained the last of his glass and poured himself another.

"We need to go there," Canby said quietly.

Vernon shook his head. "No point in it. We sealed the bombproof up after we removed her body. That hillside's been grown over with ivy for ten, fifteen years."

"I think that's where we'll find John Drew."

"Good God, in his mother's tomb. Dead or alive?"

"From what the bishop told us before he passed," Underwood said, "the boy might be alive."

Vernon drained his second glass of whiskey. "This thing is inconceivable."

"That's how Billingsley has tricked us. His modus operandi *is* the inconceivable."

Canby saw Underwood's expression change again. He saw that the black man bore the trace of a smile on his face. "Now you coming around," he said.

Then Underwood seemed to be working to return his expression to a neutral one.

"Sir," he added.

November 15

ON THE HILLSIDE THEY STOMPED THE EARTH IN widening circles, their feet tangling in the ivy, then tearing free to stomp again, their motions like a pagan dance to the rising sun. Canby marked the cardinal points of the compass as they canvassed the hillside, from the sun cresting over Kimball House to its farthest light on the foothills in the west, where the Chattahoochee wound its way southward. Above the hills a line of clouds was coming on, gunmetal-gray. They looked to be bringing heavy weather with them.

Vernon's boot sounded on a dull hollowness. "Here," he said. He stomped again, sounding out the perimeters of the bomb-proof's door. Canby and Underwood joined him, the three of them kneeling. The ivy had been cut along the left side of the charred door. Underwood pushed the vines clear of the rusted handle, looked at the others for a second, and pulled the door open.

A set of stairs led down into the darkness. "John!" Vernon called.

There was no answer.

"A light, Vernon?" Canby asked, and Vernon struck a match and handed it to him in a cupped hand. Canby started down the stairs, with Underwood behind him and Vernon squatting in the doorway holding the door open to let in as much light as it could. Canby could make out an unmade double bed and a nightstand with a lamp on it. He lifted the globe and touched the match to the wick. When it flared, he set the globe back in place.

"I feel it here," Underwood said.

At first they saw nothing amiss. There were shelves of canned goods on one wall and a washbasin and water pitcher sat on a small table beside a small pile of dirty washcloths. Beneath the table was an old peach crate full of cans that had been opened raggedly, as though in haste or by an unpracticed hand. Among the rumpled linens on the bed rested a little pickaninny doll, the eyes bulbous, red ribbons plaited into the kinky hair that Canby guessed was fashioned from cotton dyed black. The skin darker than night. They saw in a corner a slop jar that, from the smell of the room, needed emptying, and beside it a set of marbles that the boy had apparently abandoned mid-game. It was this that drew their eyes to the floor.

The boy had drawn off chalk circles for his marbles but alongside them and winding through the circles and across the floor were drawings of such vileness that Canby felt his breath coming short. The figures were human, but barely so, contorted into acts of deviance Canby could not have imagined, a bacchanalia of sadism and sexual congress that wound and crept across the entire floor in whorls of chalk. Most of the figures were Negro men and women, crudely caricatured, suffering as many types of assault as the floorboards' span could accommodate. Each time Canby or Underwood moved their feet, they were greeted with more of the nightmare visions.

"No boy could have done this," Canby said.

"He ain't a boy no more."

"'In time, everything will be made vile.' That's what Billingsley said, isn't it?"

"Looks like he's working on it." Underwood scraped his heel across the floor, smearing an image of two black children conjoined. "You take a good look at that door? Wasn't no lock on it. The bolt's on the inside. Someone's been coming and going as he pleased."

"I thought he'd have been held captive here." Canby saw among the figures a phrase scribed in bold letters, *Vexilla regis prodeunt inferni.*

"That's Latin, isn't it?" Underwood asked.

"It is." Canby studied it a moment. "'The banner of the king of hell advance.'"

Underwood snorted. "Sounds about right."

"I can't conceive of a boy being capable of this."

"You'd better start conceiving," Underwood said. He looked again at the pickaninny doll on the bed. "If you don't kill this thing, I will," he said. He bent and swatted the doll to the floor.

Canby did not reply. His eyes were fixed on what lay on the bed where the doll had been. Lying on the sheet was the severed hand of a man. The skin of it was a shade lighter than Underwood's. It was withered, nearly mummified.

"Sweet Jesus," Underwood said.

Canby drew his knife and poked at the hand with the blade. The palm was bloodless and dried, leathery. The knife's tip did not penetrate it. "Vernon," Canby called, "Dempsey and Lewis—you told me all that was done to those bodies?"

"Of course."

"None of them missing a hand?"

"You know whose hand that is, Mister Canby," Underwood said.

Canby looked up at him sharply. "Now, how would I know whose hand it is?"

"Because he told us. In Spot Twelve. That's a Hand of Glory. The left hand of a hanged man."

"And?"

"That old Saul they hung on the Billingsley plantation. Think that ain't his hand?"

Canby looked down at the hand, its lined palm, trying to gauge how old it might be.

"Hand of Glory has got all kinds of power, any hand does. How much power you think is in a conjure-man's hand?"

Canby shook his head. But he was thinking about what he'd read in Billingsley's feverish memoir, what Billingsley wrote about the slave he claimed had started him in this business of voodoo, then black magic. About Billingsley watching the slave hanged. How he, still a boy, had looked to him as a teacher.

"And now he's got Johnny Drew wrapped up in this shite." Canby started toward the stairs. "Vernon," he said as he began to climb, "Johnny Drew isn't one of Billingsley's victims. He's an apprentice."

"We could wait here," Underwood said. "Ambush him."

"No time," Vernon said from the doorway above them. Vernon's bearded profile was dark in the chiseled-out doorway, silhouetted by the morning sun. He was looking north. When Canby reached the top of the stairs he followed his gaze. Saw the plume of steam trailing into the depot, heard the keening whistle of the morning's first train.

SHERMAN HAD NEVER been one for small talk, Grady reminded them as the general stepped down from his train and made his way quickly through the crowd gathered at the depot to greet him. Grady was at the general's heels as he moved toward the waiting carriage, nodding curtly at men in the crowd and exchanging quick handshakes while Grady did all the talking, apologizing to Sherman for the morning's unseasonable cold that had come in with the storm clouds from the west.

"Fine Ohio weather," was all Sherman said in reply as he signed an autograph for one of the boys who rushed in and out of the crowds of grown men, scuttled under the ladies' parasols. Canby and Underwood searched each of the boys' faces as they neared, looking for some resemblance to the ferrotype of John Drew they had seen, Canby hoping Vernon was keeping good vigil as well. He knew Underwood was at his keenest, given this chance to guard the man the Negroes called the Great Liberator. He could not blame him. Still, the boys darted out of the crowds and back into them boisterously, waving their autographed scraps of paper like trophies. "The nonchalance of boys is the proper attitude of life," Canby remembered from one of Emerson's essays. This morning, he thought ruefully, that nonchalance could be covering something more sinister than anything the Sage of Concord ever accounted for.

"A speech, a speech!" someone yelled from the crowd. Sherman turned as he mounted the steps to his carriage and looked out over the men, his face as fierce as though an insult had been called out.

"Come hear it at the exposition!" Sherman shouted. Then he smiled through the red beard now flecked with gray and ducked into the carriage, Grady and the mayor just behind him. Vernon climbed in last and looked at Canby before he pulled the door shut.

"I'd intended him to ride in the hansom with Maddox yonder," he said.

"Closed carriage is safer anyway."

Vernon nodded. "But it won't be a closed carriage he's in at the exposition. Follow us close, and when we get there I want the two of you on him like ticks on a dog." He shut the carriage door with a click of its handle. "Ticks on a dog, Thomas."

The carriage pulled away and Canby and Underwood waited as Maddox brought the police hansom around. As they climbed in, Maddox leaned down, grinning, his elbows on his knees and the reins loose in his grip. He said, lowly, "You still aim to kill him, Thomas? Today'll likely be your best chance."

Canby glared at him a moment, then turned to face forward in his seat.

"Lighten up, Thomas, I'm only kidding you," Maddox said as he cracked the reins. "You never were any fun."

THE PROCESSION TRUNDLED under the towering iron
gate at the entrance of the I.C.E. and rolled to a stop beside the
fountain that shot a column of water nearly as high as the gate
into the November air. Beside it, Director General Hannibal
Kimball stood, hat in hand, shivering in the fountain's spray
and the steadily dropping temperature of the morning.

His greeting, however, was warm as he shook hands with
General Sherman and the other dignitaries, lastly with Vernon. With Canby and Underwood flanking Sherman, Kimball
commenced immediately to lead the group on a walking tour
of the exposition.

"I cannot hope to show you all nineteen acres, General,"
Kimball said, "but I can give you a taste of what has been
accomplished here in less than one hundred and fifty days."

"The extent of the building is remarkable."

"We have a knack for building and for rebuilding, General,"
Grady said. "We attribute that in part to your being kind of
careless with fire."

Sherman turned to look at Grady and there was some nervous laughter among the men.

Grady grinned at him. "Our city is a phoenix risen from
those ashes, General."

A trace of a smile played across Sherman's face. "A New
South indeed, Mister Grady. Glad to contribute my portion."

Sherman walked on and Kimball resumed his talk of the
I.C.E. facilities, pointing out the two-story restaurant con-
structed for the fairgoers, the Judges' Hall, the Exhibition
Halls and the Arts and Industrial Pavilion, and the model

cotton factory at the center of it all, noting that each building had been fitted for steam and water lines and wired for electric light. The smell of boiled peanuts and popping corn had already begun to fill the morning air.

"You'll note the foreign exhibitors, General," Kimball said, gesturing down the long row of booths and tents that stretched to the west. "They have come, as have men from across the country, to display their wares. We intend for this exhibition to banish the last traces of sectionalism from our great nation. And thus are doubly honored by your presence."

As the group wended its way through the crowds they came to a cotton patch, perhaps an eighth of an acre, that had been set up alongside the factory. In the rows, two black women bent under the weight of nearly full burlap sacks slung over their shoulders, pulling the white tufts from the stems of the plants and stuffing them into the sacks.

"Planted expressly for the exhibition," Kimball said. "What you see there, General, is the beginnings of your new suit."

Sherman arched an eyebrow and Kimball fairly beamed.

"We aim to demonstrate for you just how far southern industry has progressed. That cotton being picked will make its way this morning to the gin. It will be carded and spun and—if you'll permit our tailor to measure you—woven into fabric that will be cut for a suit we invite you to wear to this evening's banquet."

"All in a day?"

"A single working day, General. Picked, carded, spun, woven, dyed, dried, cut, and sewn."

"From the plant that, as you see, General, dangles dewgemmed from the stalks this morning," Grady added. Canby rolled his eyes.

"Capital," Sherman said, nodding. "I have no desire to slow the progress. We should hasten to your tailor."

The Rich brothers had set up a small shop in a corner of the cotton factory and Canby saw that Morris Rich himself stood in the doorway, a yellow measuring tape draped over his shoulders. He shook his head as the party approached. "Gentlemen," he said, "will you all be crowding into the fitting booth? Please, General Sherman only."

"Let me send one man in with him, Morris," Vernon said.

Rich shrugged. Canby looked to Sherman and saw that the general's bright eyes were fixed on him. "This man," Sherman said.

Inside the shop, Sherman shucked off his overcoat and handed it to Rich, then removed his field coat and held it out to Canby. Canby could not look Rich in the eye, he so reminded him of Greenberg and his failure there. Canby took the coat, looking down at its epaulettes embroidered with a gold eagle flanked on either side by a silver star. "I did not catch your name, sir," Sherman said.

"Thomas Canby."

"Well, Mister Canby, tell me what grievance you bear toward me. I am a soldier. I know that look in your eye."

Canby's mouth opened but he seemed unable to find the right words to speak.

"If it's about the Negroes you lost in the war, or your property or the crops you lost, I have no apology," Sherman said. "None. The South brought destruction upon itself. I gave

Atlanta every chance to evacuate and be spared, but she would not do it."

"I lost more than that," Canby said, anger nearly choking him. "Innocents were killed."

Sherman stepped up onto the tailor's stool. He glowered at his own reflection in the triptych of mirrors that framed him as Rich wrapped the tape around his chest.

"War is all cruelty, Mister Canby. I've said so many times."

"And so you resolved to make Georgia howl. Was that not the phrase you used yourself, to make her howl?"

"It is all cruelty and you cannot refine it."

Rich pulled a pencil from his pocket and made a notation on his cuff. Gently, he stretched Sherman's right arm out and ran the tape down the length of it. Canby looked down at the gold braid of the field coat to hide the watering of his eyes. He wanted to throw the coat to the floor and trample it.

"Women and children, General. Men too old to fight."

"A shame, then, that they died for a war begun in error and perpetuated in pride."

"I'll grant you part of that, General. Error and pride. No one fought more nobly for an ignoble cause than the Confederates. But no one fought for a just cause more ignobly than you did, sir."

Sherman fixed his eyes, burning brightly, on Canby. You could never tell, Canby thought, if that fire burned from anger or a touch of madness. "History will be my judge," he said levelly. "And when you look to the welcome I enjoyed here this morning from my former enemies, perhaps it already has been."

"Atlanta has too short a memory," Canby said. He stepped closer to Sherman and caught his own reflection in the mirrors, dozens of Canbys refracted in the glass. He saw that his face was pale, the scar on his cheek livid.

Rich, kneeling beside the stool with his tape pressed against the general's leg, rose. As he noted the last measurement on his cuff, he said, "You may help the general with his coat, please, Mister Canby. We are finished here."

Canby looked down at the coat in his hands and saw that he had twisted it upon itself, wrung it like a washerwoman. He twisted it tighter for a moment. Then he shook it out and held it for the general.

"You strike me as a fighter, Canby," Sherman said as Canby's hands trembled and the general stuffed his arms into the coat's sleeves. "I admire that. You speak frankly, and that's a rare thing in a southern man. Always talking around what they mean, parrying and sugarcoating."

Sherman squared his shoulders in the field coat, buttoned it. Rich, his eyes cast down as if in embarrassment, handed the general his overcoat. Sherman turned away from the mirrors and saw that Canby stood blocking his exit from the booth. "You'll excuse me, sir," he said.

Later, Canby would wonder whether it was the practiced command in Sherman's voice, or the habits ingrained by his own brief service in the general's army, or his years on the police force, that prompted his next action. Or whether he was moved by some innate sense of the war's being—finally—so nearly over for him. Perhaps even Angus's hand, reaching across death and time. Canby stood aside.

He watched Sherman's back as he made his way to the tailor shop's front door, then followed. But that exit was blocked. The crowds from the fairgrounds outside had made their way into the factory, their growing numbers pushing the factory workers away from their stations at the gin and the looms, stalling the operation of the machinery. Kimball and the other dignitaries had been pressed up to the door of the shop and Grady, pointing out the idleness of the factory's works, suggested that the general accede to the crowd's demands for a speech, now nearly a chant. Morris Rich was sent for the tailor's stool to give Sherman at least some semblance of an elevation, and it was from this little perch, a head taller than those in the crowd, that Sherman made his speech.

"I have come today to look upon these buildings where once we had battlefields. I delight more to look upon them than to look upon the scenes enacted here sixteen years ago. I say that every noble man and kindly woman over this broad land takes as much interest in your prosperity and in this exposition as do those in this presence, and that we are now in a position to say, every one of us, great and small, thank God we are American citizens."

Sherman lifted his hat to the audience. The crowd stood silent, apparently uncertain whether applause was yet in order. By the standards of southern oratory, what Sherman had said barely qualified as a preamble. Henry Grady cleared his throat and said loudly, "Perhaps, General, you could say a few words about the Atlanta campaign?"

Sherman looked down at him. After a moment, he nodded and turned back to the crowd.

"It was a shame that a city so fair as Atlanta stood in the way of victory and Union. And perhaps even more of a shame that Joe Johnston's defenses were so entrenched and extensive. But as I had seen at Vicksburg, the best hope for breaking those defenses was a feint to draw him out."

"A feint," Canby said aloud before he could catch himself. Sherman turned to look at him.

"Yes, Canby," he said, "a divertive movement. Classic warfare, taught to each and all of us at West Point. You draw your enemy's attention to one part of the arena—a conspicuous movement, but a small one. Then you strike at his heart with the greater part of your force."

Sherman turned back to the crowd and resumed talking, but Canby could make no sense of his words. A dark face loomed close in Canby's vision and he felt himself being guided back into the tailor's shop. The face pressed him down into a chair and he realized after a moment that it was Underwood.

"Catch your breath, Mister Canby," he said.

"God, Underwood. That's it."

"That's what?"

"That's what this," Canby said, waving an arm, "what all this, is. A feint. Billingsley won't be here, especially not in daylight. One look at him in the shape he's in would raise the alarm. John Drew may be here, but Billingsley surely isn't."

Underwood looked at him, confused. "You think he's not with John Drew?"

"He knows where to cut me where I'll bleed the most. Christ, I need to be in Vinings."

THE SCHOOLHOUSE was empty. Canby scanned the room for sign of struggle, his eyes roving over the desks, the chalkboard, the floor. No blood slung across the pine planks, nothing overturned. The children's tablets and books were neatly stacked on the desks or tucked into the shelves beneath them. He heard a settling in the woodstove and crossed the room to it and drew open its door. It was banked high against the early cold, the half-consumed wood lengths spaced evenly as Angus had taught him, had taught Julia and the other scholars, every winter morning. He shut the door and latched it, looked around the room once more. Everything in order except that the children, and Julia, were gone.

Out front, he untied the mare's reins from the porch post and put a foot in the stirrup. The horse shied away from him and he saw the foam around the bit and realized he had nearly ridden her down. Leading the horse by the reins, he started down the School Road to Stillhouse Creek, patting her neck. He looked up the peeled-bark white trunks of the sycamores that grew on this part of the mountain and saw that the gray sky above was beginning to clear. He could just make out the peak of the mountain through the thinning clouds. Then he heard the creek and felt the mare step up her pace at the sound of water.

At the edge of the woods the horse ducked its head toward something on the ground. Canby bent and picked it up. An apple mostly eaten and tossed aside. He studied the bite marks on it and saw that they were small, the size of a child's mouth. The parts of the fruit that were left were not yet browning.

He scanned the path for signs of recent traffic, the prints of little shoes or the imprint of a lady's bootheel. But the trail was full of the prints of all in the village who did not have wells and used the creek for their domestic water. He could not tell the fresh tracks from the old. The apple was a good sign, but still he could not hear the din of children. Over the soft murmur of the creek, he should have been able to track them with his ears alone. He fed the apple to the horse, who chomped it greedily, then he led it at a quicker pace to the creek.

They came down the hillside to where the road terminated at the water, at the bend where the creek turned east to wend its way down the last of Vinings Mountain to the Chattahoochee at Pace's Ferry. The mare dropped her head to the creek and began to drink noisily. Canby saw that in the shaded eddies of the creek, under the patches of granite that jutted out from the woods, scrims of ice had formed at the edges of the water.

He thought he heard something like a cry come from over the little falls that terminated his line of vision upstream, the sound muffled by the other sounds of falling water and the horse's drinking. Quickly, he moved alongside the stream to the waterfall's base, then started upward, clutching at the mountain laurels for purchase on the steep slope. He could feel icy spray from the falls on his face as he climbed.

At the top of the incline he peered out from the laurel leaves across the broad pool that formed at the head of the waterfall. He saw no children, but as he looked upstream he saw Billingsley, shirtless and streaming water, sitting on one of the boulders at the creek's edge. Julia was draped across his lap, her hair hanging lank and her clothes clinging to her. Her head was thrown back, limp, and cradled in the crook of Billingsley's left arm. Billingsley reached around to his hip and drew a knife from his belt and pressed it to Julia's wan brow. A skinning knife, Canby thought, as he ripped the Bulldog from its holster. Meant for animals.

He fired and saw a chip of rock leap from one of the boulders behind them. Billingsley looked up at the sound of the shot. Canby had his thumb on the hammer of the pistol and was drawing it back to cock it when Billingsley dove into the creek with Julia still in his arms. They disappeared beneath the surface of the pool.

Canby holstered the Bulldog and pulled himself over the crest of the incline. He leaped to the nearest boulder, then the next, making his way as quickly as he could to the head of the pool where they'd gone under. He slipped and fell on one of the moss-covered rocks and brought himself up, cursing, and saw Billingsley pulling himself out of the creek on the far bank, his back dripping water and his pants in tatters, ribbons of the black fabric dangling like drooped feathers over his calves. Canby's hand was rising toward the Bulldog when he caught a trace of movement in the pool.

It was her skirts, billowing in the currents out from her body where she hung in the deepest water, suspended just above the rocks at the bottom of the pool. He saw that the stream was spinning her slowly, drawing her in drifting arcs closer to the falls. He cried out and leaped from the laurels into the water, firing at Billingsley as he dropped.

He hoped that his shot had not gone wild but as the breathtaking cold of the water reached his chest and he heard the second report from the Bulldog just before his head went under he knew that he was hoping against certainty. He dove and reached for Julia and saw the pistol sink to rest on the creek bed as he gathered her into his arms. He slipped an arm around her neck, his elbow coming up under her jaw, and kicked for the surface.

When they broke back into the cold November air Canby saw that Billingsley still stood on the opposite bank, watching them, half concealed behind the trunk of a sycamore. As he pulled Julia across the creek Canby tried to retrieve the pocket revolver from his boot. The motion was awkward and each time he stopped kicking and reached downward, his and Julia's heads sank beneath the water's surface. He saw that Billingsley had begun to smile at his struggle—his indecision, his helpless anger. Billingsley reached out an arm, fingers splayed, as though in delectation of what he was witnessing.

Once Canby could feel the rocks beneath his feet he ducked under the water, one hand pushing Julia's jaw above the surface and the other drawing the pistol from his boot. He surfaced, leveled the pistol at Billingsley, and pulled the trigger. The hammer fell with a dull click. Billingsley's lips stretched wide, opening on the mouth full of broken teeth in a leering smile, then he disappeared into the leaves of laurel.

Canby stretched Julia out facedown on the bank on the flattest spot he could find. He turned her head to one side, laying it gently against a rock, and began to push and knead her back between the shoulder blades.

After some time he saw that creek water had begun to flow from her mouth with each push against her back but her chest was not rising with breath. He felt his own breath quicken and he pushed harder, shivering. When he saw that no more of the water would come out of her mouth he gathered her in his arms and rose with her dripping form clutched tight to his chest.

"Is he gone, mister?"

Canby turned and saw a girl of perhaps nine or ten standing at the edge of the trees. She stood wringing her hands and her eyes cut from him to Julia and to the laurels on the far side of the creek.

"Yes."

She looked behind her and children began to emerge, singly and in pairs, from the sycamores. Most were younger than she was, and nearly all of them were crying quietly. "Miss Julia brought us up here to see the ice and that man came out of the woods," the girl said. "Is she going to be all right?"

"Yes. We just need to get her warm." Canby nodded to two of the bigger boys, who had stepped up close to look at Julia. "You boys go along up to the schoolhouse and get the stove stoked up high," he said.

The boys looked to the wooded slope that led to the School Road and shook their heads simultaneously.

"All right, then," Canby said, "we'll go together."

"Was that the devil, mister?" the taller boy asked.

Canby was walking, hugging Julia close. He glanced at the boy as they all started toward the schoolhouse. "Yes," he said. "It was."

THEY'D LAID HER out on the pine floorboards beside the stove, a grammar book under her head, two of the girls chafing her hands and feet while Canby stuffed the woodstove to its capacity and watched, shivering, until the iron began to glow gray-orange from the full load of wood. Canby had stretched his jacket across the top of the stove and now that it had begun to steam he laid it over Julia's midsection. He took one of her hands and rubbed it.

He had dispatched the oldest of the girls to Julia's house for blankets and a change of her clothes and sent a group of the boys, emboldened once they'd reached the village limits, to fetch Solomon Pace from his ferry with the request that he bring with him whatever firearms he could muster. Now as he knelt and worked on Julia's arm he reckoned the time since he had pulled her from the creek and gauged it against the coolness of her flesh. He looked at the girls, working steadily though their eyes brimmed with tears, and hung his head.

"Girls," he said after a moment, "you can go on home now."

The younger girl sobbed, a barking sound coming out of her little chest. She wiped her nose with the back of her hand and said, more a statement than a question, "Is Miss Julia going to wake up?"

The lie was bitter on Canby's tongue. "Yes. We'll just let her sleep awhile yet."

He watched until they had shut the schoolhouse door behind them, then turned to look at Julia again. She was pale but still beautiful and looked indeed to be sleeping, more in repose than in death.

"I'm not fit to speak your eulogy," he said. Then, after a time, "I should go with you."

He leaned down and kissed the blue lips for how long he did not know, until he heard the sound of footsteps on the porch boards out front. The door opened quietly and Solomon Pace leaned through the frame. When he saw Julia laid out on the floor he lowered his gray head.

"Tell me it ain't so," Pace said.

Canby shook his head.

"Who was it? Them boys told me a wild story."

"Robert Billingsley."

"I thought he was dead."

"That's the going opinion. But he's not."

"Good God."

Pace stepped into the room. He had a bundle of quilts under one arm and held a Marlin repeating rifle in his other hand. He leaned the rifle against a desk and began to shake out a quilt, gently. He handed one corner of it to Canby and together they drew it over Julia's still form.

Pace hitched up the legs of his overalls and squatted on his haunches. "Haven't been in here since I was a chap," he said. After a moment of strained silence, he began to recite the Lord's Prayer. Canby joined him for the last lines of it. They sat in silence then for several minutes, until Canby rose and shouldered his way into his jacket.

"Guess you have business in town to attend to."

Canby nodded as he buttoned up the jacket, looser now that his chest holster hung empty. He picked up the Marlin.

"I hope you catch that son of a bitch."

"Not planning to catch him, Uncle Solomon. I aim for it to be pure murder."

"Well, that Marlin will do the job. It's the best rifle for deer you'll find in Cobb County."

"He's probably back into Fulton by now."

"Where's your horse?"

"Gone. I suppose he took it."

"Get yourself to the depot. Bet you can catch the five-eighteen if you hurry."

Canby took a last look at the still form under the quilt and bade his farewell to Solomon Pace and started down the schoolhouse steps, hoping, though he knew better, that Julia might have heard his words to her before her spirit left.

No fit eulogy, he thought, as he walked westward toward the little depot, his heels dragging in the road. He wondered what lines Angus might have used for a meet farewell; perhaps Ecclesiastes, or maybe something more hopeful, from one of Paul's epistles. He knew Underwood would have cast a vote for Paul. Instead, Canby remembered a line of Emerson's: "The sky is less grand as it shuts down over less worth in the population."

But he saw, as he walked toward the sun dipping behind the ridges to the west, that the usual humid haze of the southern air had been abated by the cold front passing through. The air fairly sparkled with clarity. Every crimson leaf still clinging to the branches of the trees was lit crystalline.

Saw that it was going to be a goddamned beautiful sunset.

AND SO HE found himself aboard the Western & Atlantic again, this time headed south.

They bore down, the tracks just perceptibly dropping in altitude beneath them with every mile as they descended into Atlanta, the long line of boxcars behind the engine pressing their weight forward with the dropping grade, pushing their speed. Canby looked out the cab's window to his left and saw the darkness moving in as the sun withdrew, like a curtain drawn from east to west across the flattening land.

Canby was watching the slice of moon rise in the east when the engineer touched him on his shoulder. He pointed toward the orange and white glow of Atlanta ahead and Canby saw a horse and rider cutting swiftly through the fields that ringed the city's outskirts, the rider's shirtless back a splash of white on the dark plain. Canby gave the Marlin to the engineer and began to climb up the side of the locomotive. The engineer leaned out of the engine as Canby found a hold and started up.

"Where's he heading, you reckon?"

"Just take it to the roundhouse. Don't let up."

"I can't take it into the city running full-out like this."

"Yes, you can. Stay on him."

"You gone kill somebody, you know."

"Yes," Canby said, "I know." He stretched himself out on the roof of the cab and rapped on the steel. The Marlin's barrel came up and he took it and shucked the lever to chamber a round, then looked down the barrel and through the iron sights.

"Mind that stack," the engineer shouted. "She gets hot."

Canby did not answer him. Through the sights he saw that Billingsley was hunched close over the horse's neck like an Indian rider. Steam poured from the horse's nostrils into the cold night air. He snugged the butt of the Marlin against his shoulder and tried to relax his body against the shuddering of the train and squeezed the trigger.

Billingsley rose from his crouch and sat back in the saddle. He turned and looked over his shoulder at the train and then to the roof of its cab and stretched his lips into the leer Canby had seen at Stillhouse Creek, the white stumps of his cracked teeth just visible as the train closed the distance between them. Canby shucked the lever for another round and as he did Billingsley stood in the stirrups to his full height and raised an arm, fist shaking above it, into the night air.

Canby fired again and Billingsley twisted quickly in the saddle as though shoved by an invisible hand. Canby chambered a fresh round and sighted and saw that Billingsley had begun to pull the reins to his left, away from the railroad tracks. He saw that the horse's eyes were walled and the bit pulled taut in her mouth was coated and dripping with froth. How the poor mare could be running at speed through this, the second of her day's journeys, Canby could not imagine. Still, she ran at full sprint as though she believed her speed could outdistance herself from the creature clinging to her back.

He squeezed the trigger and the horse shuddered and side-stepped. A burst of blood, slick-black against the dark hide, bloomed on her shoulder. Billingsley bent down over her neck again and pulled harder to the left, his heels kicking into her sides. The train was gaining ground on them. The moon was rising and it shone down on the plain, where patches of ice glinted silver in its light. Canby looked ahead as the train pulled nearly alongside horse and rider and saw that the northernmost of the city's foundries was looming on the horizon, where it split the railroad tracks from the beginnings of Marietta Street.

Billingsley seemed to have seen it as well. As the horse veered farther from the tracks he flashed another of his broken smiles at Canby and Canby fired again and saw that blood was flowing down Billingsley's side. The train had pulled ahead now and Canby sat up and turned to take his aim alongside, backward. He leaned against the engine's stack, feeling the steam heat come through his jacket, burning, as he levered again and his shot went wild, the rifleman having lost count of the rounds he had left, and he fired again and saw another bloom of blood on the horse's haunch and Billingsley's fist rising into the air, and then as Canby raised the rifle his vision was truncated by the corrugated tin walls of the foundry and its loading docks, the dark tin hulk of it severing him from Marietta Street and his target, where Billingsley was now, he knew, making headway down the broad thoroughfare to the city's center.

The engineer pulled down on the steam whistle to warn the city of the missile entering its limits and Canby howled with it, the rage and frustration that billowed forth from his windpipe shaking his rib cage. He pounded the roof of the cab with the butt of the rifle until he dented the steel. He looked again to his left and could see, periodically, in the yards that marked gaps between the houses that lined Marietta Street, glimpses

of horse and rider making their own way south. In the moonlight and the flickering light of the street-corner lamps, both
were glistening with free-running blood.

Then he was conscious of the pain in his back. He pulled
himself away from the smokestack and felt the skin peeling
away. He screamed again, his voice mingling with the shriek
of the whistle. He leaned over, eyes smarting with tears, and
pressed a fist to his forehead. The chill of the night air washed
over his wounded back and when he trusted that he could
stand again he tossed the Marlin into the cab, then, climbing
down, followed it.

The engineer had one hand on the brake lever and the other
hung on the strap that sounded the whistle as though he meant
to pull it loose. If he had heard the rifle clatter to the floor he
gave no sign of it, his eyes were so intently fixed on the tracks
ahead and on the pedestrians hustling off the tracks. But he
cut his eyes away from the tracks when Canby bent to pick up
the Marlin.

"Christ, mister! I warned you about that stack."

Canby rose with the rifle in his arms, wavered, then straightened. "Any whiskey on this train?"

Without looking aside again, the engineer took his hand off
the brake and fished it into the front of his overalls. He pulled
out a flask and held it for Canby to take.

"You may as well drink it all. They'll call me on the carpet
in the morning, no doubt. Better it's you who wakes up with
fumes on his breath than me."

Canby turned it up and gulped the whiskey like water. He
took a breath and turned it up again, pulling on the flask until

it was empty. He moved to drop the flask in the man's back pocket, but the engineer shook his head.

"Keep the flask. I'll get me another if I ever have another payday with the W&A. Can I slow it down now, captain?"

Canby looked out ahead. The gulch of the rail yard was ahead and beneath them. He could not see, but knew, that in a few blocks this single track would split into two, with two more splitting off those in turn, to make up all the siding lines that formed the yard before they whittled back down to the single set that entered the roundhouse from the north. There the trains could be turned, and repaired if need be, and spun around on the great wheeled machinery of the roundhouse either to go back in the direction from which they had come, or else turned onto the tracks running northeast and southwest, or southeast to Augusta or due west to Birmingham.

But all this, on the unlighted rails, he could not see. He saw instead the lighted grids of the city's gaslights, brightest at the center, subdivided out and diminishing into darkness at the borders. Saw, too, a set of brighter, clearer lights that clustered in the few blocks around Calhoun and Kimball streets, where the superior electric light originated, then ran in a straight westward line out to Oglethorpe Park, glowing in a white aura above the exposition.

"'The darkness is mine,'" Canby said.

"What's that you say?"

"'The black sky is mine and I will see you in it.' That's what he said. Hell if he will."

"Not following you, captain."

"You can slow it down at Calhoun Street. Stop it there, in fact. Get me as close to the Dixie Light station as you can."

"That's close by the roundhouse."

"Then I guess you'll have made your run for the night."

"What's the power station got to do with that crazy bastard on the horse?"

"He owns Dixie Light. And he's going to try to shut it all off."

CANBY WAS ACROSS Calhoun and midway up the steps of Dixie Light—hurrying through the white light and grateful to hear the slender lines still humming above him—when the power was cut off. He thought he could hear the crackle of the electric current running past him, dying, chased by the silence racing in its wake down the lines from the station and out to the farthest reaches of its circuit as the lines went dead. He turned and looked out toward Oglethorpe Park, which was now as black as the countryside beyond it. He imagined he heard a collective gasp as the exposition went dark, but he dismissed the notion. But a few seconds later he heard, no questioning it, screaming, then more screams, a crescendo of them, coming from the park.

Yet the windows of Kimball House still glowed with the mellow cheer of gaslight, as did the blocks fanning out from the hotel to the roundhouse. Canby paused at the top of the steps, listening. He heard a grating sound, metal on metal, coming from the basement of Dixie Light. He was reaching for the building's door when the lights at Kimball House flickered, then went out in a quick succession from the street level to its top floor. Grid by grid, the city's streetlights shut down in waves of spreading darkness. In a moment Atlanta was darker than he'd seen it since the nights of the siege.

He felt his way down the side of the building, counting out six paces away from the door, willing his eyes to adjust to the darkness and wishing the scant moon would rise higher. He was crouching down, the Marlin raised in front of him, when the door to the building burst open.

What emerged from Dixie Light was blacker than the darkness around it. For a moment Canby did not recognize the figure as human. But he saw as it moved into Calhoun Street that it was indeed a man, upright and walking on his toes, completely black, glistening in the faint light. Canby's hands shook as he raised the rifle, but he steadied the sights on the center of its back and fired.

It stopped and turned in the center of the street and Canby saw its eyes. They were the only points on the blackened body that gave back any light. Covered in the horse's blood, Canby thought, figuring that Billingsley had smeared himself with the dark matter for camouflage, concealment in the night's dark. As he shucked the Marlin's lever he saw, too, a flash of the broken teeth, white against the inky blackness, then the figure wheeled and plunged down Marietta Street toward the roundhouse. He fired once more then took off after it.

The night-shift mechanics who had gathered outside the roundhouse scattered before the dark apparition barreling up Marietta Street toward them. Only one remained when Canby reached the great building. The man pointed to its cavernous interior with a shaking hand.

"What the hell was that, mister?"

"We need light. Is there any light?"

"There's the furnace."

"Throw it open. Fire it full-out," Canby said as he moved into the shadows.

"What the hell *was* that?" the man said again.

Inside the roundhouse was a cacophony of unseen motion. In spite of the darkness, the building shook with the vibrations of the rails and the tonnages of steel that groaned on them, locomotives and boxcars grinding to a stop as the blackout stalled them, the smell of hot metal mingling with the acrid scents of creosote and cinders. Canby picked his way over the rails and crossties, every footstep in the gravel seeming to announce his position, until he made his way to the plank floor that formed the edge of the mechanics' workshop. He moved more slowly now, remembering the pit that marked dead center of old Terminus, where the rails came together in a pentacle of steel. It was here that the trains were turned and in the dugout beneath the center that the mechanics accessed the undersides of the cars and engines. The men had left their tools scattered in disarray across the floor when the gas had been shut off and he nearly stumbled over a toolbox as he circled the pit and he heard a movement below him and fired at the sound of it.

In the muzzle flash he caught sight of Billingsley crouched and blackened in the pit and saw that his shot had gone wide. He chambered another round and fired again, the rifle at his hip now, and saw that Billingsley was closing the distance between them. He fired again and saw in this flash that one of Billingsley's arms hung limp at his side, and as he worked the lever again he felt his ankle grasped as though in a vise and his leg was pulled out from beneath him.

Canby hit the boards with force enough to knock the wind from him and the burns on his back sang out in pain. He worked the rifle down along his leg and fired it again, then rolled onto his stomach as he felt the hand on his ankle begin to pull him downward. His fingers played across the boards, seeking purchase, and he had nearly caught his fingertips in a gap in the boards when he felt something tear into his leg.

Canby screamed and the pain intensified, a clamping and wrenching, twisting. He felt the hand moving over his leg and realized that his calf was being chewed by the broken teeth. He felt something give in one of his muscles. For a second the pain lessened, then the ripping came again, higher up this time, and Canby was writhing on the boards. His hands flailed and as he felt himself beginning to go over the lip of the pit his right hand settled on a wooden handle and he lifted it and swung it into the source of his pain.

The grip on his ankle and the tearing went away. He sat up on the edge of the pit, legs dangling over it, and gathered his weapon in his lap. He felt of it. Some kind of mallet. One end of its head was peened and the other, flatter side was slicked with blood. He was raising it to strike again when he heard the squealing of hinges and the hulking forms of the engines and boxcars sprung forth from the dark roundhouse. He looked behind him and saw that the mechanic had flung open the furnace and was shoveling coal into it, showers of yellow sparks and orange light pouring out of the furnace door.

The pit was bathed in flickering light and shadow. Billingsley was down in it, down on one knee, his good hand pressed against his blackened face. Freshets of blood poured from his open mouth. Canby dropped into the pit and began to circle him. Billingsley was trying to work his jaw, but the mallet had broken the bone past functioning. The left side of it hung loose in the ripped flesh as though it had been shot away. With every clenching of it came a clicking sound and another spurt of blood. He looked up at Canby, his jaw working its strange new circuit, guttural sounds coming from behind the cracked and broken teeth. His eyes flashed in anger and pain.

"Speak, Malthus," Canby said.

He brought the mallet down with both hands gripping its shaft and the full force of his weight behind the blow. Billingsley's head came apart at the stitches the doctors had sewn into it, the plates of the skull separating. Canby raised the hammer and struck again. And again.

His arm had begun to waver, flagging with fatigue, when the mechanics pulled him off Billingsley's ragged body and carried him to the roundhouse office. There, under the light of the yardmaster's green-shaded lamp, they doctored his wounded leg with kerosene and wrapped it tightly. Then wiped the blood from his face and arms. After some time, nursing the pint of whiskey they'd given him, Canby was aware that the gaslights had come back on and that the trains were moving through the roundhouse again, the iron horses that graced the city's seal rumbling through Terminus and back out into the southern night again. He watched the trains come and go, watched the nimble hustle of the mechanics and flagmen and signalmen stepping lightly over the rails and

crossties, moving unscathed among the steaming and clanking machinery that dwarfed them. All of them going about
their business as though the bloody-sheeted corpse laid outside the office were not there, had never been there.

Atlanta, he thought, just before the fatigue and the wounds
and the whiskey claimed him, his head nodding. *Restored to her
timetables.* It did his soul good to see it.

VERNON THOUGHT that the evening's breeze, though cold,
held all the elements of a perfect Georgia night. It carried on it
the reassuring tide of people-noise above the crowded exhibits,
the music of the calliope piping from the east end of Oglethorpe
Park, the myriad good odors that the food vendors sent up into
the night air. And he savored, best of all, what was not in it:
the shrieking of police whistles, cries of alarm.

Yet still there was this crowd of gawkers that surrounded
Sherman and the entourage like a cloud of mosquitoes. Vernon hung close to the general's elbow, but Underwood had
been pushed back now to the periphery by Grady and the
men of prominence. Every one of them wanted a word with
Sherman. Grady making sure that none of Atlanta's or the
I.C.E.'s virtues escaped the general's notice; Kimball and his
circle leaning close to the man's ear, no doubt pressing further investment ventures. All of them flushed by close prox-
imity to this celebrity, faces lit up like jack-o'-lanterns. And
the autograph-seeking boys dashing up out of the crowd con-
stantly, dozens of them.

They passed the last of the industrial buildings. Ahead of

them, at the park's western edge, lay the racetrack. It was now ringed by what Kimball had dubbed "Horticultural Avenue," a collection of flowering plants and shrubbery of which only the azaleas were native, and many of which, Vernon thought, would not likely survive this night's frost. A brass band of a dozen musicians was lined up on the track, in the blue and green uniforms of the exposition staff. The conductor, spying Sherman in the crowd, raised his baton above a braided shoulder and the band broke into "Dixie." Knees raised high, the band members began a prancing circuit around the track. Apparently the conductor had an ironic sense of humor, Vernon thought. Or an ax yet to grind. But just a few bars into the song the man signaled again and the horns segued into "The Star-Spangled Banner." Vernon did not need to turn his head to see that Grady was smiling.

Then it all went dark.

The sounds followed the light. Behind him, Vernon heard the calliope wheeze into silence, and out front the brass horns fell off, one after another, in sputtering decrescendo. Then there was scattered noise: the nervous laughter of the women and the muttering of men fumbling for matches. The procession halted.

Vernon pulled a match out of his jacket pocket and struck it with his thumbnail. Other matches began to flare and he saw a new face working its way through the ranks of the autograph-seekers. Vernon felt some stirring of his memory as he regarded the boy, sorting through the inventory of faces he'd stored over a long career. The boy smiled at Vernon and he realized that though the boy's hair was black as pitch, the eyebrows were white. He studied the distinction as the match's flame ebbed down into a steady glow, and he was watching the face as a bead of sweat ran down the side of its forehead, in spite of the night's chill. The sweat ran black as a woman's makeup through tears.

The boy stepped closer, and as he raised a hand with a paper in it the smile on his face twisted into a snarl of rage beyond his years. The breeze lifted the paper away and Vernon saw that it had covered a derringer, which the boy raised higher as he pressed through the crowd toward Sherman.

Underwood stepped forward.

WHILE THE SHOT was still echoing in Grady's ears, and his eyes were fixed on the black man on the ground, the others of the Ring were in his face, at his ear, his elbow.

"We can't let this get out, Henry."

"God, this is worse than Greenberg."

"What will Chicago say?"

"We are so *close*, Henry."

And above it all he could hear Hannibal Kimball shouting to the crowd: "Just a child's popgun, ladies and gentlemen! No cause for alarm!" over and over while the Negro detective whose name he could not remember lay bleeding on the exposition turf. It was the first serious violence Grady had ever seen close-up and the amount of blood that was flowing from the black man's upper arm was staggering. And the expression on the child's face—the *grimace*, Grady thought—just as he let off the shot and as he turned to run through the crowd with one of the policemen behind him. Grady felt overwhelmed.

"We still have a month to go, Henry. Think about attendance."

"You can bury the story, or not run it at all."

"It doesn't have to get out."

Grady looked around him at the faces of Atlanta's first citizens, the expression on his own face like that of a man pulled abruptly from an unpleasant dream.

"An ambulance," Grady said.

"What?"

The crowd was now, at Kimball's urging, moving away. Bearing with it General Sherman away from the scene, to safety. No one had moved to assist the black man where he lay writhing on the ground.

"An ambulance, I said."

The others looked at him in bewilderment.

"Gentlemen," Grady said, waving a hand at the backs of the departing crowd, then at Underwood where he lay, "is this what we want for our Atlanta?"

IT WAS THE silence that woke him. Canby started from the chair and then winced at the burst of pain from his calf, looked around the roundhouse, and saw that it was still, the trains mute hulks on the tracks. The body was still where it had been laid out but all the railroad workers were gone. Nothing in motion but the pulsing glow of the great furnace. Then he caught the scent of cigar smoke on the night air.

"Found you sleeping on the job, didn't I?"

"Vernon?"

Vernon stepped out of the darkness at the edge of the W&A platform. "I hear you got our man."

Canby nodded. "Where is everyone?"

"On break until the eleven o'clock trains come through. Courtesy of the Atlanta P.D. You and I have one last bit of business here." He moved through the shop with his cigar clamped in his teeth, sorting through the tools and oil cans, until he found a pair of railroad gloves. He pulled them on and walked to the furnace, pulled its door open.

"What do you aim to do?"

Vernon walked over to the body and squatted beside it. He lifted the sheet and stared down at the broken face for a moment, his expression stern, chewing on the cigar.

"You gave him hell, didn't you?"

"He had it coming."

Vernon nodded and dropped the sheet. "In spades. Come help me with this."

Canby found himself loath to touch the corpse. He took an ankle in each hand and hoisted and they lurched with it to the furnace. At the open door, Vernon looked at Canby and nodded, wincing at the blast of heat. They heaved the body in.

It crumpled upon itself as the head went into the coals, bending nearly double. The sheet caught fire and the flames began to lick around it and the outline of the body came clear, blackening, the blood smeared on it beginning to crackle and peel. When they could smell burning flesh Vernon shut the door and latched it.

"And that's an end to that," Vernon said. He took off the gloves and dropped them to the ground. He tapped the ash from the end of his cigar and looked at Canby. "Probably headed for the exhibition when you got him."

"Likely so."

"Johnny Drew was there."

"According to plan," Canby said.

"In the flesh. Right after the electric cut out. Little black-haired boy like any other. Came out of the crowd as they do, out front of the Exhibition Hall. Black-haired, I said, or else I'd have known the bishop's son. But, Thomas, as this boy comes closer, I see his brow is slick with sweat, spite of the cold, then a bead of it runs down his cheek, black as coal. Underwood saw it, too.

"Little single-shot derringer, it was. Popped off a round meant for General Sherman but Underwood was there. He took it in the arm."

Vernon saw the concern in Canby's face. "Underwood will be all right. I sent him down to Doctor Johnston's clinic."

Canby nodded. "What about John Drew?"

"Disappeared into the crowd. Maddox was right behind him."

"Maddox better be careful."

"Always is. He's got him collared by now, I wager."

"And how will the prosecution of that case be handled?"

Vernon looked weary. "God knows," he said. Then he raised his eyes to Canby's. "You've not mentioned Julia."

Canby shook his head.

Vernon took in a long breath. "I don't know what to say."

"There's not much to be said. She's gone."

Vernon took Canby's shoulders in his hands.

"It's all a bunch of shite in the end."

"No. It is not. That's no fit benediction for that good woman's life."

Canby felt his throat hitch. He fought it back by thinking of the body in the furnace. "I've got nothing left."

"Yes, you do. There's the difference between you and Julia. And Angus. And that bastard," he said, jerking a thumb toward the furnace, "whose name I'll not speak aloud. You're alive."

He clapped Canby's shoulders, softly. "I'll wait for you outside."

Canby watched his old friend walk out of the roundhouse, feeling certain that Vernon would have the hansom waiting at the curb, that he'd be able to sleep for a week, if he needed it, at the house on Butler. Then he picked up the gloves Vernon had dropped and opened the furnace. The flesh was burning away from the body. Its skull was now peeled of skin, the broken dome of it blackening in the bed of coals. Malthus subsiding to ash.

He shut the door and walked out into the night.

THE YOUNG PRIEST STRUGGLED TO RAISE HIS VOICE over the wind on the mountain. "'I am the resurrection and the life, saith the Lord,'" he read, the wind snatching the tail ends of each of the words. "'He that believeth in me, though he were dead, yet shall he live; and whoso believeth in me shall never die.'"

The priest stood with the open prayer book in his hands, Julia's coffin before him and the great expanse of Georgia sky behind. Canby listened with the others gathered in the little cemetery, where Uncle Solomon Pace had dug out a grave for her among his own people, his father Hardy and the rest. The coffin was heaped with flowers and the wind caught them up and lifted them until they dropped and mingled with the fallen leaves of the mountain's old oaks and hickories. Canby, lost in the rhythms of the service, heard the trace of a brogue in the priest's voice, noted the ruddy complexion over the white collar, and felt his eyes water yet again.

They were all here: Vernon and Maddox, Uncle Solomon,

even Henry Grady. Underwood standing a bit off to the side, his right arm hung in a cotton sling. He'd brought an old Negro woman with him who nodded along with the liturgy, her hands held out with the palms upraised. Mamie O'Donnell seated in the lone chair that had been brought up the mountainside, dressed as demurely as she could manage. Mamie the patroness of this affair, whore's money lavished on the funeral and its crates of flowers, the casket with its glass viewing window, the embalming done by Patterson's downtown, where the undertaker's art had frozen Julia in time.

"'If I say, peradventure the darkness shall cover me, then shall my night be turned to day.'"

Grady's presence here a surprise. He had called at Vernon's house the day previous, waving a special edition of the *Constitution* on which the ink had barely dried, his old vigor rekindled, to show Canby two of the day's features he had written himself. The first an obituary for Julia that began, "A new star has been added to the firmament over our fair city." The second a story entitled "Atlanta and Her Friends," in which Canby's name was mentioned favorably and Underwood—"a credit to his race"—was mincingly praised for an accident narrowly averted at the I.C.E. And more on the exposition's current success, where attendance had surpassed one million and Atlanta was leading the charge into the twentieth century. In between the lines of type, Canby thought he sensed the Ring's epitaph. He hoped that Billingsley's guilt had destroyed it from within, dispatched those men of power and influence into the shame of counting him one of their number. But when he had looked up into Grady's smiling face, he couldn't be sure. Canby had spread the paper out on Vernon's kitchen table and cut out Julia's obituary with his Case knife. Then he had folded the rest of the paper, neatly, twice, and opened the door of Vernon's woodstove and placed it inside.

"'In the midst of life we are in death; of whom may we seek succor, but of thee, O Lord, who for our sins art justly displeased?'"

Mamie had pressed her tear-streaked cheek to Canby's shoulder before the service, and the scent of her perfume yet lingered on him. He looked down the mountainside, past the Negro settlement and the green-shingled roofs of Vinings, saw a locomotive smoking in on the Augusta line, heading toward the roundhouse, there at the center of the teeming city.

"Rest eternal grant to her, O Lord, and let light perpetual shine upon her," the priest said, and Canby replied, with the others, *Amen.*

THEN THERE HAD been hands to be shaken, the protracted ceremony of condolences, a haze of faces before him that Canby only half perceived. "Fortitude, Thomas," Vernon had said in parting, then clapped a hand, very gently, on Canby's shoulder.

He stood over the open grave for a time he could not have determined, could perhaps only have reckoned by the wind. He saw that the Chattahoochee, a mile off to the east, had begun to glow orange with the sunset. Saw Uncle Solomon still standing close by with his head bowed, patient as though he would bide an era here with Thomas before he took up his shovel for the last thing that there was to be done. And that Underwood and his friend were still there as well, that the old woman's hands were now clasped together at her waist. Canby bent and took up a handful of loose earth and held it over the grave, let the rocky soil sift through his fingers onto the casket. He nodded to Uncle Solomon and turned away.

At the edge of the slope he heard footsteps behind him and turned to see Underwood walking toward him, the old woman hooked on his good arm like a bride with her escort.

"This is a thin place now, isn't it, Mister Canby?"

It took Canby a moment to catch the meaning of the question. "Yes," he said.

"Even more so now."

Canby almost smiled, in spite of himself. *My black Celtic friend*, he thought. *Honorary member of the tribe.*

"I suppose it always was."

The old black woman stepped away from Underwood and took Canby's hands in hers. Old hands, gnarled with rheumatism, trembling with age or nervous energy. She hummed a hymn under her breath and kneaded his hands as she would have, he guessed, a child's. Then she looked up into his eyes and smiled. "She *is* the mountain, now, son," she said.

CANBY AND UNDERWOOD sat on the mountainside watching the dusk deepening down in the valley. All the others were gone, Vernon and the rest back in the city on the W&A by now, Uncle Solomon and Lettie Lee down the mountain. Now the two men sat, passing between them the bottle of Jameson that Underwood had brought up from the city, watching the lights of Atlanta coming on, and arguing quietly.

"Superstition again, Underwood," Canby said. "Maddox saw him fall."

"Maddox saw *something* fall off that trestle. But you don't know it was Johnny Drew."

"If it wasn't John Drew, what was it?"

"If it was Johnny Drew, how come they haven't found a body? Been dragging the Chattahoochee for days."

"He'll turn up."

"You got that right. One way or another." Underwood stared out to the trestle, miles to the west, where Maddox's pursuit had ended. The boy, Maddox said, had jumped the W&A freight on the tracks that ran past Oglethorpe Park. Maddox just behind him had climbed on and over cars, crawling atop them until he saw the splash in the dark water. Maddox had jumped off on the river's other bank, where the tracks twisted into the woods, and walked across the bridge back into town. Underwood could not admit that was the end of it.

Underwood took a deep drink from the Jameson and passed it to Canby. For a long time, neither of them spoke. Canby studied the valley, marking the increments of night shutting down the day.

He remembered the bottle in his hand and took a pull from it. As he did he saw that Underwood had turned his head to look at the top of the mountain, the Pace Cemetery on its summit.

"If you're thinking to say more about Julia, I'd prefer you didn't," Canby said, his throat tight. In the fading light,

Underwood saw that his jaw had clenched and the scar on his cheek was dark as a bruise.

"You know, I've been thinking about something I read a while back."

"Underwood is thinking. Watch out."

Underwood adjusted his arm in its sling, wincing. "'Evil exists in the world not to create despair, but activity.'" He watched Canby's profile until Canby, slowly, began to nod.

"Maybe there is something to that. But despair seems to be the order of the day. Where did you find it?"

"It was in Malthus's *Population* book. Right there at the end."

Canby nodded again. "Activity or despair. I guess that's the choice to make."

"It's the choice you need to be making."

Canby cut his eyes to the black man angrily. After a long moment his expression softened, just perceptibly. "Thomas Malthus," he said. "Better philosophy than superstition."

"I'd have figured you'd be giving superstition more of a fair shake by now," Underwood said.

Canby thought of what he had seen emerge from Dixie Light, the transformation of Billingsley in the roundhouse pit. He took another drink. "I'll grant you some of that, Underwood. What took Julia and the others—that was evil."

"Absolute evil?"

Canby thought a moment before he spoke. "Yes," he said finally.

"Supernatural evil?"

Canby was slower to answer. "Possibly."

"Don't that leave it open that there might be absolute good?"

"No. Not in mankind. I cannot see that."

"I mean supernatural good."

"I believe the theologians call what you're getting at a Manichean duality, Underwood."

"Call it what you like. I call it good sense."

"My quarrel with God is unresolved, Underwood."

As Canby tipped the bottle up he thought he saw Underwood's teeth flash in the dark. "What is it?" Canby said.

"You said it, not me."

"Said *what?*"

"God."

"Underwood," Canby said with a sigh.

"Just study on it some. All I ask."

"All right, then. I'll study on it." Underwood and his perpetual catechism, Canby thought. He sipped from the whiskey again and watched the night gather its shadows over the valley, saw the stars beginning to emerge overhead. It really was beautiful; there was no other word for it. Or other way to see it. He said, before he could quite catch himself, "I'll grant you that there are two kinds of darkness."

Underwood looked at him. He seemed to be trying to think of what to say, then he nodded solemnly. Canby passed him the bottle.

They sat in silence long enough to watch the valley slip into full night. In the cold clarity of the November air the lights of Atlanta wavered, the gas and the electric, all the way out to the exposition at Oglethorpe Park. And above them the stars shone brightly, like an immense scattering of diamonds cast against the black sky.

"I read somewhere once that we don't see the stars," Canby said. "Not really. They're out every night and we look right past them, take the sight for granted. That if the stars came out just once in a thousand years, we would call it a miracle and record it for all time. That we'd declare it was the city of God revealed to us. I think there's a lot of truth to that. Do you?"

Underwood looked up at the pinpricks of light in the velvety darkness. "I think there is," he said.

Canby leaned his head back, trying not to group the stars into constellations, trying not to think of them in any order imposed by man. "Look up, then, and see them.

"There they are."

What else to do when a man—younger and more sure of himself—calls your hand? I gave my proper notice to the county judge and he and I saw to it that Ringgold had a new sheriff by month's end. A man off the Chattanooga force eager to get himself some land and a better position just over the state line. Nearly ten years' experience; a good man, plodding but conscientious. He will do well there. Handed him the keys yesterday, paid my respects to Anse's grave, and did not look back.

Galling, Underwood's conviction. Not content just to be Atlanta's first Negro detective—better still, decided to be the first Negro detective to resign voluntarily from the force. Turned his badge in to Vernon and headed west when the Constitution *ran the wire report on the second killing in Birmingham. Of course, found himself completely shut out of the Birmingham department, as he ought to have known beforehand. Convinced that the Alabama murders are the continuance of what we saw in the fall of '81. Certain that it was not Johnny Drew that fell from the trestle over the Chattahoochee, that the boy got out of Atlanta. Deeply suspicious of Maddox and his testimony. He may be right there.*

Got myself on board this train at the Vinings station, a long silent visit to the mountaintop this morning. The marker in place now, paid for with what Mamie loaned me years ago. A ring traded for a stone. Despair is the one unforgivable sin, Angus told me once. But the new Bulldog hung heavy against my chest.

Saw that the sycamores around the cemetery were beginning to bud; dogwoods blooming white in the valley. She'd have pointed that out. I headed down the mountain to the depot.

Birmingham smokes in the distance ahead, iron mills running shifts through the night, steam rising toward a crescent moon. And Johnny Drew there, Underwood says, taking up where his mentor was shut down. The corpse they found in the mine shaft on Red Mountain proof of it, he believes. I'm to meet him at Five Points. More work to be done, he says. We will see.

Even here at the outskirts, one of the Irondale foundries is running a third shift. So close by the tracks that it lights the conductor's face bright as noon as he walks through the car announcing the Birmingham depot. Men laboring around the mill and its looming stack like ants on a mound aflame. An echoing boom of metal as they drop the chute for a pour and the molten iron sluices down it. Bright as a sun, bright enough to blind a man if he looks at it for long.

A collective gasp from the travelers as the white-hot metal runs down the chute into its cast. Some turn away from the windows. I shut my eyes. But the glare is in them now, red and white motes lingering, lights flaring out of darkness.

Historical Note

Writing a historical novel is a bit like a tightrope act—with the wire as story, and the long distance below it studded with razor-sharp errors of fact. With that peril in mind I have attempted to write with careful attention to accuracy in twining fact and fiction together.

Yet I confess to a bit of dancing on the wire. I have deliberately altered two points of Atlanta history, and reworked a third, hoping that the reader will indulge that willfulness in the service of the story.

The first liberty is the presence of electric light at the I.C.E. of 1881. Electric streetlights were not a fixture in Atlanta until 1885, though Mayor James Warren English's home, the first in the city to be equipped with both electricity and a telephone, was completed in 1880. The second is Fulton Tower, which was not built until near the end of the century. Having come across Fulton Tower—with its winding, Gothic stairwell and its grim old cell Spot 12—in Franklin M. Garrett's *Atlanta and Environs*, I could not bring myself to leave it out. And the lynching in *The*

Scribe is of course a reworking of the infamous Leo Frank trial that came years later, in one of Atlanta's very darkest moments. These elements served the story well enough, I believe, to justify some reimagining of history. And certainly the eruption of evil that was the Frank case warrants reiteration as a cautionary tale. I hope the reader will concur.

Those wishing to learn more about nineteenth century Atlanta can do no better than the first two volumes of Garrett's magisterial *Atlanta and Environs* (University of Georgia Press, 1954). Principally composed of reprinted contemporary accounts from local newspapers (including the *Constitution*), it shows Atlanta's history unfolding in something very close to real time. It is a compendium all things Atlantan—which is to say, two thousand pages of the wonderful, the strange, the outrageous, the disgraceful, and the delightful.

—*M.G., October 8, 2014*

Acknowledgments

THANKS FIRST, AS EVER, to Kristen Sulser Guinn, who makes all of it possible, and to our remarkably patient children, Braiden and Phoebe Guinn.

For their friendship and support, I am grateful to Andre Dubus III, Chris Offutt, Michael Farris Smith, Michael Kardos, Jim and Frances Zook, David and Rebekah Moulder, Pam Sultan, Kelly Boutwell, Mechelle Keeton, Charlie Godbold, Park Ellis, Scott Sutton, Dick and Kay Largel, and my parents, Wendell and Jane Guinn.

To my friends Joe Hickman, Jason Shelby, Chris McMillin, Paul Rankin, and Steve Yates, thank you for continuing to be invaluable readers.

My stalwarts of legal and medical expertise, Floyd Sulser, Jr., and Keith Stansell, M.D., have once again aided me with their insights.

For their knowledge of wing shooting, thanks to Jeff Bowling, Jim Carruth, Randy Freeman, and Bill Porch. For medical arcana shared on a cobalt-blue-sky day of quail hunting outside Meridian, I'm indebted to Ed Carruth, M.D., and Bob May, M.D.

To Johnny Evans and his incomparable Lemuria Books, thanks for being the best friend a writer could have in this business.

Grateful acknowledgment is due to Mary Ann Caws for permission to reprint from her translation of Victor Hugo's *Et nox facta est* and to the Cornell University Press for reuse of the passage from Jeffrey Burton Russell's *Mephistopheles*.

Alane Salierno Mason has once again graced my work with her keen vision, and it has come out the better for it. Thank you, Alane.

Finally, a much belated thank you to my graduate professors at the University of South Carolina, especially David Cowart, Joel Myerson, Keen Butterworth, and the late James Dickey, all of whom taught me, as Mr. Dickey put it, that "Wild hope can always spring / From tended strength." Everything is in that.